Pr...

"Humphreys's s... ay...
You will feel as... her
world... This series is getting better with each book."
— *RT Book Reviews*, 4.5 Stars

"Compelling... Deft world-building and sensuous love
scenes make this paranormal romantic thriller an enjoy-
able journey."
— *Publishers Weekly*

"The sizzling chemistry, drama, and suspense were
enough to make me a fan of this series."
— *Fresh Fiction*

"The characters are well-developed, the twists and turns
of the plot are well-crafted, and the situations are alter-
nately funny, action-packed, and sensual."
— *Fresh Fiction*

"Strong, admirable characters, a sizzling love story, and
a seat-of-the-pants action plot."
— *Star-Crossed Romance*

"Humphreys bends suspense and sensuality into a delec-
table spicy mix."
— *Night Owl Romance* Reviewer Top Pick

Praise for *Untouched*:

"Incredible world-building and a fast-paced plot pulled me in right away, and I was instantly hooked on this fascinating new world."

—*Long and Short Reviews*

"Outstanding… Red-hot love scenes punctuate a well-plotted suspense story that will keep readers turning pages as fast as they can."

—*Publishers Weekly* Starred Review

"Full of fast-paced action and complex characters."

—*RT Book Reviews*

"Fast-paced mystery, twist and turns, lots of passion and romance. The last two chapters of this book will have you in awe!"

—NetGalley Reader Review

"Another sizzling, passion-filled book that will keep you engrossed."

—*RomFan Reviews*

"This book will have you crying, turning the pages for more, and loving the characters."

—*Book Lovin' Mamas*

"Fast-paced, full of plot twists and turns and great characters. Definitely a great read!"

—*Star-Crossed Romance*

Praise for *Unleashed*:

"A stunning new shifter series that will thrill paranormal fans… A fascinating world… Spectacular."

—*Bookaholics Romance Book Club*

"A moving tale that captures both the sweetness and passion of romance."

—*Romance Junkies*, 5 Blue Ribbons

"A fast-paced paranormal romance with fantastic world-building. I can't wait to read more from this author and in this series."

—*The Book Girl*, 5 Stars

"A well-written, action-packed love story featuring two very strong characters."

—*Romance Book Scene*, 5 Hearts

"The characters haunted my dreams and I thought about this book constantly."

—*The Long and Short of It Reviews*

"The love scenes are steamy… The plot is intriguing… The reader will be entertained."

—*Fresh Fiction*

"I loved this book. A paranormal top pick, and I'm looking forward to many more in this series."

—*Night Owl Romance* Reviewer Top Pick, 5 Stars

Also by Sara Humphreys

The Amoveo Legend

UNDONE

SARA HUMPHREYS

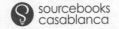
sourcebooks
casablanca

Published by Sourcebooks Casablanca, an imprint of Sourcebooks, Inc.
P.O. Box 4410, Naperville, Illinois 60567-4410
(630) 961-3900
FAX: (630) 961-2168
www.sourcebooks.com

Printed and bound in the United States of America
VP 10 9 8 7 6 5 4 3 2 1

"Chains do not hold a marriage together. It is threads, hundreds of tiny threads which sew people together through the years."

—Simone Signoret

For my husband, Will.

Chapter 1

WHITE LIGHT PULSED AND FLICKERED THROUGH THE club in time with the gritty dance music. The crowd of writhing bodies throbbed with the unmistakable energy of lust as they clamored for a connection—any connection. Hands wandered, looks were cast, and figures melded together, almost becoming one.

Maybe living like a human wouldn't be that bad.

Marianna leaned back in the horseshoe-shaped VIP booth and watched the humans as they danced. The scene before her flickered rapidly between darkness to blinding, artificial light as the strobes flared. She observed couples as they disappeared into the crowd, losing themselves in the music, the sex in the air, and in the moment.

No conversations. Eyes closed.

No past. Bodies touching.

No future. Hips swaying.

No consequences.

Just now.

She sipped her champagne and crossed her bare legs as she witnessed the mating rituals that they participated in with relentless energy. They spent their lives looking for someone to ease the loneliness, with no idea who or what they were looking for. No predestined mate. No clan. No telepathy. No shapeshifting. No powers of visualization. Aging and eventually dying.

On second thought, living like a human was going to suck.

Marianna shuddered and took a swig of her champagne. As a pure-blooded Amoveo female from the Bear Clan, she should have found her mate by now, or he should've found her, but he hadn't. Having past her thirtieth birthday, she could already feel her Amoveo abilities waning, and if she didn't find her mate soon, they would disappear altogether, and she would have to live, for all intents and purposes, as a human.

Mateless. Powerless. Alone.

Yup, she thought, sighing heavily, it was going to suck.

The bass beat vibrated the tabletop beneath her fingers. Hayden sat next to her with his arm draped behind her, wearing his usual air of irritating arrogance. She wanted to tell him where he could stick it, but instead, opted for ignoring him as much as possible.

He hated this place—most Amoveo did because it was owned and operated by vampires—but of course, that's exactly why she came here. Up until tonight, hanging out at The Coven had been a surefire way to keep Hayden and the rest of the Amoveo out of her hair. Apparently, his desire to try and get her to mate with him overrode his innate disgust of vampires.

"I have to admit, Hayden," she said over the music. "I'm more than a little surprised that you came to The Coven tonight."

Marianna glanced at him over the rim of her glass and offered him a tight smile. She could still connect with any Amoveo telepathically, but didn't necessarily want to. She didn't care for being next to him in the booth, so the last thing she wanted to do was invite him into her head.

"You practically live here now." He drained the rest of his scotch. "Although I can't fathom why."

He didn't look at her, but leveled his dark eyes at the humans who passed by their table. Marianna noticed how hard and unforgiving his features were. Hatred and contempt oozed off him like bad cologne and stuck in her throat. She knew most women found him hand-some, but she thought he was far too much of an asshole to be attractive.

Hayden was a self-entitled tool who rode his father's coattails with obnoxious ease and made no secret that he wanted her for himself. He wasn't her predestined mate, and he knew it as well as she did, but that didn't stop him from trying. Unfortunately.

"Olivia is my friend, Hayden. If I'm going to go club-bing in the city, then I may as well go someplace where I'm friends with the owner." She narrowed her eyes and struggled to keep her voice even. She didn't want to fight with him. She just wanted him to go away. "I like sitting at the VIP booth and doing a bit of people-watching."

"Your *friend*? She's a vampire," he said with con-tempt. "Vampires are dirty, disgusting creatures. They drink the blood of humans, which makes them no better than humans. In fact, it makes them worse and puts them far below us on the evolutionary chain. If it weren't for you, I would never step foot in a place like this."

At that moment, a young human girl with dark, heavy eye makeup sauntered by the table and gave Hayden what was surely her most seductive look. Clad in a tiny black dress, fishnets, and several tattoos, she looked like a regular here at The Coven. She ran one hand through her long dark hair and winked at Hayden as she swayed to the music.

Hayden promptly looked away and inched closer to Marianna. The girl shot him a dirty look and turned her attentions to another clubgoer who had almost as many tattoos as she did. Moments later, they were absorbed into the dancing mob.

"As for your *people-watching*," he sneered, "I could do without it. I may as well be at a farm watching pigs wallow in mud."

Your friend looks a tad uncomfortable. Olivia's voice touched her mind gently, and Marianna suppressed a grin. She scanned the club and found Olivia behind the bar with her two bartenders—both vamps. Her bright red hair made her easy to spot in the sea of black. Olivia was the owner of the club, the head of this all-female vampire coven, and one of Marianna's best friends.

He's not my friend, and you know it, but I'm thrilled that he's squirming, Marianna thought back with a smirk. *You have to come over here soon. It will annoy him and hopefully get him to leave.*

He's not bad looking, but you obviously loathe him, and you already told me he's not your mate, so why even bother? Olivia continued to make drinks and tend customers without missing a beat. *Tell him to fuck off.*

Let's just say it's politics. She gripped her champagne flute and gave a slanted glance toward Hayden. *I have no interest in picking sides in this stupid civil war that my people started. However, I'm getting tired of playing nice. Now be a good friend. Get your ass over here, and flash him your fangs.*

Olivia's laughter jingled along her mind. *Now, come*

on. If any of my human customers got wind of my wiles, we'd have a serious problem on our hands. I don't feel like fending off silver, crosses, garlic, and wooden stakes—that's so last millennium.

I thought that garlic couldn't hurt vampires?

It can't, but Hollywood keeps perpetuating the myth. I really don't care for garlic, and it takes forever to get rid of the stench. She threw a wink from behind the bar. *I'll be over in a second.*

Another song erupted loudly, and the startled look on Hayden's face made Marianna want to bust out laughing. If he insisted on chasing her, then she was going to make it as uncomfortable for him as possible.

"I love this freaking song!" Marianna raised her arms in the air. "I think it's just about time to dance."

"I don't think so." He grabbed her arm and yanked her toward him, preventing her from leaving. "Aren't you almost finished with your champagne?" He shouted over the music and looked at his watch for the tenth time in as many minutes.

"Oh dear, I hope you're not leaving yet." Olivia's voice cut into their conversation, and Marianna smothered a giggle when she saw the look of surprise flicker briefly over Hayden's face.

"Hey, Olivia," Marianna said with a big smile as she tugged her arm free of Hayden's grasp. "The club is packed tonight, so thanks again for hooking me up with the VIP booth. I would tell you that you don't always have to give me VIP status, but I'd be lying. However, as much as I adore it, I don't want to wear out my welcome."

"Anything for you, Marianna. You know that," she

replied without taking her emerald green eyes off of Hayden. Olivia folded her arms over her chest, and her lips lifted at the corners. "I don't believe I've had the pleasure."

"Hayden," he bit out. He kept a neutral expression on his face, but his energy signature—the spiritual finger-print that all Amoveo had—pulsed with nerves and fear in the air around her.

Holy shit. Marianna arched one eyebrow and touched her mind to Olivia's. *I think he's afraid of you.*

Marianna had expected him to be uncomfortable. To climb up on his high-horse of superiority and look down his nose at Olivia, but never, in a million years, did she think he was *afraid* of vampires.

Slap my ass, and call me Sally. A smile spread across Olivia's face. *This is going to be more fun than I'd hoped.*

I thought you didn't want to do anything to draw attention to yourself. Marianna rubbed her thumb along the edge of the champagne flute as she surveyed the humans who brushed by the table. Clad in her Armani suit, Olivia may as well have been wearing a sign that said, "I own this place and could buy you free drinks if I wanted to."

Don't worry. I'm just going to see how easily his buttons are pushed. Her voice dropped low as it wafted along Marianna's mind. *Besides, I don't like the way he put his hands on you. This guy isn't just a dick; he's violent. I can see it in him as clearly as I can see his hideous taste in clothing. No man—Amoveo or otherwise— should be caught dead wearing a T-shirt like that. He looks like a* Jersey Shore *reject.*

Marianna almost spit out her mouthful of champagne on the last comment.

"Where the hell is the waitress?" Hayden flicked his cold gaze back to Olivia and slid his glass across the table. "I need another Scotch."

In a blur of inhuman speed, Olivia leaned on the table with both hands and got right in Hayden's face. "I'm sorry," she said innocently. "I couldn't hear you over the music. What did you say?"

They all knew that was bullshit. Olivia's hearing was better than any Amoveo's. Members of the Fox Clan had extremely acute hearing—the best of all ten clans— but not better than a vampire. She was just messing with Hayden, and he knew it.

"A Scotch," he seethed. "On the rocks."

"Are you sure you wouldn't like something with a little more *bite*?" Olivia's green eyes flicked down to Hayden's throat, which worked as he swallowed. "Our signature drink is very popular." Her grin broadened. "The Bloody Mary."

Hayden's lip curled in disgust, and sweat broke out on his brow. "Scotch."

"Of course." Olivia sighed and pushed herself off the table, while keeping her attention on Hayden. "I suppose there's no accounting for taste, but who am I to argue with the customer?" She flashed her fangs so quickly that Marianna almost missed it. However, based on Hayden's pasty complexion, he didn't. "I'll be right back," she said with a wink.

Hayden's energy signature calmed down as Olivia increased the distance between them and went behind the bar to collect his drink. Marianna studied him more

closely and scolded herself for not seeing it before. She
wondered how many other shifters were afraid of vampires like Hayden was. It made sense. Most prejudice
was rooted in fear, wasn't it?

"It's time to go, Marianna." Hayden threw a wad
of cash on the table. "This place is making me sick to
my stomach."

"You're welcome to leave anytime you like, but
I'm not going anywhere." He tried telepathy again,
but she held up a mental barrier to prevent it and
was certain that bothered him more than the ear-
shattering music. "Besides, Olivia will be back soon
with your Scotch."

"I ordered another just to get her the hell away from
me. I can't abide the stench of vampires." He looked at
his watch again, and she suppressed a smirk. Vampires
didn't smell bad. Maybe he was smelling his own fear?
"It's well after midnight, and we still haven't discussed
the subject at hand."

"There's nothing left to discuss." She sighed without
looking at him. "You aren't my mate, and I'm not yours,
so I don't know what else there is to talk about."

"Marianna," he growled. "This isn't just about us."

She let out a short laugh and shook her head. "There
is no *us*."

"You still haven't declared your allegiance to the
Purists," he said, ignoring her last comment. "My father
is losing patience. You are a high-ranking member of the
Bear Clan and served on the Council before it dissolved.
I don't understand what the holdup is." He waved at
Susie, the only human waitress at the club, but she
failed to see it, which increased his level of aggravation.

"Since you're obviously not siding with your brother and the rest of those human-loving traitors—"

"Don't," she ground out. Marianna leveled a deadly glare at him. The space suddenly felt too small, and if she didn't get control over her emotions, she was going to shift into her Kodiak bear form and tear off his head off right there in the middle of the club. "Don't you dare say a bad word about Dante. He is *not* a traitor, and you can tell your father that I said as much." Her dark eyes narrowed. "We may be part of the same clan, Hayden, but that doesn't mean much these days, now does it?"

"Really?" Hayden let out a harsh laugh. "Your brother is mated to a half-breed freak. He and the others like him are breeding human weakness into our race." He grabbed her upper arm, pulled her close, and growled into her ear. "Your father knew this and tried to wipe them out. He's dead because of the hybrids and the other Amoveo who have the nerve to call themselves Loyalists. How can you consider soiling the Coltari name any further?"

"Stop it." Marianna squeezed her eyes shut and flinched as his fingers dug into her bicep. He was as strong as he looked. She struggled to keep from letting him know how much he was hurting her. Causing her pain would only get him off. His Scotch-tainted breath puffed along her cheek and made her want to puke. "Get your hands off me," she hissed.

"Is there a problem?" Pete's voice washed over her, providing instant relief.

Marianna opened her eyes to find him standing at their table with a lethal stare locked on Hayden. His intense eyes, the ones that made her stomach flutter every time she looked into them, were fixed on Hayden, and he looked ready to pounce. His broad-shouldered frame cut an imposing figure and towered over them with surprising authority, especially since he was only a human.

Even if he weren't dressed in that dark gray suit, he still would've stuck out like a sore thumb at the nightclub. Pete Castro was strikingly handsome in a wholesome, Midwestern way and lacked the piercings and tattoos that covered most of the patrons. At the moment, he looked just like a cop, which wasn't all that surprising, because up until a couple of years ago, that's exactly what he had been.

"Ms. Coltari?" His lips barely moved, and if it weren't for her acute hearing, she wouldn't have heard him above the pulsing music. His eyes didn't move from Hayden's face. "I think it's time to leave."

"We'll leave whenever Marianna wants to," Hayden bit out as he met Pete's stony stare. He released Marianna from his grip and slipped his arm over her shoulders with unwarranted possessiveness. "Now, why don't you be a good boy, and go back and wait in the car like you're supposed to. You're her chauffeur, so run along, and she'll let you know when *we're* ready to go." He leaned back in the booth, picked up his empty glass, and waved it at Pete. "I requested another Scotch, but that *woman* seems to have gotten lost. Find out where my drink is on your way out, would you?"

"I'm fine, Pete." Marianna mustered up a smile, but Pete continued to stare down Hayden. She rubbed her arm as she glanced back and forth between the two men. Pete didn't flinch, but his energy waves, which were remarkably thick for a human, fluttered violently around them. He was one hundred percent tuned into Hayden. One of the girls at the club could've run past him stark naked, and the guy wouldn't have flinched.

"I think we should go." He turned those piercing blue eyes on her, and her stomach did that odd fluttery thing again. He must've sensed her apprehension because his features softened, and his energy waves shifted subtly. "I'm ready to take you home whenever you've had enough." He glanced at the empty champagne bottle on the table and then back at her.

The fluttering in her stomach was swiftly replaced by a knot of anger as he gave her a scolding look. What the hell? Yet another man who felt he had the right to judge her, tell her what to do, and monitor her choices? Apparently, Amoveo men hadn't cornered the market on being bossy and butting their noses into what doesn't concern them. Pete may be human, but he could be as alpha male and overbearing as all of the men in her clan put together.

She wondered whether he'd be this bold if he knew she could shapeshift into a bear and tear him a new one. She smirked. He was just a human, and if he knew what she was, he'd probably piss his pants.

"Really?" Marianna's eyes narrowed. She placed the champagne flute on the table and held his gaze as she slid to the edge of her seat. She smiled as she noticed his attention instantly went to her bare legs and admittedly short hemline. "Well, I'll be the judge of that—not you. My brother hired you to be my driver… not my babysitter."

"Yeah?" he scoffed harshly. "You could've fooled me."

She rose slowly from the table and stood to meet his

challenging gaze. She kept her eyes fixed firmly on his as she moved her body close, but he remained motionless. In her stilettos, she was just a few inches shorter than he was, and she noted that his heart beat faster as she closed the distance between them.

Her intent was to intimidate him and unnerve him, but something far more surprising happened.

Heat wafted from his muscular body and flowed over her erotically, which sent her heightened senses into overdrive. She took a deep breath to steady herself, but the instant his distinctly male scent filled her head—it had the exact opposite effect. Her eyes tingled, and she struggled to keep them from shifting into those of her Bear Clan. It was common for an Amoveo's eyes to shift into the eyes of their clan animal during moments of extreme emotion. Like lust. Red-hot, fuck-me-blind kind of lust.

Right now, Marianna was more turned on than she had ever been before. It was as though he was tuned directly into her energy, her soul, and her body. Suddenly and inexplicably, she was connected to this man—*this human*—more than she had been to any other creature she'd encountered.

For a second, she forgot where she was—where they were—and she had the ridiculous urge to kiss him. Forget that Hayden was sitting right next to them and would flip his lid—nothing mattered but the man standing in front of her and how he made her feel.

Her eyes wandered over the hard planes and angles of his face, his strong jawline with late-night stubble, the high cheekbones, and strong dark brows that framed those ice-blue eyes flawlessly. It seemed for a moment as if they were the only two people in the entire place.

All she could see was him.

Her body moved to the music, subtly at first, and willed her toward him almost imperceptibly. She inched nearer, until their lips were just a breath apart… and then she heard him.

What in the hell is this woman doing to me?

Marianna blinked, breaking the spell as the rest of the club and the crowd came roaring into focus. She stepped back as if he'd slapped her—and in a way he had. She'd heard his voice in her mind, which made absolutely no sense. Not only had she been actively shielding her mind to keep Hayden out of it—but Pete was human, and there was *no way* she should've heard him like that.

"I—I want to dance." Her confused eyes searched his equally befuddled ones as she backed away toward the dancing mob. "This is a nightclub after all," she shouted. Marianna strutted into the writhing crowd, hoping that neither Pete nor Hayden was aware of how rattled she was.

She threw her hands up and swayed to the beat amid the sea of bodies, but kept her sights fixed on Pete. A handsome, young human male sidled up behind her and began to bump and grind to the pulsating tune. Marianna danced with him as though she didn't have a care in the world, a facade she prayed that both Hayden and Pete would buy.

Pete glowered from his spot by the table as she dirty-danced with the stranger. Then he said something to Hayden, and he stalked out. Marianna watched him go and wondered if he even knew what he'd done. She'd heard his deep, gravelly voice in her mind, and he'd touched her in a way that only one person on the planet could… her mate.

Chapter 2

PETE STUFFED HIS HANDS INTO HIS SUIT PANTS POCKETS, wondering exactly why he gave a shit. He was only doing his job, and no job should be this goddamn irritating. His blood pressure rose by the second, and tension settled in his neck as one person after another stumbled out of the nightclub, all but the one he was looking for.

He was still fuming at the way she had dismissed him in the club earlier.

Pete swore under his breath and leaned against the black Mercedes as he continued to keep a lookout for his uncooperative charge.

"Any sign of her yet?" Pete called to the bouncer.

"Nope," Damien said in a deep baritone voice that rivaled James Earl Jones. He shrugged his bulky muscular shoulders. "But you know how Marianna is. She'll be in there until closing." He ran a hand over his head and grinned. "That girl can party like a rock star." He laughed. "She's an animal."

"You have no idea." Pete sighed and shook his head as the pedestrians brushed past him. It was almost two in the morning, but the city sidewalks were always bustling. He loosened his tie and undid the top button of the collar, which had been strangling him since he put it on. He hated wearing a tie. It was almost as irritating as this job.

Pete ran a hand through his short dark hair and let

out a slow breath, which puffed a cloud of mist into the crisp January night. No sense in trying to bullshit himself because it wasn't the job that was irritating. It was the woman at the center of the job who had the ability to piss him off more than anyone he'd ever met, and she stirred up other uncomfortable emotions that were less than professional.

When Dante had asked if he could look out for his twin sister and keep an eye on her while she was staying in New York, what the hell could he say? Dante was his boss, but he'd also turned into more of a friend, so obviously, his answer was going to be yes.

Keeping an eye on a regular guy's sister would be a no-brainer for any ex-cop, but Dante and his sister were anything but the usual folk. They were Amoveo— shapeshifters—and until a couple of months ago, he was like the rest of the human race and had no idea that they existed.

Sometimes he longed for that blissful ignorance.

He watched a few more clubgoers wander into the dark, city night. They had no idea that an ancient race of dream-walking, telepathic shapeshifters lived side by side with them right under their noses.

When Dante asked Pete to take on this glorified babysitting job, he neglected to mention how ridiculously hot his sister was. Hot wasn't adequate enough. The woman was stunning. Long, curly waves of espresso-colored hair almost perfectly matched the unique shade of brown in her hypnotic, almond-shaped eyes. Those eyes, the ones that seemed able to see right through him, made Pete more nervous than the fact that she could shift into a bear.

He'd been around plenty of beautiful women in his life. Hell, since working as a driver for Inferno Securities, he'd been exposed to some of the hottest women around, but none came close to turning him on like Marianna did. He wondered, more than once, if it was because she was Amoveo.

He'd met several Amoveo since he found out about their existence, and every one of them was gorgeous, so he figured Marianna would be as well. However, nothing could've prepared him for the lightning storm of lust that washed over him when he first laid eyes on her. The mere memory of that day sent blood rushing from his head to his crotch and made him hard as a rock. When her exotic brown eyes latched onto his, every coherent thought was driven from him, and all he could do was picture her long, curvy body wrapped around his.

The cell phone buzzed in the breast pocket of his jacket, tearing him from thoughts that were too dangerous to entertain. His face heated with embarrassment when he saw Dante's number scrolling across the screen.

"Shit." He knew Dante was telepathic, but he didn't know if that was the same thing as being a mind reader. If he could read his mind right now, he'd want to rip his head off for thinking dirty thoughts about his sister.

"Hey, boss." Pete cleared his throat, hoping like hell that his friend had zero idea what he'd been thinking. "What's up?"

"Where's Marianna?" Dante's curt voice cut through the line abruptly.

A tickle of awareness tripped up Pete's spine, and the all-too-familiar alarm bells started ringing in his mind. Call it a sixth sense or a hunch. He'd had it his whole life, but ever since he'd hooked up with the Amoveo, it had happened with far more frequency and intensity.

Something bad was coming.

"She's inside with that douche bag, Hayden."

"Hayden's at the club?" Dante asked with surprise.

"Yeah, why?" Pete stilled, but his gaze remained fixed on the door of the club. "What's going on?" Dread clawed at him.

"There have been rumblings from our informants that Artimus has Marianna at the top of some kind of acquisition list." Silence stretched for a beat or two. "Artimus is Hayden's father."

"I see." Pete continued tracking the entrance for any sign of Marianna. "What the hell is an acquisition list, and why is she on it? Do you think Hayden knows about it?"

"It looks like Artimus and the Purists have compiled a list of pure-blooded Amoveo who have yet to declare allegiance to either side. We have word that Marianna is at the top of that list, which is no surprise. She was a member of the Council before it dissolved, and it would be a real victory to have her side with him." He sighed heavily. "And yes. I'm sure that Hayden is privy to his father's business dealings. My guess is that he's doing his best to convince her to side with them."

"Artimus is part of the Grizzly Bear Clan right?" Pete's jaw clenched as he kept his voice low. The last thing he needed was someone to overhear his conversation. "Is there anything special that I should know about him or his clan? Aside, of course, from the fact that he can shapeshift into a grizzly bear, travel at the speed of thought, and break my neck like a twig?"

"No," Dante responded humorlessly. "Except that he'll stop at nothing to get my sister to side with him, especially because she is part of the Bear Clan. Granted, she's descended from the Kodiak Bear Clan, which is a different branch, but at this point it's semantics."

"He won't touch her." Pete adjusted the gun holstered discreetly beneath his jacket. "If I remember correctly, you shapeshifter boys may be tough, but you're still not bulletproof," he said wryly.

"No, still not bulletproof." Dante laughed. "I just wanted to give you a heads-up. I'd like to go over a few more things, so come by our place tomorrow afternoon before you pick up Marianna for the benefit at the Waldorf, okay?"

"Consider it done, boss."

"Hey Pete, she's not giving you a bad time is she?"

"Not really. It was definitely a smart idea to let her think I don't know about the Amoveo and that I'm just another clueless human. Otherwise, every time I annoy her, she'd pull that disappearing act you guys can do." He sighed loudly and muttered "Or shapeshift into a bear and kick my ass."

"Agreed." Dante laughed.

"See you tomorrow." Pete hit the end button and slipped the phone back in his pocket as a familiar feminine laugh captured his attention.

He looked up to see a rather tipsy Marianna being escorted out of the club by the owner, Olivia Hollingsworth. Pete eyed the tall redhead warily. There was something off about this chick, but he couldn't put his finger on it. She wasn't an Amoveo, not a pure-blood like Marianna or a hybrid like Dante's wife Kerry, but she was definitely not a normal person.

She made him uncomfortable and gave him an overall hinky feeling.

However, as she helped Marianna out of the club and over to the car, he couldn't deny that she was good people. She might have a weird vibe, but it wasn't dark or evil… it was just *different*. Marianna was draped over her like a limp noodle, and it looked like she was only staying on her feet because of Olivia's assistance. Her dress, or the small scrap of fabric she called a dress, was riding up to dangerous heights. Her bright red coat had fallen off, or never been put on quite right in the first place, exposing her smooth bare shoulders to the winter air.

"You're going to sleep well tonight," Olivia said quietly. She turned her sharp green eyes to Pete. "You're gonna have to walk her up to her apartment."

"Oh, he's such a poop." Marianna giggled and attempted to pull her coat on properly. "He's so fucking serious and doesn't ever want to have any fun." She pushed a mass of dark, wavy locks off her face and narrowed her eyes at Pete. "You and Dante are always taking the *F* out of fun. Isn't that right?" she asked, waving her manicured hand in his face.

Before Pete could respond, she swayed forward and would've fallen on her face if he and Olivia hadn't been there to keep her upright. Pete looped one arm around her waist and gave a nod to Olivia. "I got her," he said.

She allowed all her weight to lean into him and

hooked her arms around his neck so that her lips were inches from his. He was just over six feet tall, and those ridiculously high heels she wore made her almost his height, which was a turn on. He liked women with some meat on their bones, and this beauty fit the bill.

He held her under her arms, attempting to put some kind of distance between her body and his—but no such luck. That luscious fragrance she wore, the one that smelled of peaches, wafted off her skin and filled his nostrils like it had in the club earlier tonight. He tightened his grip, telling himself it was so he could keep her from falling on her ass, but the truth was he wanted to get closer.

Much closer.

He glanced at those full, red lips and couldn't think of anything but tasting them. It had taken herculean strength not to kiss her earlier when she'd brushed her long, lush body against him—almost daring him to try. Her pink tongue darted out and moistened that gorgeous mouth as if in invitation. God, he wanted her, and if he leaned down just a bit more…

What was he thinking? Pete yanked his head back.

The woman was drunk as a skunk. Trying to kiss her now wouldn't *only* be unprofessional, but it would be a total scumbag move to try something while she's shit-faced and he's stone-cold sober.

"Pete," Marianna whispered. "Take me home please." Her voice, almost childlike, was edged with desperation. Her dark brown eyes, tinged with sadness, latched onto his. "I need to go home."

His gut clenched at the needy edge to her voice. "Yes, you do." Pete softened his grip and nodded curtly.

"Come on. In you go," he said as he helped her into the backseat and closed the door behind her.

"She's a hot mess," Olivia said bluntly.

Anger flared, and his protective instincts kicked into overdrive. Who the hell did this chick think she was? She had some goddamn nerve talking about Marianna that way. Fuming, Pete turned to give the weird broad a piece of his mind, but the look of sadness on her face stopped him cold. She looked at Marianna with pity.

"I care about her too, you know." She crossed her arms over her chest. "We've been friends for a long time, and I've never seen her behave this way."

"What?" He stuffed his hands in his pockets, feeling uncomfortable by the fact that she'd seen right through him. She knew how he felt about Marianna. Shit. Was he that transparent? Pete cleared his throat and decided to ignore the first part of her comment. "Are you kidding me? Dante said she's the original party girl, and based on what I've seen, he's right."

"I'm not talking about the clubbing or even the drinking." Olivia shook her head. "She's acting like someone who has nothing left to lose." Her gaze flicked back to the car, and her voice softened. "That's a dangerous way to live."

Before he could respond, an angry male voice cut into their conversation.

"Where the hell did she go?"

Pete looked over to see Damien trying to restrain the guy. It didn't take more than two seconds for Pete to realize it was Hayden, the Amoveo dickhead from earlier. Instinctively, he reached inside his jacket for his gun even though it was unlikely he'd pull it out. It made him feel better to have the cold steel beneath his fingers while he stared down a guy who could shapeshift into a grizzly bear. Truthfully, he reminded Pete more of a snake.

Olivia let out an exasperated sigh and turned to deal with the ruckus developing outside her club. "Let him go, Damien," she said with surprising authority. "Hayden, what exactly is the problem?"

Damien released Hayden, who immediately muttered something rude, but Damien smirked and maintained his post by the door. Hayden straightened his jacket and smoothed back the strands of brown hair that had fallen over his face. Pete's bad-vibe hunch was back in full force as he recalled the acquisition list Dante mentioned. He kept his sharp sights set on Hayden but didn't move one inch from the car door. There was no way he was getting anywhere near Marianna again.

"I'll tell you what the problem is," he spat. "I buy her drinks all night long, she dances with everyone but me, and as soon as I go to the men's room, she cuts and runs. Not even so much as a good-bye." He slipped leather gloves out of his pocket and put them on hands that looked like they'd never seen a hard day's work. "Where I come from, that's bad manners."

"Yeah," Pete interjected. "Where I come from, it means you're not getting laid."

Olivia stifled a giggle and gave Pete a look of approval.

Hayden, who up until this point had been completely ignoring Pete, turned his beady eyes right to him. "Really? Well it's a good thing we aren't cut from the same cloth." He sniffed and looked Pete up and down as if he were dog shit on the heel of his expensive shoes. "When Marianna sobers up"—he glanced at the car and sneered—"tell her that I'll see her at the fundraiser tomorrow night at the Waldorf. We'll continue our discussion then." Without another word he turned and walked away.

"Don't bet on it, you smug asshole," Pete murmured as he watched the scumbag disappear around the corner. "You know that guy?" he asked Olivia.

"No. I just met him tonight, and I only know what Marianna told me. He's been trying to get her to hook up with him, but she's not interested. I've never seen a guy try so damn hard after a woman has made it abundantly clear that she wants nothing to do with him. I asked her why she doesn't just tell him to get lost, and she said something about not wanting to pick a fight or some nonsense like that."

Pete knew exactly what kind of *nonsense* Marianna was talking about, and that bad feeling was growing by the second. Could it be possible that Hayden was her mate? Was she actually supposed to… he didn't finish the thought or couldn't. Either way, he would be damned if he let her get mixed up with a shit bag like that.

"Yeah." Pete shrugged and fished the keys out of his pocket. "Well, you know how Marianna can be."

"Mmm-hmmm," Olivia murmured and walked to the door of the club. Before she went inside she threw one last comment over her shoulder. "She can be a real bear."

Pete stood in the open door of the driver's side and watched Olivia and Damien go into the club. He couldn't help but wonder if good old Olivia knew more than she was letting on.

———

He pulled up in front of Marianna's brownstone on 89th Street, and much to his surprise, she was awake. She'd been dead silent the entire ride home, and the few times he'd glanced in the rearview mirror, she looked completely passed out. Pete got out and opened the door for her and told himself that he was only opening it because it was part of his job—but that was a lot of crap.

He did it because it was the gentlemanly thing to do, and he couldn't help but hear his grandmother's voice in his head. *A real man always opens a door for a lady.* She'd been gone for over ten years, but her voice was still there. Pete wondered what his grandmother would say if she knew this lady could change into a bear. Would the rule still apply?

Every single thought was driven from him as a pair of long, shapely legs slid through the open door, and her stiletto-clad feet rested on the curb. He extended a hand as his gaze wandered leisurely from the tips of her black painted toenails, along the curve of her calf, all the way up her firm looking thighs, and finally landing on the hem of that barely there, little black dress. His mouth went dry, and his cock twitched as every cell of his body tuned into hers.

He was in an enormous amount of trouble.

"It's as I suspected." Her voice ripped him from his thoughts, and he forced himself to look her in the face. Her eyes smiled mischievously as she slipped her warm hand into his. "You're a leg man."

"What?" Pete blinked. He tightened his grip on her fingers and stepped aside so she could get out of the car. He cursed himself for getting busted ogling her like some kind of horny kid. What the hell was the matter with him? "No," he added quickly, as he looked away. "I was just wondering how it is that you're not freezing your ass off in that dress."

"I'm warm-blooded. The cold doesn't faze me in the least." She stood on surprisingly steady feet as he helped her from the car. Twenty minutes ago she'd been stumbling drunk, and now she's stone-cold sober? Perhaps she wasn't as drunk as she let on.

Interesting.

"Uh-huh." Pete narrowed his eyes and looked her up and down.

"Walk me up to my apartment?" A smile played at her lips as she sashayed to the steps of her building.

Pete shut the car door and joined her at the foot of the steps as he surveyed the surroundings. It was the cop in him. He never could breathe easy, especially in a city like New York. However, at the moment, everything looked clear, and there wasn't a soul on the street except the two of them. Why would there be? This Upper West Side neighborhood may have been one of the only areas in the city that wasn't still populated at three in the morning. However, if the Purists really wanted to get to her, they could blink their asses here in a matter of seconds—hence the gun.

He caught her studying him with an impish smile. She linked her arm through his and peered at him with a look that screamed trouble—and sex. Pete swallowed the lump in his throat and willed himself to keep his hands in his pockets.

"C'mon," she whispered. "You're my bodyguard and my chauffeur. You have to guard my body and chauffeur me all the way to my apartment."

Pete cleared his throat and started up the steps with her delicate arm still linked through his. He said nothing as she keyed into the building, and they walked up one flight to her apartment. For a brief second, he wished it was a fifth floor walk-up, just so he would have an excuse to keep her body brushing against his for a little while longer. He tried to keep his mind on the job and to remember that this woman's safety was his job—and that she's his buddy's sister.

You don't nail your buddy's sister. It's unbreakable guy code.

Her hip bumped enticingly into his as they climbed the last couple of steps at the top. Pete used every ounce of willpower to keep from looking at her legs or her spectacular cleavage. Sweat broke out on his forehead, and he tried to think of something else—anything else—except the woman on his arm.

"You know," she sighed as she slid the key into the lock of her apartment door, "you've been driving me around town for the past two months, but I don't think you've ever been inside my apartment."

"Nope." Pete stepped back, kept his hands in his pockets and both eyes on her. What was she up to? First she pretends to be wasted and bails out on that Hayden guy, and now, she's hitting on him. What is her endgame with this?

Marianna flipped the lock and arched one eyebrow. "Care to break that streak tonight?"

He swallowed the urge to scream, *hell yes*, and instead bit out, "I don't think so." Pete shook his head even though his body was screaming yes.

"Are you sure?" she asked as she grabbed his tie and

twirled it playfully around one finger. Her large dark eyes clapped onto his. She tugged the annoying garment and pulled him closer.

"Yes," he whispered. Pete willed his body not to move, to be strong and hold his ground, but it was no use.

The enticing scent of peaches wafted over Pete as she held him captive. His hands curled into fists in his pockets as he struggled to keep from touching her and resisted the urge to lace his fingers through that silky looking hair. Pete bit back the driving need to taste her. His entire body hummed with arousal and awareness as the heat from her body radiated along his.

Her mouth hovered dangerously close, and her eyes glinted back with the unmistakable glaze of desire. It would be so easy to dip lower and take just one taste.

"Come inside," she whispered.

Everything seemed to move in slow motion, and somewhere in that odd displacement of time and space, his mouth settled over hers. A rush of sweetness flooded him as her lush, gorgeous lips fused with his.

She tasted like peaches too… and champagne.

Marianna ran her tongue along his. He yanked his hands from his pockets and slipped his fingers into that long wavy hair that did indeed feel like silk. He moaned as she linked her arms around his neck and pulled him closer. Devouring her lips, Pete pinned her against the door and drank greedily from her soft, pliant mouth. Her full breasts crushed against his chest, and all he could think about was getting closer.

His body, taut with desire, sensed every single spot where her heated skin touched his. However, amid the haze of lust he heard the voice of reason screaming at him to stop, listing all the reasons why he definitely shouldn't be doing this.

She's your friend's sister.

She's Amoveo, and you're human.

She's got some predestined shapeshifter mate out there, and you're not it.

She can't ever be yours.

"I can't do this," he murmured against her lips.

Pete squeezed his eyes shut and leaned his forehead against hers. Breathing heavily, he pulled her arms from around his neck and stepped away. But as her hands slipped from his, he noticed with more than a little disappointment how quickly cold replaced warmth. Her tousled hair that just seconds ago had been tangled between his fingers spilled over her bare shoulders as she looked at him through confused eyes.

He wondered if she could sense his heart pounding. It felt like it was about to burst through his rib cage, and the wounded expression on her face only made it beat harder.

"Fine," she seethed. Hurt and embarrassment flickered over her features as she turned her attention back to the keys dangling from the door. She looked at him like she wanted to kill him, or at the very least, kick him in the shin. "Forget it."

"Shit." Pete sighed in frustration and ran his hands over his face. "It's not that I don't want to, believe me," he said softly. "But half an hour ago, you were completely shit-faced and hanging out with some other guy at the club."

His jaw clenched as he fought for a plausible reason as to why he wouldn't take her in that apartment and feast on that gorgeous body until sunrise. The truth was that all he wanted to do was spend the rest of the night showing her just how badly he wanted her, but that simply wasn't in the cards.

"Forgive me if I don't shift gears as quickly as you do," he snapped. Looking into her stormy eyes, a potent mixture of pent-up lust and frustration boiled over and made him sound harsher than he intended. "Besides, I don't think Dante would appreciate it."

It was a low blow to turn the tables, but he needed to find a way to put out the flames as quickly as possible, and ticking her off seemed like the most efficient way.

It was a shitty thing to do, and he knew it.

"Typical." Marianna glared at him through furious eyes. "First of all, that guy at the club is a *complete* asshole, and I pretended to be drunker than I was, so I could get out of there and get away from him. Secondly, you have done nothing but ogle me and flirt with me from the moment you laid eyes on me, so don't act innocent and shocked by my proposal." She poked him in the chest with one finger, which hurt more than he expected. "And lastly, my brother doesn't get one damn bit of say about who I bring into my apartment or my bed."

Pete opened his mouth to say something, but Marianna slammed the door in his face before he could say anything else. Nothing killed a hard-on like having a door slammed in your face—except maybe that wounded look in her eye when he rejected her.

Pete swore under his breath and headed back downstairs. He needed a cold shower and a few hours of sleep before he'd have the strength to face her again. He wasn't sure if she'd cool off anytime soon, but there was one thing he knew with absolute certainty… now that he'd had a taste of her, he only wanted more.

Chapter 3

THE INDIGO AND SILVER HAZE OF THE DREAM REALM surrounded her like a warm blanket, but this time it was different because she wasn't alone. Marianna wandered through the fog of the dream realm, as she'd done count-less nights before, but tonight another energy signature permeated the air.

Pete was here.

Her heart raced as dozens of questions swarmed her mind, but her volatile stream of emotions made the fog thicken and the colors pulse vibrantly. She stood for a moment, struggling to get her bearings amid the swirling clouds.

All Amoveo walked the dream realm in search of their predestined mates because the spiritual connection was a crucial part of the mating process. She'd spent endless hours searching for that one person the universe selected for her, and she had practically given up...but he was here.

Marianna closed her eyes and sent her own energy signature, her spiritual fingerprint, in search of his, hoping she could pinpoint where he was.

In the club, she'd heard his voice clearly in her mind, but she suspected he had no idea what he'd done. He didn't know what she was or that the Amoveo existed, so how could he possibly be aware of how significant that telepathic contact was?

What puzzled her most was why hadn't it happened sooner. She'd spent a good deal of time with him over the past two months, so why now? If he really were her mate, then why wouldn't the connection have been made when they first met?

Frustration clawed at her. She shook her head, trying to clear out the confusion and litany of questions, and refocused her energy on finding him. If Pete were her mate, whether he was human or Amoveo, they would have to connect in the dream realm. The mental connection was more crucial than the physical one.

Physical? Damn it. That's about all she could think of since that kiss. Her mind wandered to the sinful taste of him, and she bit her lip. He tasted like a warm summer night. Hot. Desperate. Urgent. Intense. Over far too soon.

Her plan was to kiss him and prove that this man, this human, couldn't possibly be her mate. However, the instant his mouth touched hers, she knew that he was. There was no denying it, but she still couldn't wrap her brain around it.

Her mate was human.

She knew that the only way to absolutely, positively prove it once and for all would be to find him in the dream realm. Hybrids could dream-walk, at least that's what she'd heard from her brother. But she'd never heard of a human dream-walking before.

What the fuck is going on? Who's there?

The deep timbre of his voice cut through the cobalt-hued mist that pulsed and rippled. Marianna's heart raced as his mind connected with hers. The fog dissipated, and in seconds the dreamscape clearly revealed itself—but it was not at all what she was expecting.

The realm she stood in wasn't created by her. For the first time, she'd been pulled into someone else's dream plane—Pete's.

They stood in a heavily wooded area, which reminded Marianna of the Catskills, where her brother had a cabin. The impossibly tall pine trees were dappled with snow, which continued to fall around them in fat, lazy snowflakes, and Pete stood in the middle, looking bewildered. Clad in jeans and a plaid flannel shirt, with an ax in his hand, he looked like a lumberjack. The poor guy gaped as if she'd materialized out of thin air—which she probably had as far as he was concerned.

His dark eyebrows flew up, and a smile cracked his handsome face, as he looked her up and down. Now this is what I call a dream. *He swung the ax, lodged it in the hunk of wood he'd been chopping, and stalked slowly toward her, but she held her ground, uncertain of how to handle the situation.*

When, exactly, was she supposed to tell him what she was? Or what they were to each other? Is she supposed to just blurt it out in the middle of a dream? Probably not. Wouldn't he simply dismiss it as only a dream? Why didn't all this mate crap come with instructions?

Pete closed the distance between them until his body was just inches from hers. His heated gaze skimmed her up and down as his thick energy signature circled her like a rope and willed her closer. It was even stronger here in the dream realm and more intoxicating as well. She almost felt stoned and willed herself not to jump his bones like the sex-starved woman she was.

Really? *Marianna cocked one eyebrow.* What does that mean? I'm the woman of your dream or something like that? *she asked playfully, realizing that this defi-nitely wasn't the time to tell him who she was. She de-cided to let him take the lead and see where things went.* So now that you have me here in your dreams, what are you going to do with me?

Pete trailed one finger up her bare arm. Anything I want, I suppose, *he murmured seductively. Marianna shuddered and let out a sigh as his skin sizzled along hers. He slipped his fingers beneath the thin strap of her nightgown and brushed his thumb along her col-larbone, all the while never taking his eyes off hers.* But you know what I really want?

No, this is your dream... so why don't you tell me?

I want to know what turns you on. *He caressed the sensi-tive skin along her neck as he whispered to her.* Tell me.

A smile crept over Marianna's face, and her libido went into overdrive. He wanted to know what turned her on? He was more concerned about her needs and desires, even though this was his dream. Now that was sexy... and the answer was simple.

You, *she breathed.* The way you look at me. It's as if you can see right through me, and somehow, I know that even if I wanted to hide from you—I couldn't.

Marianna licked her lower lip as her eyes wandered over the hard planes of his face. Goddamn she wanted him, and if he didn't make a move soon, dream or no dream, she was going to lose her senses and maul him. But since one rejection a night was all her ego could take, she let him maintain control.

You're right, *he whispered.* I do see you. *Pete slipped his arm around her waist and tugged her up against his rock-hard frame.* You're the most spectacular woman I've ever laid my eyes on. You're gorgeous, tough as nails, smart, and you don't take crap from anyone. *He pushed the strap of her nightgown down, traced the curve of her shoulder, and blazed a trail of kisses along her throat.* I know the secrets you keep, Marianna, *he said between kisses.* I know what's underneath this satiny skin.

You do, do you? *Amused and turned on, Marianna arched back, allowing him access to the sensitive skin. Her eyes fluttered closed as she sank into his firm embrace. The snow fell gently, and Marianna could swear she heard it sizzle as it hit her heated skin. Her hands found their way underneath his shirt, and she ran her nails along his lower back.* So, what is it that you see?

Pete kissed his way back up her neck and nibbled on her ear, but before he could answer her, the low, menacing growl of a bear rumbled through the dream realm. Pete spun around and instinctively shielded Marianna's body with his. What the hell? *He glanced over his shoulder at her.* That's some rotten timing.

Marianna clung tightly to him as a pair of familiar, glowing black eyes glared back from the shadows of the trees. Only one person had ever looked at her with such unmistakable disdain—Artimus.

His massive furred body lumbered out of the shadows while keeping that deadly glare locked on Pete. His clawed paws left craterlike footprints in the once pristine snow, and his dark energy signature soiled the serenity of the realm.

Before she could utter a word, Artimus stood on his hind legs and bellowed triumphantly into the air. To Pete it was just a bear in his dream, but Marianna knew it meant far more—Artimus was gloating. He'd invaded Pete's dream realm with ease, and Marianna knew that if Pete were attacked in the dream plane, he wouldn't have a fighting chance.

A mortal wound in the dream meant he was a dead man.

Holy shit, *Pete said under his breath.* I know this is only a dream, but that is one big goddamn bear.

You have to wake up, Pete. *Marianna gripped his arms and shook him.* Right now!

Artimus bellowed louder, but Pete laughed. It's only a dream. Right, Yogi? *He laughed harder.* Where's Boo Boo?

Marianna spun him to face her. I mean it, Pete. Wake up! *She glanced at Artimus, who had dropped to all fours and was advancing with slow, deliberate steps. Fear clogged her throat, and she shook him harder.* Wake up, you stubborn son of a bitch!

Artimus growled louder and started running toward them. In one last-ditch effort, Marianna hauled off and slapped Pete across the face as hard as she could. Wake up, *she screamed.*

The mist swept in and swallowed Pete's shocked face from her sight. Shaking with fear, relief, and fury, she searched the swirling clouds for Artimus. Come out, you coward. How dare you try to assassinate a human in the dream realm?

I came out tonight looking for you, but imagine my surprise to find a human man here with you? *His gravelly voice barreled around her like a storm.* I am wondering how it's possible that you're dream-walking with a human? How and why?

Silence surrounded her as Artimus's question hung in the air. Panic swamped her. He knew. Artimus knew that Pete was her mate, and he was going to kill him—dream or no dream. She had to say or do something, something to make him think that Pete was of no importance to her.

He's just some clueless human that works for Dante. He's been insisting I have him around, but I can't imagine why. I was curious to see what a human's dream might be like, so I did a little peeking. *She kept her voice light and playful, hoping to keep him away from the truth.* You went to all this trouble to come and find me in the dream realm, so why are you hiding? What's the matter, afraid to face me?

Don't flatter yourself, Marianna. *His rumbling baritone filled her mind, but he remained hidden.* And if you think, for one minute, that I don't believe that human is important to you, then you're not as smart as I thought you were. One more word of advice, I think it would be wise not to dream-walk with this human. It won't end well for either of you.

Is that a threat? *she shouted to the blackening clouds, hoping her fear wasn't as obvious to him as it was to her.*

No, my dear. You know as well as I do that it's simply the truth. *A gritty laugh rolled around her as she spun in circles, struggling to find him in the stormy realm.* I'm two hundred years old, and killing you would be as easy as breathing. I have far more *productive* plans in mind.

Thunder rolled and lightning flared in the gray clouds as his energy signature vanished in a blink. Standing alone amid the now-empty dream plane, Marianna shuddered at Artimus's ominous message. She didn't know what the sick bastard had in mind, but she was relatively certain it was a fate worse than death.

———∙∙∙∙∙———

Pete snagged the gun from under his pillow, sat straight up in bed, and pointed it at every corner of the studio apartment. Blinking the sweat from his eyes, and breathing like he just ran a marathon, he scanned the messy space as though his life depended on it.

Nothing. No woods. No fucking bears, and unfortunately, no Marianna.

He let out a long breath, flipped the safety back on his Beretta, and flopped onto his rumpled bed with a combination of relief and embarrassment. He hadn't had a nightmare like that since he was a kid, and it would be fine and fucking dandy if he never had another one like it again.

A smile crept over his face as he remembered the beginning of the dream. Well, he thought, the first half was great, and the whole thing was on a fast track to one sexy-ass dream—until that stupid bear showed up. He frowned. Why would he do that? Why would his subconscious sabotage such a hot dream about Marianna with a bear?

"Probably because you know she's an Amoveo in the Bear Clan, and you can't have her," he said out loud. "Must be some kind of self-preservation mechanism or something, but it still sucks, and now I'm talking to myself."

Pete glanced at the clock and swore loudly. It was almost noon, which meant he'd practically slept the day away. What the hell was wrong with him?

He put the gun on his nightstand, swung his legs over the side of the bed, and rubbed his face in an effort to wake up. He winced and touched the left side of his face.

His cheek was tender from where Marianna had slapped him in the dream, and if he didn't know better, he'd think she'd smacked him for real.

Pete rubbed the early morning scruff along his jaw, grabbed a probably dirty towel from the chair, and made his way into the tiny bathroom. He glanced at the tuxedo in the plastic rental bag that hung from his closet door and grimaced. Putting on that monkey suit for the benefit at the Waldorf was going to suck—he'd almost prefer to get smacked. A grin cracked his face as he turned on the shower, *especially by Marianna*.

—⁓—

Pete rode the elevator up to Dante and Kerry's penthouse apartment and tugged at the collar of the tuxedo shirt. He could swear the bloody thing had gotten tighter by the second, or maybe it was his guilty conscience that was strangling him. He'd not only made out with Dante's twin sister, but he'd also had a dirty dream about her, and hadn't been able to think about anything else since he woke up. He'd tried everything. A cold shower. A five-mile run. Another cold shower—but nothing worked.

He couldn't get away from the taste of her. Peaches and champagne lingered along the edge of his senses since that kiss last night. *That kiss*. Holy hell, all he'd done was kiss her, but it felt like she'd put him under some kind of spell, and the only thing he could think about was *her*.

The ding of the elevator brought him back to reality and the foyer of Dante and Kerry's spacious penthouse apartment. Grateful to find the hallway empty, he willed himself to think about something other than Marianna. He opened the white-paneled French doors at the end of the hall and found Dante and Kerry snuggled up together on the red sofa.

"Jesus," he teased with a big smile. "Don't you two ever stop mauling each other?"

"Pete!" Kerry's face turned as red as their sofa as she sat up and straightened her long ebony hair.

"We didn't hear you come in," Dante said quickly.

"I'm not surprised." He smiled and sat in the over-sized chair across from them.

"You look absolutely gorgeous." She whistled and wiggled her eyebrows as Dante pulled her into the crick of his arm. "You clean up very well. Maybe you should wear tuxedos more often."

"Yeah, well, I feel like a waiter."

Kerry laughed loudly and hopped off the couch. "I'm going to grab a glass of wine. Would you like some?"

"No thanks." He waved. "I'm driving."

"Of course, be right back." She sauntered toward the kitchen and threw a wink to her husband as she disappeared around the corner.

"She's right," Dante said as he looked at Pete more intently than usual. "You seem… different."

"It's the tux," Pete said abruptly. He pulled at the stupid collar again and adjusted his position in the chair. He was busted. Dante knew something was going on. "You know I hate wearing these things."

"Mmm-hmm." Dante narrowed his eyes and studied him. "It's more than that. Did something happen with Marianna?"

"Like what?" Pete started to sweat.

"I'm not sure," Dante said quietly. "But I'm getting the sense there's something going on that you're not telling me." He leaned both elbows on his knees and peered at Pete over laced fingers. "Your energy signature is practically nonexistent, invisible almost. Yours has always been unusually strong for a human, but now, it's almost gone."

"Don't ask me. Energy-whatever-you-call-them, are your specialty. Not mine." Pete shrugged and desperately wanted to change the subject. "You said that you wanted to talk to me about something. Did you find out anything else about this list that Marianna is on?"

"Not exactly." Dante shook his head and sat back, but didn't take his sharp eyes off of Pete. "However, I am concerned that Hayden is so persistent in his pursuit of Marianna. He even went to that club. He and Artimus are getting bolder, and that worries me."

"Yeah, well, they're both going to be at the benefit tonight." Pete's gut clenched, and those all too familiar alarm bells started ringing again.

"I know." Dante grabbed a folder off the table and handed it to Pete. "Pictures of Artimus, Hayden, and few other Purists from the Council. I included a list of the top clan members who have declared themselves Purists."

Pete flipped through the folder and stopped at Hayden's picture. "This guy is bad news. I don't like the way he speaks to Marianna. The son of a bitch acts like he owns her or something," he bit out. Pete knew he sounded like a jealous lover, but he didn't care. All he cared about was Marianna's safety.

Dante leaned back and smiled. "I dare him to try. My sister is not a woman who would allow herself to be owned by anyone. I pity the bastard who attempts it," he said with a laugh. "If her mate ever does turn up, the poor guy has his work cut out for him. I tease Marianna that maybe he did find her, but decided she was too much of an unpredictable handful and split."

"Uh-huh." Pete tried to ignore Dante's comments about Marianna's mate. The mere idea of another man touching her made him want to punch someone's lights out.

"She can't get out of her own way sometimes." The smile faded from Dante's lips. "I am particularly worried about the latest development."

"What is it?"

"We have at least five more pure-blood females who have gone missing—all from different clans and all un-mated." He ran a hand over his tired face. "One is a friend of Marianna's from grade school—Courtney Bishop. She's a member of the Coyote Clan. She disappeared a few days ago. Like Marianna, she never declared a side. Her family hasn't been able to find her anywhere. Her energy signature has vanished, and they can't connect with her telepathically."

"I see," Pete said grimly. He tried to squelch that bad feeling, but it only grew stronger. "Could she be dead?"

"No." Dante shook his head. "When one of us dies, our energy signature flashes brightly, and it's sensed by our family members. It's like a bolt of lightning that goes directly to the hearts of those you're most connected with." His features darkened. "I felt it for the first time when my father was killed."

"I see." Pete kept his attention on the contents of the folder, knowing that Dante wouldn't want to linger on unpleasant memories. "Were these women on this acquisition list you're referring to?"

"Yes." Dante nodded and pointed to the folder. "The missing women's pictures are in the back of that folder, and I want to be sure we don't add Marianna to this group."

"Not gonna happen." Pete flipped the folder open on the table and looked through the photos as he wrestled with his anger. "You think Artimus and the Purists are behind their disappearances?" He locked eyes with Dante. "Don't you?"

"Yes," Dante replied grimly. "But I can't for the life of me figure out why they'd target these women. By the way, don't tell Marianna about this. I'd rather not worry her more than necessary."

"What's this?" Pete asked, pulling out a list of names. He didn't relish the idea of keeping anything else from Marianna. He already felt like a shit for pretending that he didn't know about the Amoveo.

"It's a list of Amoveo men who mated with and had children with human women. As far as we can tell, the numbers indicate how many children they had, and we think the initials are the states they were raised in. For example, Kerry's father's name is there, and it has a one and R.I. next to it. She's an only child, and she grew up in Rhode Island. The same pattern fits for Samantha and Layla, who are both hybrids as you know."

"I see," Pete said quietly as he studied the list. "I'm not sure what use it is to me."

"I just want you to have as much information as possible while you keep an eye on Marianna. Artimus is far less likely to make a scene around humans, so I'll feel much better knowing that you've got her back."

"If Artimus and Hayden really want to get to her, they'll find a way." Pete closed the folder and leveled a serious gaze at Dante. "I think we should get her the hell out of the city. It's too difficult to protect her here. There are too many nooks and crannies where one of these bastards can hide. Besides, they can blink in and out of any place that they fucking want." Anger and resentment flared fast. He hated feeling like he was somehow handicapped against these guys, but he was.

"We had one of our elders place a shield around Marianna's apartment building," Dante said seriously. "No one can use their visualization skills to enter, except for her. So we know she's safe in her apartment."

"Great," Pete bit out. "What about the stuffy-ass event tonight? Any *shields* going on over there?"

"No." Dante shook his head. "I wasn't planning on attending the event tonight, but maybe Kerry and I should go."

"Not necessary." Pete shook his head and took a small plastic tube out of his pants pocket. He held it up and smiled. "I've got a backup plan."

"Is that what I think it is?" he asked warily.

"Yes sir," Pete said with more than a little satisfaction. He wiggled the small bottle, full of the precious silver powder. "I got myself some binding powder."

"Well, I'll be damned." Dante laughed loudly and pointed at his friend. "I knew I liked you for a reason."

"What?" Kerry asked as she came back in and handed Dante a glass of red wine. "What reason? Well, of course, aside from because he's one of the only humans on the planet who know about the Amoveo?" Kerry resumed her place on the sofa next to her husband.

"Pete is one of the smartest and prepared men I know. Which is exactly why I hired him," Dante said as he draped one arm over his wife's shoulders.

Kerry sipped her wine and glanced at the bottle Pete was holding. "Is that what I think it is?"

"Yes," he said as he slipped it back into his pocket. "This silver powder will bind a shifter in their *human* form for one month with no other powers. No shifting, no telepathy. Zip. Supposedly it makes a shifter a regular person for about a month. This is only for emergencies anyway, but I'll tell ya, I feel better just having it in my pocket. It's kind of like having my gun." He adjusted the weapon under his jacket. "I'd rather have it and not need it, than need it and not have it."

"Are you sure you don't want us to go with you to-night?" Dante asked again.

"Absolutely." Pete tried not to let his pride and ego take over, but he wasn't having much luck. He may not be some supernatural being, but he was a damn good cop, and he wasn't going to let either Hayden or Artimus get their hands on Marianna. "I don't think they're going to try anything in the middle of the Waldorf Astoria, and if they do, they're going to get a face full of this shit or some lead in their ass."

"Understood," Dante said firmly. "I'll let you know when I hear more about this list that Artimus has put together. Prince Richard has an informant in Artimus's camp. He won't tell any of us who it is, but this individual is gathering information. From what I understand, this person can rarely use telepathy to contact Richard for fear of being discovered, so the information is coming in small doses." Dante smiled at Kerry. "But at least that's something."

"Good." Pete stood from the chair and saw Kerry looking at him curiously. He cleared his throat and looked away. "I better get going. Marianna will be pissed if I'm late."

He suspected that Kerry knew something was up. If he didn't get out of here soon, he would confess everything and risk getting fired or getting his ass kicked. Neither sounded appealing.

"Take good care of her, Pete, and watch your back. She's a member of the Bear Clan, and they're known for their unpredictable behavior." He shook his head. "You never know what she's going to do."

Pete started to go, but stopped short. "Wait a second. I thought you two were twins. Why isn't she a fox like you are?"

"My mother is from the Fox Clan, and my father was from the Bear Clan. We don't know which clan our children will favor until they go through puberty."

"Lovely," Kerry mused. "As if puberty isn't crappy enough."

"Huh." Pete shook his head and chuckled. "You Amoveo are full of surprises." He turned on his heels and headed out. "I'll call you tomorrow and let you know how it went," Pete said.

Kerry followed him into the hallway. The penthouse elevator was open and waiting for him, as if conspiring to help him escape.

Pete stepped into the elevator, hoping to make a quick exit, but Kerry threw one arm out and prevented the doors from closing. She arched a dark eyebrow at him and wordlessly extended her other hand toward him.

"No way," he said firmly and crossed his arms over his chest. "You're not peeking into my brain."

Kerry had the gift of second sight, and with one touch

she could see right into a person's soul, stripping away all facades and uncovering buried secrets.

"Pete." She sighed. "Cut the crap, and give me your hand. Don't make me shift into my panther and claw up that handsome tux," she said sweetly. "I can usually read your energy signature, but it's—"

"Yeah, Dante said it's not there—or something."

"Well, gimme your hand, and let me see what's going on," she persisted. "Dante may be lots of things, but he's not psychic—I am."

"You're something else." Pete couldn't help but chuckle. Kerry was nothing if not direct. "You don't have to use your super-secret whammy powers, okay."

"Ooookaay," she said as she leaned against the elevator doorway. "Start talking. What's going on with you and Marianna?"

Pete cursed and looked past her to make sure Dante was nowhere in sight.

"No way," she whispered, before he even had a chance to say anything. "You mean the two of you...?" She clapped her hands over her mouth and stifled a giddy giggle.

"Shhh! Now what the hell are you laughing at?" he said in an exaggerated whisper. "It's not very damn funny. First, she kisses me like... like—I don't even know how to describe it," he sputtered. "And then, as if that's not enough, I can't get her out of my head, and I had a dream about her last night that—"

"What?" All the color drained from Kerry's face, and the smile vanished. "You dreamt about her?"

"Yes." Pete stilled, immediately alarmed by Kerry's obvious discomfort. "Why are you acting like you just saw a ghost or something? I had a dream. What's the big deal?" A smile crept back over his face. "Actually, it was a pretty nice dream until a bear showed up—weird."

"Give me your hand," she said firmly. "Now!" Her brown eyes flickered and shifted into the bright, glowing yellow eyes of her panther.

"Shit. I hate it when you guys do that weird thing with your eyes."

Kerry said nothing, but wiggled her fingers at him impatiently.

"Fine," Pete growled with frustration and yielded to her request.

He placed his hand in Kerry's and waited. Her eyes fluttered closed and moved rapidly behind the lids, almost as if she was dreaming, but her body remained motionless. They stood there for almost two minutes before she finally opened her eyes, which were back to normal, much to his relief. She looked at him with genuine awe and something else he couldn't identify.

"What?" he said hesitantly. "What did you see?"

"I don't believe it," she whispered in a shaky breath and removed her hand from his. "I just don't believe it."

Pete shoved his hands in the pockets of his tuxedo pants and fiddled with the bottle of precious powder. Was she really that stunned that Marianna would kiss him? Was being a human that freaking bad?

"What the hell did you see?" he barked.

"You are Marianna's mate."

Chapter 4

Marianna pushed the food around her plate and smiled politely at the other guests, all human, who were seated at the large round table. The conversation centered on the financial meltdown and how it was affecting the children's charity they were there to support. To her surprise, Pete had no trouble joining in, and he had become the superstar at the table. He regaled them with stories from his childhood and how this charity had personally helped him and kept him off the streets as a kid.

The man could charm the pants off anyone— including her.

She was doing everything within her power not to drool over Pete, who looked far too handsome in his black tuxedo. Dante had insisted that Pete attend the event with her, but when she protested and questioned exactly how a human man could be of help to her, he reminded her that it would keep Artimus and Hayden in line.

God, she hated when her brother was right.

So far, having Pete with her kept the two away. They couldn't start a troublesome conversation with a human date at her side.

She glanced around the enormous ballroom of the Waldorf Astoria and scanned the multitude of tables for the Amoveo men. It didn't take more than a minute to spot them. The two sat at their table, which was on the opposite side of the room, as fate would have it. A moment later, she picked up another Amoveo signature.

There was a man who looked vaguely familiar to Marianna, and based on his energy signature, had to be an elder. He was seated on the other side of Artimus, and Marianna studied him as she tried to remember where she'd seen him before. Artimus raised a champagne glass to her, interrupting her train of thought, and offered her a disingenuous smile. Marianna narrowed her eyes and looked away quickly, refusing to acknowledge his phony gesture.

"What's wrong?" Pete whispered.

Marianna straightened her back and shook her head quickly. "Nothing," she said before taking another sip of wine. She hated lying, but she couldn't tell Pete that the dream he had last night wasn't just some dream. That look in Artimus's eyes last night was one she wouldn't easily shake. He looked at Pete as though he was nothing more than a bug that needed to be squashed.

Pete draped his arm over the back of her chair and leaned close, so that only she would hear him. "You're shaking, and it's hot as hell in here, so don't try and tell me that you're cold." His warm breath puffed enticingly along her neck. "What gives?"

Before she could answer him, the band struck up a rousing number from the forties, signaling the obligatory phase of dancing. Marianna simply gave him a tight smile and shook her head.

"Oh, my goodness." The elderly woman named Alice, who sat across the table from them, clapped her wrinkled hands enthusiastically. "This music takes me back. If I were your age," she said to Marianna, "I'd be asking this handsome young man to take me on the dance floor."

"No reason this handsome old man can't take you out there." Her husband, Leo, stood from the table and extended his hand. "Come on, my lovely. Let's dance."

Alice giggled as her husband led her gingerly onto the dance floor. Marianna watched the elderly couple as they danced together and couldn't help but smile. How many years had they shared? What secrets did their hearts hold, and how much time did they have left before it would end? Marianna swallowed a surprising lump of emotion.

If two people truly loved each other, was there ever enough time, or would they always want one more day?

"So, how about it?" Pete asked with a lopsided grin. He tossed his napkin on the table, stood, and extended his hand. "Let's go out there and give Alice and Leo a run for their money."

"You can dance?" She looked at Pete through wide eyes and couldn't stop the smile that spread across her face. "I don't believe it."

"Are you kidding?" He took her hand and helped her from her chair. "My grandmother made me take dancing lessons at the Boys and Girls Club every week during middle school." He linked her arm through his. "My cha-cha is second only to my Lindy."

Marianna picked up the small train of her gold, formfitting gown as they wove their way through the sea of tables, chairs, and people, until they reached the dance floor. Before she could say a word, Pete swept her into his arms and onto the dance floor. He held her tightly against his strong body, and the two danced as if they'd been partners for years, as opposed to minutes.

They fit together like they'd been made for each other—and they had. How on earth was she supposed to explain the whole Amoveo-mate thing? But when he cracked that dazzling smile, all her worries floated away with the music.

Tonight she wouldn't worry… she would just dance.

She wasn't sure if she was breathless from dancing or from being close to Pete, but frankly, she didn't care. Pete was right. He could dance—really dance—not that bumping and grinding crap they did at The Coven, but real, old-fashioned dancing. He twirled her until she was dizzy with laughter, and she couldn't remember the last time she'd had this much fun. His captivating blue eyes twinkled mischievously as the song came to an end, and he dipped her dramatically before whisking her against his muscular body.

The orchestra shifted to a gentler melody. Pete pressed his hand against her lower back, pulling her tighter, and she could feel his heart pound in time with hers. Breathless and flushed, she smiled as his warm fingers curled around her hand, and they moved with the music. She couldn't take her gaze off his chiseled features, but those fierce eyes looked down at her intensely and with more confidence than she'd seen before.

Maybe confidence wasn't the right word… possessiveness, perhaps?

She narrowed her eyes and studied him carefully as his body melded perfectly with hers in all the right places. Something about him had changed, and she couldn't put her finger on what it was. As they moved

between the other couples on the dance floor, Marianna
tried to tune into his energy signature to see if she could
decipher what was going on, and then she heard him.

*What if Kerry's right, and I really am Marianna's
mate? I'm only a human.*

He knew. Marianna stilled. He *knew* about the
Amoveo. Pete knew what she was and that he was
her mate?

Her jaw clenched, and a knot of anger formed in
her belly. All of this added up to one big, fat lie. Pete
hadn't been hired as some clueless human to be a shield.
Apparently, she was the clueless one, and her brother
took it upon himself to manipulate her because he didn't
think she was capable of taking care of herself.

Marianna had never been so furious in her life, and it
took every ounce of self-control to keep her eyes from
shifting into their clan form. Pete looked at her with
confusion and concern, sensing her sudden change in
demeanor, but before either could say a word, Hayden
tapped him on the shoulder.

"May I cut in?"

Pete didn't take his eyes off Marianna and pulled her
closer. "No, you may not." Pete steered her away from
Hayden, but kept his gaze fixed on her.

Marianna peered over his shoulder to see Hayden,
Artimus, and the other Amoveo man standing at the
edge of the dance floor watching. Their disdain for Pete
was evident in the dark energy waves that rippled across
the room. They hated Pete for getting in their way, but
Artimus grinned like the cat that ate the canary. He was
up to something, but at the moment, all she cared about
was teaching Pete and her brother a lesson. She was

more than capable of handling herself, and it was about time to demonstrate it.

"I don't think you've made a friend of Hayden," she said tightly.

"Then it's a good thing I don't give a shit," Pete said through a laugh as he waltzed with her through the crowd. "Do you?"

"Not especially. But I don't like people making my decisions." She slipped out of his arms and leveled an angry glare at him. "I'll decide who I dance with, thank you very much."

Without another word, she cut through the crowd and made a beeline for Hayden. She glanced over her shoulder to see Pete stopped by Leo and Alice on the dance floor. She smirked. Based on what she'd witnessed earlier tonight, the chatty twosome would hold him up for a while.

Marianna steeled herself against the heavy darkness of their energy signatures and mustered up the nicest smile she could manage.

"Hello gentlemen." She gave Hayden the obligatory kiss on the cheek, smiled, and stuffed down her instinct to run. "Good to see you again."

"Yes," Artimus hissed. He flicked his gaze toward Pete, escorting a slow-moving Alice back to her seat. "I see you're still enamored with your plaything."

Marianna ignored his comment and extended her hand to the elder. "I don't believe we've had the pleasure."

"Charmed, Ms. Coltari." The tall slim man took her hand and kissed it regally. "I haven't seen you since you were a child, and you've grown to be quite a gorgeous woman."

"Forgive me," Marianna smiled tightly and swiftly removed her hand from his cold grip. "I thought I recognized you, but you'll have to pardon me for not remembering your name."

"This is Dr. Moravian," Artimus interjected. "He was a good friend of your father."

"I see," Marianna said as she fought the urge to look for Pete. Instead she kept her attentions fixed on the doctor. His dark brown hair was gray in some spots—unusual, even for an elder—and his goatee was streaked as well. She tuned into his signature and knew he was from one of the birds of prey clans. "You are a member of the Falcon Clan? Gyrfalcon, like William Fleury."

"Yes." His features darkened at the mention of William's name. "It's too bad that he's chosen to disgrace our clan by mating with that half-breed," he sneered.

Marianna suppressed a grin. She'd hoped that mentioning William's name would irritate him. Good. *Prejudiced son of a bitch.*

"Dr. Moravian," Artimus said in an effort to placate him. "Let's focus on more reputable men. Shall we?"

"Of course." He took a sip of what looked to be a glass of whiskey. "Forgive me, my dear, but sometimes my frustration gets the better of me. Your father was an honorable man, and I was saddened to hear of his death." Dr. Moravian kept his voice low, wanting to keep any nearby humans from overhearing. "He was a true patriot, and his death was a great loss to the cause."

"Yes," she said evenly. "My father's death *was* a great loss, especially for my mother."

"I meant no disrespect," he added quickly, as they walked from the dance floor toward one of the alcoves along the wall. "But you know that we are at a crucial time, and the future of our race depends on devoted Amoveo like your father. Men like Artimus and Hayden." He made a sweeping gesture to the two other men.

"Don't forget about the women," Hayden said as he slipped his arm around Marianna's waist. It reminded her of a snake, coiling around her unwelcomingly. "The women are a pivotal part of the plan, aren't they, Father?"

"What plan are we talking about exactly?" Marianna asked, without really wanting to know the answer.

"Well," Artimus began. "Let's just say that while I don't want to mix our bloodlines with humans, they have made significant strides when it comes to overcoming their own reproductive problems."

Marianna stilled, and her nausea grew. "Reproductive problems?"

"Dr. Moravian has been studying reproductive therapies for humans." Hayden tightened his grip. "It's actually quite impressive—the solutions they've come up with."

"I don't know why we didn't think of it sooner." A smile spread over Artimus's face. "Just because you and Hayden aren't mates doesn't mean we can't genetically engineer offspring from the two of you."

"What?" Marianna breathed. "That's ridiculous. You know that our people can only have children with our mates."

"Think about it, Marianna." Hayden leered. "We'd make some gorgeous pure-bloods for the Bear Clan."

"We're not mates, Hayden." She tried to pull away, but he held her in his iron grip.

"Maybe not, but it would still be fun to try the old-fashioned way." He looked down at her cleavage and grinned. "I'd like to try that first, you know, before we give medical science a shot."

"This is sick." Marianna wanted to visualize herself away from this entire situation. She swallowed the bile that rose in her throat. "You are suggesting that we genetically engineer pure-blood children from Amoveo who aren't mated? That's—that's disgusting," she sputtered. "It goes against the very fabric of our society."

"Not as much as mixing with *humans*," sneered Artimus.

"It really doesn't, my dear," said Dr. Moravian. He put a hand on her arm in an effort to calm her, but all it did was make her skin crawl. "And I can assure you that it's perfectly safe, but it is imperative we find the right match. We suspect that it would be best to keep it within the clans. Since you and Hayden are both a part of the Bear Clan, albeit different branches, it makes sense that we try with the two of you."

"You're crazy," she whispered. Marianna looked at their faces and saw that they were dead set on this idea—and on including her in their ridiculous plan. "Forget it. I do not want any part of this."

"It would be much easier if you would cooperate." Artimus's stony gaze stayed fixed on her. "Besides, you're already thirty, and no Amoveo mate has claimed you." He shrugged casually. "You really have nothing to lose by trying."

Marianna opened her mouth to correct him, to tell this sick bastard that her mate had indeed found her, but she snapped it shut without saying a word. If Artimus knew with absolute certainty that Pete was her mate, he'd kill him without hesitation.

"Your father would want you to help your race and your clan." Artimus's jaw clenched. "It's much easier when the participants cooperate. It's not as messy. Besides, I don't relish the idea of… convincing you."

Utter dread washed over her at that last statement. She wanted to ask him what in the hell they'd been doing, but Pete's unmistakably angry voice sliced into their conversation.

"Convincing her of what?"

"Pete," Marianna said far too brightly in an effort to change the subject. She was still pissed that he lied, but she could overlook it for the time being. All she wanted right now was to get the hell out of there, away from Artimus and his ridiculous plan.

"I'm so glad you could join us." She smoothed her hair back, amazed her updo was still in place after all that dancing. "Pete, you already know Hayden. I'd like you to meet his father Artimus and his friend, Dr. Moravian. They were both friends with my father."

Pete didn't even spare them a glance, and no one tried to shake hands with him. The tension in their small circle was off the charts. Marianna glanced at the humans at the nearby tables, but none seemed remotely aware of the tense situation developing. They were too busy enjoying the five-hundred-dollar-per-plate event.

"Nice to meet you," Pete said, clearly not meaning it. He didn't take his furious eyes off hers. "It's time to go, Marianna. *Now*."

He stepped between them, grabbed Marianna's hand, and pulled her from the circle. The two practically ran from the ballroom and through the doors to the empty hallway with the outdated pay phones. He pulled her up to the coat check window but still didn't look at her. He slapped the ticket onto the counter and passed her the small gold clutch that she'd left on the table before their dance. Pete tossed a tip into the tip basket, grabbed Marianna's hand and they headed down the grand staircase to the extravagant lobby below.

He didn't say a word as they walked to the parking garage, but there was no mistaking how he felt. The man was irate. *He* was pissed at *her*? Well, fine. She was pretty goddamn mad herself. Not only did she have to contend with Hayden and Artimus propositioning her, apparently, she couldn't trust Pete or her brother.

Would *every* man she knew try to control her life?

The parking attendant pulled the car up, and Marianna got into the backseat without a word. Pete said something under his breath, slammed the door behind her, and got into the driver's seat. He peeled out of the lot and turned onto Park Avenue.

"You and my brother have a lot of damn nerve, you know that?" she spat. "I almost expect it from my brother. Dante was always bossy." Marianna slammed her purse onto the seat. "But I have to admit, I'm more than a little disappointed in you."

"What are you talking about?" He didn't even look in the rearview mirror but kept his eyes trained on the city traffic. "I don't know why you're so ticked off. I'm the one who got ditched on the dance floor so you could talk to that douche bag, Hayden."

"Really?" Her voice rose. "He may be a douche bag, but at least he's honest about it."

"What the hell does that mean?" Pete flicked a glance in the mirror as he turned onto her street.

"It means that I don't like being lied to." She leaned forward and visualized the living room of her apartment. The familiar scent of vanilla filled her nostrils, and static flickered around her. "Good night, Pete."

As Marianna vanished from the car and visualized herself back to her apartment, she heard Pete curse and the screech of tires on the pavement. Marianna threw her purse onto the couch and smiled triumphantly as she walked to her bedroom. "Put that in your pipe, and smoke it."

Chapter 5

"Son of a bitch!" Pete bellowed.

He slammed on the brakes and gaped at the now-empty rearview mirror. The Mercedes skidded to a halt, and Pete spun around to see that she was actually gone. Marianna must have used that disappearing act the Amoveo could do—what did Dante call it? Visualization? She used that to blink her ass out of there, most likely back to her apartment.

"That's it," he bit out. Pete floored it down the next few blocks until he came to Marianna's brownstone. He double-parked, not giving a crap if he got a ticket or towed. He was so fucking mad right now that he thought his head was going to explode.

He got to the door of the building as one of the other residents was leaving and slipped right in. As he stormed the steps to her floor, he tried to figure out when exactly she'd realized that he knew what she was. She said that she'd been lied to—damn it.

They were trying to protect her, mostly from herself. She'd only proved their point when she marched up to that asshole Hayden and his father with absolutely no regard for safety. He'd never met the doctor, but he'd seen his picture in that file that Dante had given him.

"Open up, Marianna." Pete pounded on the apartment door. "I mean it. Open this door right now. I know you're in there."

Silence.

Pete banged on the door again, but still she didn't respond. He knew she was in there. He could feel it. Just when he was about to start banging again, Marianna swung the door open, but once he laid eyes on her, all the blood rushed from his head directly to his crotch. She stood in the doorway barefoot and clad only in a short, red satin robe. Her long hair was loose, the way he liked it, and spilled over her shoulders in inviting waves.

"Something wrong, Pete?" A satisfied grin cracked her heart-shaped face. "You seem a bit upset."

Marianna turned on her heels and waltzed into her apartment as if she hadn't just vanished from the backseat of his car. Pete followed her and slammed the door behind him. He took a quick look around the small apartment and noticed it was decorated simply, but tastefully. The whole place smelled like vanilla and peaches—or maybe that was her.

"Can I get you a nightcap?" she asked as she poured herself a glass of wine.

"No." Pete undid the stupid bow tie from his tuxedo and opened the top button of the collar. It didn't do much to squelch his anger, but it gave him something to do with his hands. "I'm too pissed."

"Why on earth would you be angry?" she asked innocently. Marianna sipped her wine and sidled up to him. He tried not to notice the seductive sway of her hips or that come-hither look in her eyes.

"Oh, come on, Marianna." Pete whipped his tie off and stuffed it into the inside pocket of his tux jacket. "Let's just cut the crap, okay?"

"By all means." She raised her eyebrows and peered over the rim of her glass. "You first."

Pete took a deep breath and let it out slowly. Apologizing wasn't his favorite thing to do, but she was right. He hadn't been truthful, but he wasn't a liar. He wasn't like his father.

"I'm sorry I wasn't honest with you," he said quietly. "I've known about the Amoveo ever since Dante and Kerry got together."

"Why?" Marianna's eyes grew stormy. "Why wouldn't you tell me that you knew what I am?"

"Why? Are you freaking serious?" he asked incredulously. Pete went to the wine bottle on the counter and poured himself a glass. "On second thought, I do need a drink."

He took a swig and tried not to look at her long, tanned legs and perfectly pedicured toes as she sat on the arm of the oversized chair. She sipped her wine, but kept those dark eyes on him as he made his way back into the tiny living room.

"Okay, you've got your drink… why did you lie?"

"If you knew that I was hip to the Amoveo, then it would be impossible to keep an eye on you. If you got pissed—which you seem to do a lot by the way—you'd just pull that disappearing act like you did tonight." He raised his glass. "So thanks for proving my point."

"Really?" Marianna narrowed her eyes. She stood from her spot on the chair and placed her drink on the glass coffee table. "For your information, *Mr. Castro*, I'm perfectly capable of taking care of myself without you or my brother meddling in my life."

Her eyes flashed and shifted into the glowing black

eyes of her clan. Pete was mesmerized as images of a
moonlit sky filled his mind. Usually, when one of them
shifted eyes into their clan form, it freaked him out, but
it had an opposite effect with Marianna. They glittered
like black diamonds and held him captive.

He hadn't thought it would be possible for her to be
more breathtakingly beautiful than she already was—
but he was dead wrong. She moved toward him, and
something whisked through the air, like static, or a heat
wave. Whatever it was, it turned him on, but he was
determined to keep his composure and not jump on her
like some horny kid.

"After what I saw tonight at the Waldorf, you are
trouble with a capital *T*," he said evenly. "You went
looking for it with Hayden and Artimus, but I can't for
the life of me figure out why. I know you can't stand
Hayden, and there's obviously no love lost between
you and Artimus, so why in hell did you run over to
them tonight?" His jaw clenched. "You know that
they're Purists."

As the words flew out of his mouth, one possibil-
ity fell on him like a ton of bricks. What if that's how
she felt? *Holy shit*. What if she sympathized with the
Purists and would never in a million years want him for
her mate? She was attracted to him. He wasn't blind or
stupid, but what if that's all it was for her? What if she
loathed the idea of having a human for a mate? He knew
she wasn't a big fan of Kerry's, but he thought that was
some kind of sibling jealousy; he never dreamed that she
could be a Purist.

"I know exactly who they are and what they're all
about." She poked him in the chest. "At least they're

straight with me, which is more than I can say for you or my brother. If those guys want to find me, then they'll find me. They can sense my energy signature and get to me *anywhere* but this apartment. However, if they do come after me, then I can take care of myself, and I don't need a human babysitting me!"

"Well, sweetheart," he ground out. "It was the presence of *this* human who's kept those dicks away so far." Pete's jaw set as he struggled to keep his temper under control, but it was no use. "I may not be able to shapeshift into a bear or a squirrel or a what-fucking-ever, but I've managed to keep an eye on your fine ass for the past couple months without so much as your hair getting mussed."

Marianna didn't take her furious eyes off his. Hands on her hips, she inched closer, and her breasts brushed against his chest. "My fine ass and everything else on my body is no longer your concern," she whispered. "I can take care of myself because I *can* shapeshift into a bear, among other things. By the way," she added sweetly, "you're fired."

Frustrated, turned on, and at a loss for words, Pete slugged back the rest of his wine as if it were a shot of bourbon. He tried not to notice the way her bare legs brushed against his pants or how the heat of her skin wafted over him, but it was no use.

He'd never get away from the taste of her.

Staring into those glittering ebony eyes, he knew he was lost. Lost to a woman who couldn't stand what he was and would likely never accept him. Pete shoved his other hand in his pants pocket, and the vial of precious powder slipped into his hand easily. He squeezed it tightly, and staring into those glowing eyes, he realized what he had to do.

"That's it, isn't it?" he murmured. "They can find you anywhere because of your energy signature, right? That's part of your Amoveo abilities, like shapeshifting and telepathy?"

"Yes." Marianna looked at him with confusion and crossed her arms over her ample breasts. "So?"

Pete took the vial of silver powder out of his pocket, uncorked it, and poured some into his hand. "Then I guess we better make sure that they can't find you."

Marianna opened her mouth to undoubtedly ask him what he was talking about when Pete blew the magical powder into her face. He quickly corked the bottle and stuffed it into his pocket. Pete grimaced as she sputtered and coughed, hating himself for what he'd just done, but what choice did he have?

How in the hell could he protect her if those bastards could find her anywhere, and she could vanish from his sight at the drop of a hat?

"It should pass in a minute." He slapped her on the back as she coughed and swiped at the tears that streamed down her face. He noticed that her eyes had shifted back to human form, which gave him hope that this crap was actually working.

"What the hell?" She sputtered between coughs as she sat on the couch and put her head in her hands.

"Sorry, but it's for the best." Pete sat next to her and tried to rub her back, but she shoved his hand away. He couldn't really blame her. He'd have been pissed too.

"What did you do?" she wheezed. Marianna picked her head up slowly, and the look of fear on her face made his heart squeeze in his chest. "What did you do to me?"

She scrambled off the couch and ran to the bathroom. Pete followed and found her leaning on the oval porcelain sink, staring at her frantic reflection in the mirror above. Marianna wiped away the tears and flicked her brown eyes at him. They may not have been glowing, but now, they reflected her anger.

Pete stood in the doorway with his hands shoved in his pockets, waiting for her to say or do something. She turned slowly and looked as if she wanted to rip his head off, but since she hadn't shifted into a bear, he figured he was safe for the moment.

"I'll ask you one more time. What… did… you… do?" she seethed.

"You weren't safe as long as Artimus and the rest of the Purists could find you. I made it so they can't find you. It's a binding powder, and according to the voodoo guy I bought it from, it'll keep you bound in your human form for a month—give or take a few days."

She gaped but said nothing. He felt like a shithead.

"My human form?" she repeated, trying to make herself believe it. "That stuff you blew in my face and made me choke on, it took my Amoveo powers away."

"Basically." He struggled to remain calm and detached and act like her pain wasn't killing him. "Come on. You've got to pack a bag because you can't use that visualization thing to make stuff appear." He looked at his watch. "I want to get on the road as soon as possible." He went into her bedroom and looked around for a suitcase. He found one in the back of her large closet and tossed it on her bed. "Start packing."

"And just where do think you're taking me?" she asked incredulously.

"I have a cabin up at Schroon Lake. It's secluded, and no one will find you there." He flipped the suitcase open. "Come on. Toss stuff in here, but make sure it's warm clothes. It's January, and we'll be in the mountains."

He looked away because he couldn't stand the way she was looking at him. She probably hated him, and he'd given her every right, but as long as he kept her safe, it didn't matter. "Please," he said quietly. "The sooner we get there, the better."

"Are you crazy?" Marianna tightened the belt of her robe, which had drifted open. He tried not to look, but he couldn't help it, and it didn't escape her attention. She clutched the neckline closed and made a face. "It's not bad enough that you've made me an invalid, but you have to ogle me too?"

"Hey." He shrugged. "I'm only human."

"Exactly."

"And so are you—for at least a month," he said evenly. "And based on what I've seen over the past few weeks, a little humility will do you good."

"You arrogant jerk! I'm not going anywhere with you." Marianna stalked over and shoved him with both hands, but he held his ground. "You bastard." She shoved him again, harder this time. "How could you do this to me?"

Marianna tried to punch him, but he grabbed both her wrists, preventing her from achieving her goal. She swore and struggled against his grip, but it was no use. He was far stronger than she was now, and he had no interest in fighting. He spun her around and pinned her against the wall next to the nightstand as her robe gaped open again, exposing the curve of her full breasts.

"Stop," he said gently. Her lush, warm form melded against his as she squirmed, trying to get away, but he didn't relent. He held her hands above her head and placed his legs against hers, which was meant only to restrain her, but had a far more erotic effect. Her lips, the ones he'd tasted the night before, hovered temptingly below his, and the tantalizing scent of peaches and vanilla filled his head. "If you don't stop squirming, I'm going to do a lot more than just hold you here."

"Let me go." Marianna arched her back, which made her breasts press harder into his chest. Her eyes shimmered, and his heart broke when one big tear rolled down her cheek. "Please," she whispered.

The pleading sound of her voice combined with the touch of her body sent him over the edge, and before he knew it, his mouth was on hers. He sighed contentedly as her warm lips collided with his. Marianna moaned and opened to him, swept her tongue along his, and pressed her body harder against him, trying to get closer.

He devoured her, drank from her as if he could never get enough. She linked her fingers with his as he held them above her head. Need took over, and his basest instincts to claim her clamored. He tore his hands from hers and tangled his fingers in her long locks. Marianna wrapped her arms around his neck, draped one leg over his hip, and tugged him even closer as she kissed him greedily.

One hand trailed down her side, over the curve of her satin-covered hip, and along her thigh. He pulled her leg up and rocked against her. His hand swept the smooth skin of her thigh and cupped her bare ass. The vixen was completely nude beneath the thin satin robe, and the knowledge almost made him come.

This was heaven—this woman's touch, taste, and scent. He could drown in it and die a happy man.

The shrill chirp of his cell phone in his jacket cut through the haze of lust. They broke their kiss, but he didn't let her go. Even though he wanted to throw the goddamn phone out the window, he couldn't ignore it. It was the ring specifically assigned to Dante, and he had a pretty good idea why he was calling.

Breathing heavily and still tangled in each other's arms, he rested his forehead on hers. "I did it to protect you." *Liar,* he thought, *you did it to keep her from running away. You did it to keep her near you and needing you.* "If this binding powder works the way it's supposed to, then your energy signature will vanish, and you'll be invisible to them." He picked his head up and locked eyes with her as he released her leg, and it slid along his. "Don't you understand? You'll be safe."

Marianna looked away and clutched her robe closed. "You better answer that."

Her wounded expression did nothing to make him feel better about what he'd done. *First he binds her in her human form, and then he mauls her.* All he wanted was to shelter her and keep those bastards away. Finding out that he was her mate validated the way he'd been feeling since he first laid eyes on her and made him feel like he wasn't crazy for having fallen head over heels in love.

Pete released her and stepped back abruptly. Son of a bitch. He loved her.

"Right," he said absently as he pulled the phone from his pocket and answered it. "Hello?"

Marianna slipped away and straightened her robe. He watched her take clothes from the dresser. She tossed them carelessly in the suitcase as Dante's panicked voice filled his head.

"What the hell is going on?" Dante barked. "What happened to Marianna? Is she alright? I can't find her—her energy signature is gone. It's like she just disappeared—"

"Calm down," Pete said without taking his eyes off Marianna. "She's fine. I'm in her apartment right now. You can't find her energy signature because I used the binding powder."

A string of curses filled Pete's ear, and he could hear Kerry in the background trying to calm him down. Pete held the phone away from his ear as Dante cursed him, and a satisfied grin spread over Marianna's face at the sound of Dante's expletives.

"I hope my brother fires your sorry ass," Marianna hissed as she brushed past him to the bathroom.

He put the phone back to his ear. "If you're done cursing me out, would you like to hear why?"

"This better be good."

"First of all, the jig is up, okay. Marianna knows that I'm Vasullus—or whatever—that I know about the Amoveo. Secondly, not only did she insinuate herself into what could've become a volatile situation with

Hayden and Artimus tonight, she pulled that vanishing act that you guys can do. She got pissed at me tonight on the way home from the benefit and left me sitting alone in the car talking to myself like a schmuck."

"Why was she pissed at you?" Dante asked impatiently.

"Oh, it's not just me, boss." He laughed. "You're in the doghouse too because we kept the truth from her and tricked her into having me around."

"Bring her to my place, right now."

"Not a chance." Pete didn't like defying his boss, but this wasn't about work. This was personal.

"What?"

"You heard me," Pete said tightly. He kept one eye on Marianna while she zipped her suitcase.

"You must have a death wish." Marianna laughed. "My brother doesn't take kindly to back talk." She scooped a pile of clothes from the bed, went into the bathroom, and slammed the door.

"Hey," Dante shouted. "Did you hear me?"

"No," Pete whispered into the phone, not wanting Marianna to hear this part. He stalked to the living room and ran a hand over his face. "No, I didn't. Your sister has me all twisted up, and I don't know if I'm coming or going. Here's the deal. You know that I would do anything for you—you're my friend—but this isn't about you. It's about Marianna and me. My only concern is keeping her safe and away from those Purist bigots, and I can't do that if they can find her with that homing-device-energy-signature thing you guys have."

Silence hung heavily, and Pete paced the living room, certain he would wear a hole in the Oriental rug. If Dante didn't say something soon, he was going to hang up, and they could all be damned. He glanced at the bathroom, but the door was still shut.

"Kerry just told me," Dante said evenly. "She said that you are Marianna's mate."

"Yes, I guess I am," Pete said on a long breath. "You seem okay with it, but I don't know if she will be."

"What do you mean?" he asked defensively. "You're not suggesting that she sympathizes with the Purists, are you?"

"I'm just not sure if she—" The door to the bathroom clicked open. Pete quickly changed the subject and raised his voice to normal levels. "If she can handle slumming it as a human for a month."

"I heard that." Marianna came into the living room clad in furry boots, jeans, and an oversize sweater. She stood there, glaring, and if looks could kill... he'd be a dead man. "When I get my powers back, I'm going to kick your ass."

Pete ignored her comment and continued speaking with Dante, but he didn't doubt that she meant every word she said.

"I'll be in touch once we're settled, and before you ask—no, I'm not telling you where we're going, but I promise that she'll be safe."

"Fine—just get word to me once you're settled. Wait, Kerry wants to talk to you."

"Pete?" Kerry said expectantly.

"Yeah, I'm here." He glanced at Marianna, but she looked away and went to the closet, presumably in search of a coat. "What's up?"

"Remember the dream you had last night? Well, it wasn't just a dream, okay? Part of the mating process is dream-walking, so that really was Marianna with you, but the bear you saw wasn't her or some manifestation of your subconscious."

That bad feeling crept up his back. "Then what was it?" he asked.

"It's not a *what* that I'm worried about, but a *who*."

"Let me guess. With my luck it was Artimus or Hayden."

Marianna stilled at the mention of their names, grabbed her coat, and swung the closet door closed as she turned to face him. She was suddenly more interested in his conversation.

"My point is, Pete," Kerry continued. "You have to keep them out of your dreamscape. You can't let them in."

"Well, how in the hell am I supposed to do that?" he snapped. "I'm not like you guys. I'm just a human, remember?" He knew he sounded like a resentful dick, but he didn't care.

"You're not a regular human, and you know it. You get hunches, right? You've mentioned those before, and since we know that you're Marianna's mate, we know those are more than hunches. I've been thinking about something else since we saw you today."

"Yeah?" he asked warily.

"Remember how Dante and I noticed your energy signature was just about gone? Well, when you came over… you were hiding your feelings about Marianna and what happened." Pete heard Dante interrupting, but Kerry shushed him. "What if you created your own shield without realizing it? I know you've got psychic ability—you'd have to in order to be Marianna's mate—maybe by consciously hiding your feelings, you actually hid your energy signature too?"

"This is nuts." Pete shook his head and adjusted his gun beneath his jacket. "I'm not some kind of psycho."

"Psychic—not psycho," Kerry said with exasperation. "And yes, you are. Look, don't argue with me. Just keep it up."

"How can I keep it up?" he yelled. "I don't even know what the hell I did." He sucked in a deep breath to regain his composure. Yelling at Kerry wasn't going to fix anything. "This isn't helping. Besides, I don't think we have to worry about that right now. Isn't that dream-walking stuff part of your Amoveo powers?"

"Yes, it is, but if you don't shield your energy signature, then they can find her through you. Focus on shielding your feelings and keeping Marianna safe." She let out a weary sigh. "I hope that will work."

"Fine. I'll do my best to shield... or whatever." He fixed his sights on Marianna. "Marianna and I will be in an Amoveo-free zone for the next month, which should give you time to find out what these turds are doing and to stop it."

Marianna opened her mouth as if to say something, but snapped it shut quickly. Pete cocked his head and stalked toward her. She was hiding something—he'd bet his life on it.

"Take it easy on her, will you? Marianna not having Amoveo abilities is a weird adjustment, especially not having telepathy. She's going to feel isolated and alone—so don't be too hard on her if she gives you shit."

Pete smiled and shook his head. "You got it, Mrs. Coltari. Bye."

Marianna rolled her eyes and sat on the arm of the chair.

He was about to hang up when he heard Dante's voice. "Can I speak to my sister, please?"

"Oh—uh, sure." It dawned on him that they probably never spoke on the phone with each other. Why would they use a phone when they could use telepathy? "Dante wants to speak to you."

Marianna's mouth quivered, and her eyes glittered with tears as she took the cell phone. "Hi." She sniffled and turned her back on Pete.

He couldn't hear Dante's end of the conversation, and only muffled one-word answers from Marianna, but there was no mistaking how she felt. She was lost and reminded him of a little girl. This woman, who had been so full of bravado, energy, and life, was suddenly deflated and scared... and it was his fault. What the hell had he done?

Chapter 6

Marianna slept almost the entire ride to Schroon Lake. She'd closed her eyes and put her head back as soon as they got into the Mercedes. It was a ploy to ignore Pete, but she was so exhausted, emotionally and physically, that she'd fallen asleep before they reached the George Washington Bridge.

When she woke up, she thought it was all some kind of bad dream, but as soon as she saw Pete in his rumpled tux in the driver's seat next to her, she knew it was real. In fact, she hadn't dreamt at all. As soon as she woke up, she tried to connect with Dante and her mother telepathically, but she was met with silence. She attempted to use her visualization abilities to get back to her apartment, but still nothing.

For the next month she was going to have to live like a human.

She rubbed the sleep from her eyes and stared out the window at the falling snow as it whipped around the car. It was still dark out, but she could see that they were in the mountains. It was a moonless and starless sky, and all she could see was snow, which only served to accentuate her sense of isolation.

Her nose burned from the silver powder that Pete had used to bind her. She sniffled and rubbed it, refusing to look at him, not wanting him to see the tears that spilled freely down her cheeks.

She'd noticed the change instantaneously.

The world around her no longer echoed and pulsed the way it had all her life. The unseen energy signatures of her brother, Kerry, and her mother were no longer detectable, and it was as if the people who kept her grounded and tethered to the earth were suddenly gone.

She was alone… almost.

Marianna pulled the ski jacket tighter and glanced at Pete, who had his eyes trained on the road. His jaw clenched and flickered beneath the five o'clock shadow, which looked like it would be a full-blown beard by sunup.

His grip on the steering wheel tightened. "We'll be there soon," he said quietly. "I've had to take it slow the last hour or so. This car may be nice, but it sucks in the snow. I'll take my old, beat-up pickup any day of the week over this thing."

Marianna ignored him and looked out her window. She had no interest in making polite conversation. A few moments later, he waved a brown bag in front of her. When she didn't take it, he dropped it in her lap.

"It's a bagel with cream cheese," he said quickly. "Eat it or don't. It's up to you. But I should warn you that it's better than my cooking."

"Well, that's a ringing endorsement," she said drily. Even though her instinct was to tell him to shove the bagel up his ass, she was hungry.

"You have every right to be pissed." Pete shifted in his seat and glanced in the rearview mirror as he switched lanes. "Let's keep a couple things in mind. First, it's not permanent. You'll have your powers back in a month, and second, I hope you understand that I did what I had to do."

"Yeah, you said that like ten times." Marianna swallowed her mouthful of food and nodded. "So I hope you understand that I think you should fuck off."

To her surprise, Pete burst out laughing.

"What the hell are you laughing at?" she asked before taking another bite of the surprisingly good bagel. "I'm furious with you, and *you're* laughing?"

"I'm glad to see that the binding powder didn't take away your fire, and you've still got the nerve to chew me out." He winked. "I like a woman with some sass, but I have to admit, at this moment I'm glad you can't shift into a bear and a verbal lashing is all I'm getting."

"You're not off the hook, no matter how charming you think you are." Marianna suppressed the smile that bubbled up. He disarmed her, but she'd be damned if she was going to let him know it.

"Maybe, but I can tell that you're trying not to smile."

"Oh, shut up, and keep your eyes on the road," she said, looking out the window.

They turned off the main street and onto what Marianna could only assume was the driveway to the cabin, but it didn't look like more than a vague path through the woods. The branches of the towering pine trees drooped with the weight of wet snow, creating a canopy along the untraveled path.

"It's a damn good thing this place is along the edge of the lake and not up a hill, or we'd be walking the rest of the way," Pete said as the tires spun, and the sleek Mercedes fishtailed along the fresh snow. He gave Marianna a sideways glance as he wrestled to keep the car in a forward motion. "You'd freeze your ass off. The temperature is barely ten degrees."

"Not likely. I'm a member of the Kodiak Bear Clan, and cold doesn't faze me in the least." As the words came out, of her mouth she realized they were no longer true. "Well, it didn't," she said quietly. She gritted her teeth and bit back the anger that bubbled as she chalked up yet another power taken from her with this stupid binding powder.

"You'll find out soon enough." He nodded toward the road as the tiny log cabin came into view. "See, we're just about there."

The car's wheels spun in the wet snow, and they slowed to a stop.

"Why wait?" Marianna glared at Pete and grabbed the door handle. "No time like the present."

Before he could stop her, Marianna popped the door open and got out. As she slammed the door behind her, her feet slipped, and she landed with an audible grunt in a pile of cold, wet snow. Her breath rushed from her lungs, and her body went numb as frigid moisture enveloped her.

The jeans she'd selected (because they made her butt look good) provided little barrier from the snow, which seeped through with surprising speed. The jacket she wore wasn't as warm as she would've expected, but when she'd gotten it, it was for looks, not for protection from the weather. She'd never needed that—until now—and thanks to that damn powder, she couldn't use her visualization abilities to conjure up something warmer.

She heard Pete curse and watched as the car skidded sideways, and the back end hit a tree. Marianna scrambled to her feet, and even though she could barely feel her legs, she tromped the rest of the way to the cabin. She knew that getting out of the car like that was impulsive, childish, and stupid, and she would have a bruise the size of a coconut on her ass, but she'd be damned if she let Pete see just how much it hurt.

"What the fuck is wrong with you?" Pete yelled as he slammed the car door and slipped on the snow. "You're crazy. Do you know that? You could've gotten hurt."

His voice echoed through the silent forest, and more curses flew in her direction.

"What the hell do you care?" she yelled through chattering teeth. Marianna folded her arms over her chest and put her bare hands in her armpits. She couldn't feel her fingers. "You blew that shit in my face and took my abilities away, and now I'm freezing, so thanks. I always wanted to know what it would feel like to be a Popsicle."

"It serves you right," he barked. "The door's locked, so you can freeze on the porch until I get up there with the keys." Pete popped the trunk on the car and grabbed their bags. "*You* can explain to your brother why his expensive car will need to go to the body shop. This thing is going nowhere fast, but lucky for us, I keep my pickup truck here."

She glanced around and realized this was the place that Pete had recreated in his dream. Marianna climbed the three steps to the porch and watched as Pete stormed up the driveway. This place must be special, otherwise it wouldn't have been in his dreamscape.

Still in his tuxedo and dress shoes from the night before, he slipped a few times and almost wiped out. His ice-blue eyes flashed angrily, and he cursed under his breath. She covered her mouth to keep from giggling because she had a feeling he wasn't finding humor in his current situation.

"I don't know why you're so pissed off." Her breath puffed big white clouds into the air. "Dante's precious Mercedes can be easily fixed by him or any Amoveo—except for me, as we know—and in case you were wondering, I'm fine," she continued dramatically. "Thanks for asking."

"Did that powder suddenly rob you of intelligence?" He stormed up the steps and got right in her face, but she didn't retreat. He towered over her, and it dawned on her that she'd worn only heels around him before today. For the first time, she felt small and vulnerable. "You could've hurt yourself." His shoulders relaxed, and a contrite look came over him. "That's why I'm pissed. Okay?"

She couldn't stop her teeth from chattering or her body from shivering. "Can you please yell at me inside? I'm freezing my ass off."

A cocky grin cracked his face. "I told you."

When Pete unlocked the door, Marianna practically ran him over to get inside, but it wasn't much warmer. She rubbed her arms and looked around the one large room, while Pete flipped on the lights, tossed the bags on the old sofa, and made quick work of starting a fire in the stone fireplace.

At least the place had electricity. She glanced at the kitchen to the left and breathed a sigh of relief to see a sink—plumbing. Peeing in the woods in her human form was not something she wanted to experience. Marianna sat at the wooden table and surveyed the rest of the tiny cabin.

The walls were lined with knotted pine paneling, giving the open space a surprisingly cozy feeling. To call the decor shabby-chic would be a stretch, but somehow, it fit in a rugged-man, cabin-in-the-woods kind of way. Directly in front of the fireplace was a plaid sofa trimmed in wood, with a coffee table made from an old wagon wheel. She peeked past the edge, expecting to find a bearskin rug in front of the fireplace, but luckily, it was only a traditional braided throw.

"I think the deer head mounted above the fireplace is my favorite piece of decor," she said dryly. "Lucky for you, there's no Deer Clan."

"Don't knock it," Pete said as he put the screen in front of a roaring fire. He turned his sharp gaze back to her. "My grandfather shot that buck when he was only twenty years old, and it was one of his proudest achievements."

Marianna hopped from her seat and went to the fire. She knelt down, held her hands in front of the flickering flames, and let out a contented sigh. "Sorry," she breathed. "No offense to your grandfather. I'm just grateful there's not a bearskin rug."

"Feeling better?" he asked through a laugh.

"Yes." Marianna smirked but didn't look at him. "I'm still pissed at you."

"You'll get over it." Pete went into the kitchenette and hit his head on one of the hanging pots. "Damn," he said as he grabbed it to keep it from falling down. "My grandmother loved having these things up here, but I always manage to walk right into them."

"This is your grandparents' place?" she asked. She'd heard him mention his grandparents a few times, and his mother, but nothing about a father. Not one word, which spoke volumes. Looks like they both had daddy issues.

"It was." Pete rifled through the cabinets and glanced in the fridge as he spoke. "My Grandpa Jack died when I was in high school, but Grandma made it to see me graduate from the academy." A wistful smile played at his lips. "She was something else. A real spitfire, kind of like you."

"Thanks." Marianna stood from the fire. "I'll take that as a compliment."

"You should."

He moved from behind the counter, and it dawned on her how out of place he should look in the middle of this funky little cabin. Between the rumpled tuxedo and unshaven face, he looked as if he hadn't slept in ages. He was still sexy as hell, and oddly enough, fit into these surroundings perfectly.

"You're a spitfire alright," he murmured.

Rugged. Rough. All jagged edges.

He stalked toward her slowly, neither saying a word as he closed the distance between them swiftly and silently. Marianna hugged her arms tighter around herself, but not from the cold this time. It was the predatory look in his eye that sent her libido into overdrive and had her wanting to do all kinds of irrational things. Things she shouldn't do with someone who pissed her off at every turn—unless, of course, he was her mate.

Her mate. How the hell were they supposed to begin *that* conversation?

He studied her intently, and his dark brows furrowed as his gaze skimmed her. What was he thinking? Damn. It was like she was blind—emotionally blind. Without her ability to scan his energy signature, she was clueless as to how he was feeling.

"What?" she asked more defensively than she intended. "Why are you looking at me like that?"

He angled his head to one side and narrowed his eyes. "I was thinking about making love to you."

Her breath caught in her throat as she stared back, too stunned to say a word. She was in big trouble.

"It'll be incredible." That cocky grin spread across his face, and he trailed one finger tantalizingly along her jaw. "But it won't happen until you ask."

"You arrogant son of a bitch." Heat flashed up her cheeks, and she smacked his hand away. "Screw you."

"Ah-ah-ah." Chuckling, he wagged his finger as he stepped around her and grabbed the bags off the couch. "You have to ask me nicely."

Shaking from a mixture of adrenaline, anger, and lust, she watched him disappear through the doorway on the other side of the fireplace. She stood there for a few minutes, refusing to follow him. She figured it was probably the bedroom.

Just when she was about to shout to find out what was taking so damn long, he emerged shirtless, and for the first time in her life, Marianna was rendered speechless. She gaped at him like a stunned sheep. She knew he was fit; hell, she got a taste of how hard his body was when he'd kissed her at the apartment, but he looked even better than he felt.

The man was ripped. All muscle, bone, and sinew. The partially unzipped black tuxedo pants hung low on his narrow hips. The defined muscles in his chest flexed, as if inviting her to come on over, and the cold, hard truth was that she wanted to—but she'd be damned if she would lose this battle of wills.

Marianna's gaze met his, and that lopsided grin crept over his face. "I'm going to take a shower and have a nap because I haven't slept in over twenty-four hours. Then we'll go into town and get some supplies. If you want to change, then I suggest you do it while I'm in the shower," he said, opening the other door. "Unless of course, you'd like to join me?"

"In your dreams," she said turning back to the fire, pretending not to be ridiculously turned on by the sight of him.

"Actually, wouldn't the correct term be in *our* dreams?"

Marianna stilled, but didn't look at him. As the door to the bathroom clicked shut, she knew he was right. They hadn't uttered a word about it, but it was clear they knew they were mates and succumbing was only a matter of time.

After both of them had napped—Pete on the couch, and Marianna in the bedroom—it was midafternoon by the time they headed into town. He turned the dilapidated, blue pickup truck onto Main Street, and Marianna thought they'd stepped back in time. The quaint village street was lined with an array of shops and restaurants, and if she didn't know better, she'd think they'd time traveled back to 1965. She'd never been to a small town like this and didn't believe that hamlets like this one existed.

Smiling, she hopped from the pickup and zipped her jacket closed against the bitter wind. She glanced up to find Pete standing on the sidewalk staring at her.

"What are you grinning at?" she asked as she pulled the knit cap over her ears.

"You." He slipped the keys into the pocket of his jacket. "You look like a kid in a candy store."

"I do not." Marianna tried not to smile again. Jeez. Why could he get her to smile at the drop of a hat?

"Whatever you say," he said, placating her as he looked at the gray, cloudy sky. "We better hurry up. There's another storm coming, and it would definitely be better if we're settled at the cabin before it hits."

Marianna joined him on the sidewalk. "I thought the old girl," she said as she nodded toward the banged up truck, "could handle anything."

"Oh *she* can." Pete flicked his pale blue eyes to her. "It's you I'm worried about."

"Oh really?" Marianna closed the few feet between them and leveled a challenging gaze at him.

Pete raised his hands in defeat. "I'm just saying that you are not exactly an outdoor gal, and I wouldn't want you to be uncomfortable. Trudging through a snowstorm in the Adirondacks is an experience you can live without." His features darkened, and he stuffed his hands into the pockets of his jeans. "Trust me."

Marianna narrowed her eyes and studied him carefully. She may not have been able to read his energy signature, but it was clear that he'd had a less than pleasant experience. She was about to pepper him with questions when he brushed past her.

"Come on." He started down the sidewalk. "We'll hit the General Store first for groceries, and then I have to swing into the Towne Store for a few supplies."

As Marianna stepped into the General Store, her

senses were assaulted by the stomach-rumbling aroma of freshly baked brownies. She hadn't eaten anything since that bagel, and a brownie could hit the spot. The little bell over the door jingled happily, announcing their presence, causing the woman behind the counter to look up from her magazine and smile politely, but when she saw Pete her smile widened.

The cashier twirled her pale blond hair around one finger, and her face flushed, as she looked sideways at Pete. Marianna didn't miss it, but Pete seemed oblivious, and even though she couldn't blame the woman for staring, that didn't keep part of her from feeling territorial. Pete was gorgeous, and she knew women would desire him, but it didn't mean she had to like it.

"Hi Mindy." Pete gave her a friendly wave, grabbed two baskets, and handed one to her. "Get whatever you want. I have a house account here, so have at it."

He didn't let go of the handle as one strong finger brushed over the top of her hand. That whisper of a touch whooshed down to her toes, and her furry boots felt nailed to the worn wood floor.

He lowered his voice. "We'll probably be here for a few weeks, so stock up. There's a bigger storm coming in a couple days, after the one tonight, and if it's as they say, we could be cabin-bound for quite a while."

Marianna said nothing. She simply nodded and swallowed the lump in her throat. All she could think about was being in that tiny cabin with Pete... alone.

He walked down one of the narrow, overstuffed aisles, and she caught sight of that fine backside. How is it that a well-fitting pair of Levi's can make a man's ass look perfect? Her mind went to the sight of him this morning when he emerged from the bedroom without a shirt. Drool.

"Can I help you find something?" the woman at the counter snipped.

"No," she replied too quickly. Marianna's face heated with embarrassment because she knew she just got caught ogling his ass. Pete smirked and disappeared around the end of the aisle. "I'm fine. Thank you."

"It's okay." The cashier waved her over to the counter with a conspiratorial whisper. "Everyone gives him the once-over. Hell, the girls down at Flannagan's bar are gonna bust something when they hear he's back in town. He's the finest lookin' man that has ever set foot through that door." She stuck her hand out and gave Marianna a friendly smile. "I'm Mindy."

"Nice to meet you. I'm Marianna… Pete's… friend."

She felt like an idiot fumbling around for the right word, but what was she supposed to say? I'm his kidnapping victim? I'm his mate? Not likely. Friend would have to do for now.

"Friend?" She popped a stick of gum in her mouth with sparkle-painted fingernails and kept her voice down. "Honey, if I were you, I'd be a lot more than his friend. If I weren't already married, of course," Mindy added quickly. "A gorgeous thing like you looks like the right match for that handsome man. Brittany—she waits tables at Flannagan's bar—she's been trying to land him ever since they were kids."

Mindy sighed and peered past Marianna to make sure Pete wasn't within earshot; although the store wasn't that big, so it wouldn't surprise her if he was listening to the conversation.

"I see." Marianna looked at the jars of jam on the counter, pretending not to be interested, but making a mental note to keep an eye out for this Brittany.

"Oh yeah." She cracked her gum and whispered, "He used to come here every summer with his grandparents and his mama."

"What about his father?" Marianna hit the jackpot with Mindy, who as fate would have it, seemed to be the town crier, and she had no qualms about divulging personal information in the middle of the store.

"Nobody ever met him." She dropped her voice to a loud whisper. "From what I hear, his old man split when he was just a baby. Just heartbreaking."

"That's too bad." Marianna meant it too.

Heartbreak could mend, but it left a nasty scar.

"What's too bad?" Pete's voice cut into their conversation.

"This jam," Marianna blurted out.

"The jam is bad?" He looked at her like she'd lost her marbles.

"No." She glanced at Mindy, who was doing her best not to laugh. "It's too bad that they don't sell this jam in the city. The packaging is adorable, and I bet it would sell like hotcakes in one of those little gourmet shops." Great. Now she was babbling about jam.

"Well, stock up then." He winked at Mindy and placed two baskets of food on the counter. "I'm going to make one more pass around the store, and then we'll head to the Towne Store for fishing tackle."

"Fishing?" Marianna replied incredulously as he walked away and scooped up another basket. "It's the dead of winter. I'm not going fishing."

"Yes, you are," he shouted from the back of the store.

"Honey." Mindy gave her arm a friendly pat. "Go fishing. If you're lucky, you'll catch more than fish."

———

They made quick work of their shopping and filled the truck with their purchases. Unfortunately, Pete wasn't kidding about the fishing gear, but he was crazy if he thought she was going fishing in the frigid cold. She'd heard humans complain about the cold and always thought they were a bunch of whiners—not so much now. Every time they went outside, she felt the cold in her bones, and it was not a sensation she wanted to stay familiar with.

She stared at the passing scenery as the truck bounced along the country road. Marianna wiped absently at the fogged up window as her thoughts went to Dante and her mother. She couldn't recall ever going one day without touching her mind to theirs, and she caught herself trying to do it again—but still nothing. It had been barely a full day since the powder had taken effect, but it felt more like years.

"How do you do it?" she mused quietly.

"Do what?" Pete gave her a questioning glance and turned into the driveway as snow started falling again.

She was quiet for a few moments, trying to choose the right words. "Live in such… isolation?"

"You mean here in the mountains?" He pulled up in front of the cabin, threw the truck into park, and leaned back in the well-worn bench seat. "I don't live here year-round. It's a getaway spot."

"No." She shook her head and captured his gaze.

"Not the cabin. I don't mean physically isolated." Her voice dropped to a shaky whisper, and she closed her eyes, struggling to explain how she was feeling. "I'm talking about the emotional and mental isolation of being human, the inability to connect with another person's mind, to read their energy and to know exactly how they're feeling."

"Marianna?" Pete's warm hand cradled her cheek and brushed away one tear with his thumb, creating breathtaking friction. "Look at me please."

She sucked in a deep breath and opened her teary eyes to find that the tenderness in his touch was matched by the look on his face.

"I'm sorry." He gently wiped away another tear. "Do you really need your Amoveo abilities to know how much it's killing me to see you hurting? And because of something I did?" His voice dropped to a husky whisper. "But it's nothing compared to how I'd feel if those Purist assholes got their hands on you. They won't touch you, Marianna. You have to trust me."

His eyes searched hers for something. Trust? Forgiveness? Love? The truth was that she simply didn't know. She couldn't sense his energy, but she could most definitely feel his touch, and it was enthralling.

Pete's fingertips brushed the side of her neck as he held her face in his hand. She slipped her glove off and placed her hand over his, pressing it against her cheek, needing to connect with him—to feel another person—to feel *something*.

The sound of their breathing and the hum of the engine surrounded them in the cab of the old truck. As the snow fell silently outside, the rest of the world fell away, and it seemed that it was just them… alone… in the quiet of the falling snow.

Her gaze wandered over the sharp angles of his face, the high cheekbones and square jaw that looked like they'd been made by the gods. His most striking feature, those piercing blue eyes, reminded her of ice. Cool. Sharp. Steal-your-breath intense. And right now, they were locked on her.

His mouth was on hers in a whisper or a curse—she wasn't sure which—she didn't care. She groaned and opened, welcoming him. He tasted like sin and sex. Marianna broke the kiss, pushed him back with both hands, and straddled him in one swift move. She fit perfectly between Pete and the wheel.

His look of surprise shifted to that deliciously cocky grin as she settled on his lap and kissed him again. His hands slipped beneath her jacket and sweater, and she sighed against his lips as flesh met flesh. She'd never appreciated or needed the touch of a man more than she did at this moment—especially this man.

She held his head and kissed him as her greedy hands found their way inside his jacket and under his shirt. Marianna groaned as she ran her fingers along the washboard abs and reveled in the smooth, warm skin beneath her fingertips.

She couldn't get close enough or connect enough— she needed more.

Pete's hands rested on her waist, and his fingers dug into her hips as he pulled her against his growing erection. She licked and nibbled at his lips as she writhed seductively in his lap, seeking relief from the storm of lust building inside.

One strong hand wrapped around the side of her neck, and Marianna tilted her head, giving those talented lips access to the sensitive skin along her throat. She arched back further, and when her eyes fluttered open, she caught sight of sudden movement outside.

Marianna let out a shriek of surprise as a dog barked and launched itself against the driver's side window. Pete cursed, and in one smooth, cop-ninja move, had her off his lap and shoved protectively into the passenger seat behind him.

Breathing heavily, Marianna stared openmouthed at the goofy dog bouncing up and down at the door like it had found a bag of milk bones.

With Pete's taste fresh on her tongue, Marianna clutched her jacket closed and looked from the dog to Pete, who gave her a sheepish grin.

He shut off the engine and shook his head. "Jesus, Tramp." Pete laughed and leaned on the headrest. "You have some shitty timing."

Chapter 7

PETE SQUATTED NEXT TO THE TRUCK AND GAVE THE overzealous dog a good scratch behind the ears as the animal licked his face with exuberance.

"Where the hell did that dog come from?" Marianna asked as she got out of the truck. She walked around and eyed the animal warily. "He appeared out of nowhere."

"He's a stray, I think," Pete said as he stood. "Marianna, I'd like you to meet Tramp." The blue-eyed husky sat at Pete's feet and stared at Marianna, but didn't make a move to go near her. "At least that's what I call him. He showed up a few summers ago and comes by every time I'm here."

"Hi, Tramp." Marianna reached out tentatively, and to Pete's delight, the dog yipped and went right to her.

Smiling, she knelt in the snow and gave the husky scratches behind his gray and white ears. Her smile might have been the best sight Pete had ever laid eyes on. It lit up her face when she laughed as Tramp licked her. He grinned at the sound because he hadn't heard her laugh in a long time.

"He's adorable and looks well cared for, especially for a stray." She stroked his large body. "Are you sure he doesn't have a home around here?"

"Not that I know of. Although he could, I guess. The next closest cabin is a ways off. My cabin sits on about twenty acres." Pete gathered packages from the car. "Tramp shows up and hangs out for a few days and then leaves when he's had enough." Pete shrugged one shoulder. "It reminds me of that dog from the Disney movie, *Lady and the Tramp*. Hence the name."

The sun set as Pete put the last of his fishing tackle in the shed out back, but the snow continued to fall. He took stock of his gun and ammunition supply as well. He hoped he wouldn't need it, but knowing it was there made him feel better.

Tramp bounded happily through the snow as they headed back to the cabin, and when they got to the back porch, the dog shook off the snow as Pete kicked off his boots. His grandmother always hated it when they tracked mud or snow into the cabin, and even though she wasn't here to give him an earful, he made sure to follow her rules.

Pete grabbed an old towel from the trunk on the porch and wiped Tramp's paws off. The dog stood still and let him clean his feet, which always surprised Pete. Maybe Marianna was right. Maybe old Tramp had a family somewhere on the mountain and used the cabin as a vacation spot as much as Pete did.

When he opened the back door to the cabin, he was hit with unexpected aroma of something delicious cooking. The only thing more surprising was seeing Marianna standing at the stove stirring food in the cast-iron skillet he'd almost cracked his head open with earlier. Her long wavy hair was tied in a ponytail, and even wearing a simple sweater and jeans, she was the sexiest creature he'd ever seen in his life.

Even more striking to Pete was how right it felt to have her here at the cabin. He'd never brought a woman here until today because he'd never met anyone who'd meant enough. He'd dated and slept with plenty of women, but never for more than a few months. Eventually, the when-are-we-taking-this-to-the-next-level conversation would come up, and that's when things would end.

Pete always made it clear that he wasn't interested in anything serious, and until now, he meant it. He watched as she moved around the small space with odd familiarity. It was as though she'd done it a thousand times, and that was unsettling. She fit. She fit with him, this cabin… his life.

When did it happen? When did she slip seamlessly into his life and his heart?

"You're letting the cold air in," she said without turning around.

"Oh, sorry." Pete shook his head and shut the door. How long had he been standing there staring? "I didn't think I was outside that long." He leaned on the small island and took a deep breath. "It smells great in here."

"I hope you don't mind, but I was famished, and based on your comment about your cooking skills, I figured that we might starve to death if you tried to cook."

"A solid assumption." Tramp trotted into the kitchen and lay at Marianna's feet. "Looks like you have a fan."

"It's not me he's a fan of." She tossed Tramp a piece of chicken. "It's the food." Marianna smiled and glanced down at Tramp. "But I'm a fan of his either way."

"Oh yeah?" Pete grabbed a beer out of the fridge, closed the door, and leaned against it while he continued to watch her. "Why is that?"

"I like dogs," she said with a shrug. "I don't know. Maybe having an animal in the house makes me feel at home?" She shut off the burner, turned to face him, and leaned one hip against the counter. "Does that sound kind of nuts?"

"No," Pete replied. "It sounds kind of right."

He tucked a stray lock of hair behind her ear, and her brown eyes widened as his skin brushed over hers. Her breathing quickened, and she nibbled nervously on her lower lip as he trailed the back of his fingers along her cheek. She seemed vulnerable and unsure of herself, but for the life of him, Pete couldn't figure out why.

She may not have her Amoveo abilities, but she was still beautiful, smart, and sexy. He wanted to kiss her again—hell, he wanted to do a lot more than kiss her— but Tramp barked and jumped between them before he had a chance. Pete dropped his hand and laughed as Tramp nuzzled Marianna.

Cockblocked by the dog.

Pete smirked and shook his head. "You really need to work on your timing, buddy."

"Don't be mad at poor Tramp. He's hungry." Marianna gave Pete a scolding look and scratched the dog's ears lovingly. "We should eat before it gets cold." Marianna gently pushed Tramp down and grabbed some dishes from the cabinet.

"Right," Pete said as he took the plates and place mats from her. "Wouldn't want the food to get cold, would we, Tramp?" Pete gave the dog a look of disapproval when Marianna's back was turned, but he could swear that animal was laughing. Tramp barked in total agreement.

Marianna offered a bowl of rice and cooked chicken

to Tramp before joining Pete at the table. They ate mostly in silence, and he knew it was because neither knew where to begin. How do you start the I-guess-we're-mates conversation anyway? He still wasn't sure whether she sympathized with the Purists. What if she did? What if she couldn't really love him?

Since he had no damned idea, he let the conversations about the weather, Tramp, and the food dominate. The tough conversation would come eventually for better or for worse, and at the moment he was simply enjoying her.

Pete couldn't remember the last time he'd had a meal that good, but it had to have been cooked by his grand-mother. He threw his napkin on the table and sat back in his chair as he resisted the urge to unbutton his jeans.

"Enjoyed it?" Marianna laughed and took a sip of her beer as she looked at him through narrowed eyes. "You're dying to unbutton your jeans, aren't you?"

"Yes." Pete rubbed his belly and laughed. "Am I that transparent?"

"I have a brother, remember?" She rested her chin on folded hands and kept those big brown eyes locked on him as the smile vanished. "And, no, you aren't transparent at all. But I guess you never really were, were you? Even when I had my Amoveo abilities and could read energy signatures, you managed to keep things from me until just before the infamous binding powder incident."

"I think it's time for that conversation we've been avoiding." Pete's jaw clenched, and he saw the tension settle in her shoulders.

Weariness crept over her features, and Pete scolded

himself for being so dense. The woman had been through the ringer, and even after everything that had transpired, she had made him dinner. What a dope. The least he could do is let her take a breather before he started a difficult conversation.

"But first," he said, pushing himself away from the table. "I'm going to clean up, and you're going to take a shower and relax."

A smile crept back to her lips. "You're going to clean up?"

"Yes," Pete said as he started gathering the dirty dishes. "Why?"

"I don't know." She leaned back and watched him through serious eyes. "My father wasn't big for helping around the house and was always happy to let my mother do it. Dante's like you though. I watch how solicitous he is with Kerry, and I can't for the life of me figure out how he got that way." She let out a harsh laugh. "He sure didn't learn it from our father."

"Maybe he gets it from your mom?" Pete washed the dishes in the sink and set them in the drying rack.

"Probably." She smiled faintly as she spoke of her mother. "My mother is thoughtful, kind, and generous. I often wondered how and why the universe paired the two of them up. I loved my father, but he was a difficult man, and it was his way or the highway. Daddy was a big fan of everyone fitting into their proper role."

"What roles?" Pete shut off the water and wiped the counters while hanging on every word she uttered.

"Mother is the caretaker. Dante is the good son— well, at least until he found Kerry—I assume that Dante told you my father was a Purist?"

"Yes." Pete dried the pots off with a towel. "Dante mentioned it, but he's never discussed it with me at length. That seems like a bit of a sore subject."

"Oh, it's sore as hell. My father tried to kill Samantha—Malcolm's mate, who is also a hybrid—so you can imagine how absolutely irate he would've been to find out his own son was mating with one. And me?" Bitterness edged her words. "Well, I was the sweet little daughter who thought the sun rose and set on her father and that he could do no wrong. My job was to look pretty, find my Amoveo mate, and make him pure-blood grandchildren. Like Daddy always said, we all have a role to play. Imagine how disheartened he'd be with the latest developments."

Silence hung heavily in the air as he waited for her to continue. Her sadness at disappointing her father stabbed at Pete like a knife. Even though they hadn't said it, they both knew that she didn't have an Amoveo mate, and there wouldn't be any pure-blood Amoveo coming from her... or him.

He glanced over his shoulder, and his throat tightened at the look of sadness on her face. "Are you okay?"

"I'm fine," she responded without looking at him. Marianna got up and went toward the bedroom with Tramp at her heels. "I'm going to take your advice and grab a shower, but then I'm going to bed. I know we have to talk, but I'm just too tired tonight." She turned to face him, and that stone-cold resolute look he saw last night was back. "We never did discuss the sleeping arrangements."

"I'll take the couch... for tonight," he said with a wink.

"Yes. You will." Her dark eyes glittered with deter-
mination, and it was clear that the battle of wills was
back. "We can talk about this mate business tomorrow.
You didn't sign up for this mess, and I don't expect you
to get wrapped up any further than you already have."

Before he could respond, Marianna disappeared into
the bedroom and closed the door. Wrapped up any further? Hell, he was already gone.

"Let's go, Marianna," Pete said impatiently. "Tramp
and I were up this morning long before you were, and
we're ready to get out there and do some ice fishing.
It's noon already."

She'd taken her sweet time getting up and dressed.
He knew it was one enormous stall tactic to keep from
going fishing, but there was no way he was letting her
get out of this. He really wasn't doing it to bust her
chops, but because he wanted to share it. He doubted
that the Amoveo spent a lot of time ice fishing, and
he figured it was a human experience that he could
show her.

"I can't believe you're making me go fishing in the
freezing cold," Marianna grumbled as she pulled on a
second sweater, coat, hat, and gloves. "We have a perfectly nice cabin to stay warm and toasty in."

"Maybe." He tugged her knit hat over her ears.
"But it'll feel even warmer after we come in from our
little excursion."

Marianna and Tramp followed him down to the lake
through the layer of fresh snow, but something caught
the dog's eye, and he raced into the woods to chase it.

"Where's he going?" Marianna wondered.

"Beats the hell out of me." Pete shrugged and handed her one of the fishing poles. "Like I said, he comes and goes as he pleases."

When they reached the edge of the lake, Marianna stopped dead in her tracks and watched Pete warily as he walked onto the ice.

"Where the hell are you going?" She looked at the ice-covered lake with trepidation and tried to keep her teeth from chattering. "You can't walk on that. You're going to fall in."

"No, I'm not." Pete walked over and extended his hand. "And neither are you. Come on. The area we're walking on is totally safe. This ice is several inches thick and has been frozen like this for weeks already."

Marianna took his hand and gingerly stepped onto the ice. She kept a death grip on him all the way to the tent situated twenty yards from the edge. Pete unzipped the black tent door and let Marianna in first.

He zipped it closed behind them and smiled as he watched her survey the small space. Shivering, she sat on one of the stools and glanced at the hole in the ice. "I don't see any fish."

"Well, they don't exactly jump up and into the tent." Pete sat on the other stool and made quick work of baiting the hook on her pole. "Here you go. That's a jigger pole, so what you do is drop the line and yank from time to time—you jigger it." He took it and demonstrated. "See, it's easy."

Marianna took the fishing rod while he baited the hook on his. He dropped his line into the hole in front of his seat and jiggered in silence.

"This is quite the setup out here," she said, while she popped the line up and down a few more times. "Did you put this all up this morning?"

"Nope. A local guy sets it up, maintains it, and breaks it down every year." Pete reached over, unzipped one of the tent windows, and peered outside. "I just had to come out and break the ice in the fishing wells."

"It's actually kind of warm in here, and I've stopped shivering incessantly." She yanked the pole and made a face that made Pete want to bust out laughing, but he didn't. Somehow, he figured that would get him a fishing rod to the face. "Maybe it's just the absence of the biting wind."

"Solar heat," he said, referencing the panels on the roof.

"Impressive," she said with a nod. "I'm surprised that—"

She stopped midsentence as her line tugged downward, the unmistakable pull of a fish.

"Oh my God," she shrieked with a wide smile. "I think I got one." Giddy with the excitement of her first catch, she looked at Pete with wide brown eyes. "What—what do I do?"

"Stay calm, and reel him in." Smiling at her childlike joy, he put his rod in the holder next to his chair and coached her along. "That's it, nice and easy. If you go too fast, he could get away."

"This is awesome," she shouted as she reeled the line in slowly. The skinny pole bent in protest as the fish struggled to break free. Marianna's face was stamped with concentration as she reeled in her prize. "It's heavy." She glanced at Pete and grinned. "I bet it's a beast."

The dark shadow of the fish became visible through the ice as Marianna reeled it closer. Pete took off his gloves and got ready to help her land it. She reeled the line, leaned back, and in one last pull the fish popped through the surface, and Pete scooped it up.

"Oh my gosh! I did it." Marianna giggled as she stared at the perch that wiggled helplessly in Pete's hands. "I caught a fish!"

"You sure did, and it's quite the beast," Pete said smiling as he held up her catch. "I'm not sure if we'll be able to carry this bad boy to the cabin."

The two of them looked at the fish, then at each other, and burst out laughing. Her beast of a catch couldn't have been more than six inches long.

"I think we better let this monster go." Pete removed the hook from the fish's mouth and held it closer, so Marianna could have one last look. "Any last words before I let him loose on the lake?"

"No," she said, still giggling.

The fish slipped into the water with a plop, and Pete turned his attention to Marianna. The smile lit up her whole face, and seeing it made him grin like some kind of lovesick kid.

"That was awesome," she said breathlessly. Her twinkling brown eyes latched onto his. "Can we do it again?"

"You bet your sweet ass we can," Pete said as he picked up her rod and put more bait on the hook. "So, not as boring as you thought it would be?"

"Fine." She sighed dramatically and rolled her eyes. "You were right."

"That's music to my ears." Pete grinned broadly and handed her the newly baited rod. "See, even a simple human like me can teach an Amoveo beauty like you a thing or two."

"I don't think humans are bad, Pete." Marianna's smile faltered. "And by the way, you are anything but simple."

"Maybe," Pete said warily. He could tell that he was dancing around a land mine situation. One wrong word, and she was going to freak out and bolt to the cabin. "I'm not trying to insult you, Marianna. I'm saying that being human isn't a death sentence. I've had a great life, and I've managed it without shapeshifting, telepathy, or any of the stuff you guys can do." Pete leaned his elbows on his knees and looked at the fishing well. "Besides, you'll have all your powers back in a few weeks anyway. This is just temporary."

"No," she said quietly. "It's not."

Chapter 8

"WHAT ARE YOU TALKING ABOUT?" HIS VOICE DROPPED to a whisper. "What do you mean it's not temporary? I told you the binding powder only lasts for about a month."

"I'm not talking about the powder." She shivered and zipped her coat to her neck. It looked like now was as good a time as any to address the elephant in the room. "It's… us."

"Us?" Pete's dark eyebrows furrowed as he stared at her intently.

She marveled at the color of his eyes. They were the same color as the ice in the fishing hole—iridescent blue. He'd shaved this morning, but the shadow of a beard was already beginning to form.

"Yes." She took a deep breath and let it out slowly. "You are human."

"Yeah, that part I got."

"When a full-blooded Amoveo mates with another Amoveo or a hybrid, then there are side effects for both individuals." She studied Pete carefully, but he was riveted to what she was saying. "Their powers are amplified, they become far stronger, and they age slowly, almost imperceptibly."

"But I'm human," Pete murmured. "So none of that would happen, would it?"

"We believe that when a human bonds with an

Amoveo, then the Amoveo's powers fade, and they
age and die with their human mates. Up until recently,
we didn't know it was possible to mate with humans."
Marianna bit her lip. "I think, once we're mated, I would
become human just as I would if I'd never found a mate.
At the very least, even if I aged slowly... you wouldn't.
You will still age and die, and then when you die... I
will as well. I will live like a human and be considered
a member of the Vasullus family, the other Amoveo
who've lost their mates." Her voice wavered. "Or the
ones who never found mates at all."

Pete's features darkened. "Are you sure?"

"Yes." She nodded and looked away. "Well, pretty
sure."

"I see." Pete nodded solemnly, and his mouth set in a
grim line. "Life is full of surprises, isn't it?"

Marianna glanced at Pete, and her heart broke at the
anger and frustration stamped into his features. She
didn't need her Amoveo powers to know how upset he
was. She couldn't blame him. His whole life got fucked
ten ways from Sunday because of her.

He probably hated her for dragging him into the crazy
nightmare, and she couldn't blame him.

"I'm sorry, Pete." Marianna stood and put the fishing
pole down as she struggled to keep the tears from coming. "You don't deserve this, and I can tell that you don't
want any part of it. You are not Amoveo, and I won't let
you get hurt because of Artimus or any others. You can
have your life back."

She ran blindly out of the tent and toward the shore.
She slipped on the ice as the tears streamed down her
cheeks, and the bitter cold stung her face, cruelly adding

to her torment. The wind howled in her ears, and she could hear Pete calling, but another sound stopped her dead in her tracks. She was about ten feet from the shore when she heard a groaning and creaking noise. Marianna looked down and panicked as she realized that the ice was cracking.

"Marianna," Pete bellowed. "Don't move."

Pete's voice was the last thing she heard as she fell through the ice and into the frigid waters beneath.

Bitter cold. Darkness. Silence.

She tried to swim, but her arms and legs felt heavy and cumbersome. If she'd had her abilities, she could've visualized herself out of the water, but not anymore. Panic welled as she tried to climb from under the ice, but it was no use. Just when she thought death would claim her, one strong hand grabbed hers and pulled.

She broke through the surface, gasping for precious air, as Pete dragged her onto the ice. On his belly, he yanked her by both arms and pulled her to the safety of the shore. Pete's concerned expression was the last thing she saw before darkness closed in a second time.

Marianna sighed contentedly and snuggled into the warm, hard body wrapped around her—and then she froze.

What the hell?

Her heart raced as she struggled to get her bearings. The last thing she remembered was that Pete had pulled her out of the lake. She definitely wasn't cold anymore, but she *was* naked... in bed... with Pete... who was also *naked*.

Her eyes flew open, and she sat straight up in bed, clutching the covers over her bare breasts. Pete lay next to her, his hands folded behind his head, wearing that cocky grin and nothing else.

"What the hell is going on?" she sputtered. She looked out the window and noticed the sun was setting. "How long have I been in bed? Why am I naked? *How* did I get naked, and why the hell are you naked in bed with me?"

"Number one. You almost drowned and have been asleep for the last few hours." He adjusted the blankets, but Marianna smacked his hand away, which only made him smile. "Number two. I got you naked, and only peeked once, okay, maybe twice," he added quickly. "It was a tough job, but someone had to do it, and Tramp still hasn't come back."

Marianna wanted to punch him.

"And number three. I'm naked in bed with you because using my body heat was the fastest way to warm you up, especially since you'd passed out." He put one hand over his heart. "I promise I was a perfect gentleman the entire time, and believe me, it wasn't easy."

"Really?" she replied coolly.

"Yes, really." His heated gaze skimmed over her barely covered body. "You have no idea what you do to me, do you?"

Before she could answer him, he swung his legs over the side of the bed and grabbed his jeans off the floor. She looked away as he stood and stepped into them, but not before catching a glimpse of his perfectly formed ass.

"You are goddamn crazy, do you know that?" He

glowered as he threw on the discarded flannel shirt. Marianna wasn't sure if she was rendered speechless by his outburst or the sight of him as he dressed. "You hop out of moving vehicles. You run half-cocked onto a frozen lake you're unfamiliar with, and you make assumptions about me that are dead fucking wrong."

Marianna hopped off the bed while attempting to keep the sheet wrapped around her naked body. However, she wasn't doing a good job, and Pete didn't miss it.

"If you ask me, you deserve a good talking to." He stalked toward her, and his voice dropped low. "Bears in the wild, real bears? They're unpredictable. In fact, all those Hollywood animal trainers hate working with bears because they never know when they'll freak out and do something nuts." He zeroed in on her intently. Marianna backed up slowly, until she backed right into the wall, and had nowhere else to go. "You may not have your Amoveo abilities, sweetheart, but you've still got the bear in you."

"I scared you?" she whispered as some of the pieces started coming together. "That's why you're angry."

"You scared the shit out of me." The heat from his body wafted over her in erotic waves, and the dark, five o'clock shadow flickered as his jaw clenched. "But that's not the worst part." He placed both hands on the wall on either side of her and leaned close, trapping her, caging her. "The worst part is you drawing conclusions and *telling* me how I feel instead of taking the time to ask me."

"So tell me," she whispered. Marianna clutched the sheet tighter. Her heart thudded in her chest as he inched his lips closer to hers. "Start talking."

"No more talking," he murmured.

She nodded agreement as his mouth crashed onto hers with a groan of pleasure. Stark need clawed at her as she wrapped her arms around his neck and pulled him closer, deepening the kiss. Marianna hardly noticed as the sheet fell away and left her naked in his arms once again. Her breast crushed against the hot skin of his chest. He kissed her desperately as he pulled his shirt off and tossed it onto the floor.

His hands slid down her sides, swept over her hips, and cupped her ass. In one swift motion, he scooped her up and pinned her against the wall as she wrapped her legs around his waist and clung to him for dear life. He trailed kisses down her throat, along her collarbone, and finally, took one nipple in his mouth and suckled, sending white-hot pleasure to her core. Marianna ran her fingers through his hair with both hands and held him, urging him on.

"Pete," she murmured. Deep carnal need swamped her, and pleasure fogged her mind as he suckled her almost to the brink of orgasm. She tugged on his hair and urged him to look at her.

Pete lifted his head and smiled, still holding her firmly against the wall. "What do you want me to do, Marianna?" he whispered seductively, as his nimble fingers found their way to her slick folds and the sensitive nub within. He brushed his thumb ever so lightly over the swollen flesh, while holding her heavy-lidded gaze with his. "Tell me," he murmured between kisses, nibbling her lips. "Tell me what you want."

What did she want? *Him*. All she wanted was him. Every. Wicked. Inch.

A loud pounding on the front door cut through the haze of lust. Both were breathing heavily, and Marianna was locked in Pete's embrace. They stopped and listened again. The look on Pete's face matched her *what-the-hell* feeling perfectly.

The pounding, more insistent this time, came again.

Pete let Marianna down gently and kissed her forehead. "I'm going to shoot that fucking dog," he said between heavy breaths.

This time the pounding was accompanied by a muffled voice. Any humor in Pete's expression vanished in a blink. He threw the sheet at Marianna and grabbed his gun from under one of the pillows on the bed.

"Stay here. I don't care what you hear, don't you dare come out unless I call you. Got it?"

Marianna nodded and wrapped the sheet around her as Pete cracked open the bedroom door and peered around the edge. Gun drawn, muscles straining, he inched his way across the living room, but saw her peeking from behind the door and waved at her to get back. Reluctantly, she shut the door and waited. Silence ticked by, and just when Marianna thought she'd scream from the suspense, she heard Pete's voice.

"What the hell are *you* doing here?"

Marianna swung the bedroom door open to find Pete holding a gun on Olivia. Her friend stood in the open doorway with snow falling behind her and a look of annoyance. "Would you tell your boyfriend to get his gun out of my face and invite me in already?"

"What the hell are you doing here?" He kept his gun trained on Olivia, but glanced back at Marianna. "What the hell is she doing here?" He looked outside at the undisturbed and carless driveway. "How the hell did you get here?" He tightened his grip on the gun. "Someone better give me some answers, or I'm going to start shooting. I didn't think you were Amoveo."

"I'm not." Olivia sighed. She turned her big green eyes to Marianna. "Would you please explain before he shoots me and puts holes in my favorite suit. I just got this at Bergdorf's."

Marianna held the sheet around her and eased up to Pete, who was wound tighter than she'd ever seen him. She placed a reassuring hand on his arm. "She's not going to hurt me or you."

"If she's not Amoveo, then how did she get here?" The muscles in his chest flexed and strained as he continued to keep the gun pointed at Olivia. "There's no car."

"Oh, for christsake," Olivia said with exasperation. "I'm a vampire. I flew—*really fast*. Can I come in now?"

"A vampire?" He looked at Marianna for reassurance. "There are vampires too? Jesus Christ."

"Yup. Vampires. Demons. Angels. Witches. Fairies. Werewolves. Shifters and all kinds of creatures." Olivia ticked off the supernatural beings with her well-manicured fingers. "I'm a vampire. Now quit acting like such a baby, and let me in. If I'd wanted to drink your blood and kill you, I could've done it ages ago." She glanced at his gun. "By the way, unless those are silver bullets, shooting me will only piss me off *and* ruin my suit."

"Son of a bitch." Pete dropped his gun to his side and shook his head in disbelief. "I am gonna kick Dante's ass for not telling me."

"Sucks—not being told the whole truth, doesn't it?" Marianna smiled, but he didn't find the humor in it. "Oh, relax. Olivia and I have known each other for years. Can you invite my friend in please? The door is wide open, and this place is freezing." She shivered and rubbed at the gooseflesh on her arms.

"Fine." He waved the gun. "You're invited in... or whatever."

"Thank you," Olivia said as she stepped inside and closed the door. "Looks like I interrupted something."

She smiled knowingly at Marianna, who blushed down to her toenails, and glanced at Pete, who was shirtless, barefoot, and clad only in his unbuttoned jeans. He didn't seem embarrassed, and Marianna thought that he could've been buck naked, and it wouldn't have fazed him. He was completely focused on Olivia.

"Sorry for barging in on the two of you like this but I was worried about Marianna. I tried telepathy with you but got nothing, and on top of that, your energy signature was gone." She shrugged and sat gracefully on the couch with her legs crossed. "So here I am... but it looks like I worried for no reason. It would seem that you're safe and in *very* capable hands."

"I used a binding powder to keep the Purists from getting their hands on her," Pete blurted out. He kept his distance and grabbed a log for the fireplace, but kept one watchful eye on Olivia. "Her energy signature is hidden, so how is it that you could find her?"

"I drank her blood." Olivia's green eyes glittered.

"What?" Pete shoved another log onto the fire, sending sparks flying. "You drank her blood?" His furious eyes landed on Marianna. "You let her drink your blood?"

"Easy there, big guy." Olivia raised her hands in a truce. "I did it once and *only* so I could find her in case of an emergency. After we taste someone's blood, we can find them no matter where they are." She glanced at Marianna and lowered her voice. "But it's actually a big *no-no* that I drank *her* blood, so I'd be really psyched if we could keep this between us."

"Why is it a *no-no*?" Pete gave Marianna that scolding look as he brushed past her to the bedroom, presumably to get more clothes. "Do I even want to know the answer?"

"Shifters and vampires have had a delicate relationship. Part of the agreement between the Presidium and the Council is that there's no bloodsucking." Marianna shouted after him. "They don't suck our blood, and we don't stake them into extinction."

"What the hell is the Presidium?" Pete shouted from the bedroom.

"Vampire government," Olivia shouted back and winked at Marianna. "They're no fun at all. Very stuffy—they wouldn't like it if they found out I think their rules can be broken under certain circumstances."

"And by the way," Marianna continued. "The reason I was hanging out at Olivia's club so much was because most Amoveo wouldn't choose to go there. Olivia and her coven run it, and the Amoveo steer clear of vampire-run establishments."

"Well, that didn't last long, now did it?" Pete came out of the bedroom fully dressed, but looking no less tense. "Hayden got over it—so he could get to you."

"Our races keep the peace, and usually we stick to our own little supernatural corners of the world, but I agree with Marianna, sometimes we need to shake things up.

Actually, Amoveo blood tastes kind of funky. Some vamps think that it gives them a burst of extra power, but I didn't find that to be the case." She smiled at Pete, baring her fangs. "Then again, it was only a taste. I wanted her to have an additional measure of protection when the Purists started causing trouble. I'm glad I did." She turned her attention back to Marianna. "I was really worried about you, although, I will admit that it took me a bit longer than normal to find you."

"I knew there was something weird about you," Pete said and narrowed his eyes. Marianna watched him study Olivia, sizing her up all over again. "I just couldn't put my finger on it."

"Yeah?" Olivia scoffed and ran a hand through her long red curls. "Well, that makes us even because I think there's something weird about you too."

Pete crossed his arms over his chest and made a sound of derision. "Like what?"

"I'm not sure." She cocked her head and studied him intently. "But I can tell you're not a plain, old human. I'd have to taste your blood to be absolutely certain, but if I had to guess, I'd say you've got some demon or warlock in your blood."

"This is fucking crazy," Pete seethed. He stalked to the kitchen and grabbed his coat off the hook. "You are *not* tasting my blood, and I'm not some demon or warlock."

"Where are you going?" Marianna called after him.

"We're almost out of wood for the fire." He yanked on his hat and gloves but didn't spare a glance at Olivia. "I'm going to chop some more so we don't freeze to death."

Then without another word, he was out the back door and into the winter night.

"That boy has some issues," Olivia muttered. "Hey, are you going to put on some clothes or what?"

Marianna had totally forgotten that she was walking around clad only in the bedsheet. She ran into the bedroom, threw on the first thing she found, and quickly joined her friend by the fire.

"So he's your mate." Olivia stated. "He's a human— well, he's not *just* human because he dampens his energy signature and shields his feelings from me, by the way. You're totally hot for him, and he's got a serious hard-on for you." She looked at Marianna with confusion. "I don't get it. What's the problem?"

"The Purists will kill him if they find out that he's my mate. In fact, Artimus tried to get to him in the dream realm, and he definitely suspects something."

"Oh, that." Olivia twisted a long lock of red hair around her finger and winked. "I've got a hunch that Mr. Hottie can take care of himself."

"It's not just that." Marianna shook her head and let out a growl of frustration. "He'd be giving up his regular human life if he gets mixed up with me."

"*He'd* be giving up *his* life?" She lowered her voice and leveled a serious gaze at her friend. "Or *you're* giving up *yours*?" Marianna opened her mouth to argue, but shut it quickly. "That's what I thought. I have a funny feeling that you're also worried about giving up your life and forfeiting the future you were expecting."

Olivia wrapped her cool fingers around Marianna's and squeezed. "How are you doing without your powers, by the way? How is it—living like a human?"

Sadness flickered over her alabaster complexion. "I can barely remember."

"It's okay," Marianna shrugged and fought the tears. "It would be nice to walk these woods in my clan form, and I'm not crazy about being cold as often as I am." She laughed and shook her head. "Actually, the only thing that I really miss is the telepathy, but being with Pete has made it easier. I've never been this close with someone without touching our minds." Her lips curved. "Figuring him out is... seductive."

"Marianna." Olivia smiled wistfully. "I have one simple question. Do you love him? Forget all the pre-destined mate crap, and answer the question."

Marianna knew the answer. Deep down she'd known it from the beginning.

"Yes." She nodded. Her smile faltered, and she looked Olivia in the eye. "But I'm scared." She sniffled. "I'm scared of needing him and terrified by the idea of losing him."

"Give yourself, and him, a break, and go with the flow while you're up here away from the rest of the world." Her brow furrowed. "How long *are* you going to be up here anyway?"

"Probably a few weeks at least," she said wearily. "Ever since the Council dissolved and the Purists declared war on our people, anyone who didn't publicly declare a side is fair game." Marianna folded her feet under her and leaned on the back of the couch. "Artimus is recruiting everyone he can, and he's not taking no for an answer."

"You know," Olivia began, "I've never really asked you before. Why didn't you declare a side publicly? I mean, you told me that you're a Loyalist, but really, who gives a shit about my feelings on the subject? No one. That's who." She smiled and squeezed her hand. "Why not say it out loud to the people who matter?"

"Just stubborn, I guess." Marianna sniffled and swiped at her eyes. "I was angry. My father died because of his hatred. My mother is dying because of his actions, and all of it is because of this stupid division over breeding with humans. I guess I thought that if I didn't pick a side and stayed neutral on the subject, then I could stay out of it and avoid getting more hurt than I already was." She shrugged. "Silly, huh?"

"No," Olivia sighed and pulled Marianna into a hug. "Switzerland has been getting away with it for years." The two women laughed, and Olivia wiped Marianna's tears away with cool fingers, but the smile faded from her lips. "There's something else, isn't there?"

"Yes." Marianna nodded and rose from the couch. She stoked the fire with the last log in the bin. "Dante and some of the others have been helping the prince investigate what the Purists are up to." She laughed bitterly. "The ironic part is that they've been ferreting out information bit by bit, and the other night at the Waldorf benefit, Artimus came right out and told me what they're up to. He was actually proud of it."

"Well?" Olivia looked at her expectantly. "What is it?"

"I tried to put the whole disgusting idea out of my head and ignore it, but as we can see, the whole pretend-it's-not-happening-thing doesn't work well."

Marianna folded her arms over her breasts and rubbed her arms, trying to get warm but it wasn't working. She grabbed the iron poker and moved the logs around, stoking the flames higher. Staring into the flickering light, she shivered as she forced herself to say it out loud.

"They want to use human technology to genetically engineer pure-blood offspring." She swallowed back the bile that rose in her throat. "And they want to use me and Hayden."

"Over my dead, fucking body," Pete growled.

Marianna spun around and gaped at Pete, who was staring at her with a less than pleased expression. She was so wrapped up in her own thoughts she didn't even hear him come inside.

"Awkward," Olivia murmured. She stood and looked from Marianna to Pete. "It's been a real blast visiting with you kids. I just wanted to make sure Marianna was okay, and she is… sort of." Olivia glanced from her to Pete. "I can see you've got some things to talk about."

Pete stood still with his arms full of firewood and a fierce look that Marianna had only seen once before— that night at the club when Hayden laid his hands on her, Pete had that same ferocious glint in his eyes.

"You don't have to go," Marianna sputtered.

"Yes, she does." Pete didn't take his eyes off Marianna, and his voice was barely audible. "Isn't that right, Olivia?"

"You bet." Olivia rolled her eyes as she wrapped Marianna in a cool embrace. "This isn't going to work if you aren't honest with him," she whispered. "Facing all of this head-on will be a lot easier with him by your side. Trust me, being alone is overrated. I've been doing it for a long time."

Marianna nodded, but said nothing as Olivia went to the door and waved at Pete. He nodded and said something that sounded like good-bye as he dumped the firewood into the copper bin.

"Listen," Olivia said as she opened the front door. "It's against Presidium law for me to get directly involved in this Amoveo civil war." A smile crept over her face. "But… you know how I feel about the rules… if you need me, I'm around."

In a blur of red and a gust of wind, she was gone.

Chapter 9

PETE SAT ON THE COUCH AND STARED INTO THE ROARing fire while he waited for Marianna to come out of the bedroom. The folder Dante had given him was sitting on the table and lay open with Artimus's picture staring back at him.

The man was one cold piece of business.

Pete took a long pull off his beer and leaned both elbows on his knees as he glared at the man in the photograph. His brown eyes were flat and reminded Pete of a shark—emotionless, barren, and evil.

He knew that Artimus and the rest of the Purists wanted Marianna on their side, and until a few minutes ago, he hadn't been able to figure out why they were desperate for *her* in particular. He never dreamed that they'd try some kind of breeding program. His stomach lurched at idea, knowing that they wanted Marianna as part of their experiment.

He'd texted Dante yesterday to tell him they'd arrived at their destination safely, but he wanted to make an actual phone call to deliver the news about the breeding program. He lost his phone in the lake, and it was too late to be driving into town. He needed to hear the whole story from Marianna before he called Dante with half-baked information.

Frustrated, Pete flipped through the folder and found Hayden and Dr. Moravian's photographs amid other unfamiliar faces. He was certain now that the missing women were taken by Artimus and the Purists as part of the pure-blood breeding program, but he'd be damned if he let them get Marianna.

The click of the bedroom door opening captured his attention, and Marianna came out looking sexier than ever. Her face was free of makeup and her hair was swept up in a clip. She wore a pair of white pajamas that hugged her curvy body in all the right places and accented that gorgeous, lightly tanned skin. Barefoot, she sat on the opposite side of the couch and pulled her feet under her.

Pete was about to say something when there was scratching at the back door accompanied by Tramp's unmistakable bark.

"I should've known that dog would show up eventually," he said as he went to the back door and let him in. When he opened the door, Tramp brushed past him and went directly to Marianna. "Nice to see you too."

The husky immediately placed his head in her lap, seeking her affection. Marianna ruffled his ears and scratched, much to the dog's delight.

"I've never been jealous of a dog before," Pete said as he joined her on the couch again. He flicked his gaze from Marianna to Tramp. "But there's a first time for everything."

"I thought you liked him and dogs in general?" she said, looking at the dog lovingly.

"I do. Well, they seem to like me anyway."

"What do you mean?" She turned her big brown eyes on him and smiled warmly, which made his heart squeeze in his chest. Jesus, one look from this woman, and he was completely undone. "Tramp isn't the first stray who's adopted me." He lifted one shoulder and looked at Tramp. "When I was a kid there was a German Shepherd that used to come around here a lot, and in the city, where I grew up, there were a couple neighborhood strays that turned up now and again."

"Are you some kind of dog whisperer?"

"Hardly," he said through a short laugh. "But I will admit that they always showed up when I was going through a tough time. When I was little, my mother told me that they were my guardian angels." He sat back and took another needed sip of his beer. "I used to think it was kind of silly, but given all the recent revelations about crazy critters roaming the earth…" He didn't finish the thought, but captured those big brown eyes once again with his.

The smile on her lips faltered, and she tore her gaze away.

"What's in the folder?"

Marianna picked up the beer he'd gotten for her but avoided looking at him. He studied her carefully and noticed the strictly business attitude that she wore. Great. He'd stepped in it again.

"Dante gave it to me." He handed her the folder, which she promptly flipped through. "It's pictures of the higher-ups from different clans who have declared themselves Purists, among other things."

He watched as she sifted through the pictures one by one, but she stopped at Hayden's. Her entire body went rigid, and her mouth set in a tight line.

"It's sick," she whispered. "The notion of genetically engineering pure-blood children goes against everything we were taught. Our children are created from love, from fate..." She made a sound of disgust. "Hayden was always a spoiled child, and now he's an arrogant, self-entitled prick. I don't like being in the same room with him, let alone the idea of having children with him."

She shuddered and continued going through the folder. All the color drained from her face when she hit the last batch of photographs—they had a note clipped to them that read: *missing*. Marianna stared at the bright-eyed smile of Courtney Bishop as the folder quivered in her unsteady hands.

"Oh my God," she breathed. "This is one of my friends. Why is Courtney's picture in here?" She flipped frantically through the other women's photos before looking back at Pete through frightened eyes. "She and these other women are missing?"

"Yes." Pete's mouth set in a grim line. "Dante said that Courtney and several other pure-blood females have disappeared. He said that they found out Artimus had some kind of acquisition list—and these women were on it." His voice dropped low. "And so are you."

"That's why." Her eyes widened as she realized the magnitude of what was going on. "That's why you and Dante were so worried about Artimus. You think he took these women and that he plans on taking me." She shivered and gave Tramp more scratches, seeking solace as much as the dog was. "Have you told Dante about the breeding program?"

"No." He shook his head and sat back in the corner of the couch, needing to put a little distance between them.

"Why haven't you told Dante yet?"

"My cell phone fell into the lake when I fished you

out. I'll go into town tomorrow and use one of the pay phones. There's no phone here in the cabin, and no TV or Internet, in case you hadn't noticed."

"I noticed." She rolled her eyes. "Is there anything else that you and my brother have been keeping from me?" she asked as she closed the folder and placed it on the table. Her eyes flashed, and Tramp whined, as if he was asking her to calm down.

"No." Pete shook his head and scoffed. "But you've got some damn nerve to be annoyed with me. You haven't exactly been forthcoming. When did you plan on telling me about Artimus's breeding program?" His voice rose as his anger and insecurity got the better of him. "Or did you want more time to think it over?"

Hurt and anger flickered over her features. "How can you think that?"

"What am I supposed to think?" He slugged back another gulp of his beer, hoping it could cool his rising temper. Unable to look at her, afraid he'd see utter contempt in her eyes, he looked into the flickering firelight. "I told you why I did what I did. It was the only possible way that I could do my job."

"Being with me is your *job*?"

"Hang on." Pete put his hands up. "It was, at first." He let out a growl of frustration. Feeling edgy and out of his element, Pete stood and stoked the already blazing fire. "At first, it was just a job, and that's what I kept telling myself, every time I picked you up and drove you around town. You're my friend's sister, and on top of everything else, you're Amoveo, and I'm not. Hell, I'm not even a hybrid."

Pete paced in front of the fire as Marianna and Tramp

watched him silently. He ran one hand through his short hair and put the empty beer bottle on the mantel, before turning to face her.

"I'm only a human, Marianna. I didn't think that there was any possible way that you could be mine. I thought you were supposed to be with some Amoveo guy—even though the idea of another man touching you makes me want to rip someone's head off," he growled. Pete's voice dropped to above a whisper. "For the life of me, I can't figure out when it happened."

"When what happened?" Marianna asked quietly as her eyes searched his for answers. The amber glow of the fire washed over her hypnotically.

"When I fell in love with you."

The crackling of the fire was the only sound in the room that Pete heard, other than the thumping of his own heart. She stared back at him with wide eyes, and Pete's gut clenched with fear as he waited for her to respond. Fear. Need. Love. All of it swamped him mercilessly. He thought he'd choke on his own emotions, if she didn't say something soon.

"No." Marianna shook her head, and tears filled her eyes. "Don't say that."

"Why not?" The sting of rejection flashed over him. He'd never told that to a woman before, and when he finally does, she tells him to take it back. His eyes narrowed, and he struggled to keep his temper in check. "Don't want some pathetic human for a mate, is that it?"

"How could you think that?" Marianna rose from the sofa, her eyes glittering as she moved toward him. Tramp tracked her every move. Hands on her hips, she sidled up to him. If she were going to tell him off and rip his heart out, then he'd stand there and take it. Pete braced himself—ready for whatever she had to throw at him.

"I am not a Purist," she said quietly. "I think that my father, Artimus, and the rest are narrow-minded and twisted. I didn't tell you about the breeding program because it's disgusting, and I'd hoped that if I pretended I never heard about it, then it would go away."

She leaned closer, and the look in her eyes softened as she continued.

"I realized you were my mate the other night in the club when I heard your voice in my mind—that's when I knew. The truth is that I've wanted you from the first moment I laid eyes on you at Dante and Kerry's apartment. Based on the intensity of my attraction, I should've known that you were my mate, but because of your shielding or whatever, I couldn't sense it," she said with a wave of her hand. "Then there was the dream realm."

"I remember." A smile curved his lips at the mention of the dream.

He wondered if this was a dream. Was she really saying these things, or was it a cruel joke, and the rug would get pulled from under him at any moment? Not a chance. She wasn't getting off the hook and pretending that this wasn't happening.

"You and me, we are not a dream, and I'm not letting you act like none of this is real. I love you, Marianna. So you better get used to it because I'm not going anywhere."

"I don't *want* you to be in love with me. I don't want you to be my mate because Artimus will *kill you*. Don't you get it?" Her voice quivered as she inched closer, and the familiar enticing scent of peaches filled his head. "That night in the dream realm, the bear that tried to attack you? That was Artimus, and if he figures out that you're my mate, then he'll stop at nothing to eliminate the threat—to eliminate *you*." Tears spilled freely down her cheeks as the words tumbled from her lips. "I can handle living like a human for a month—or even forever—but what I couldn't handle is losing you. I'd never forgive myself if you were harmed, and I don't want you to give up your life for me."

"Marianna," Pete whispered her name and took her face in his hands. He smiled as he brushed his thumb over her cheek. "*You* are my life. You're unpredictable, feisty, smart, and drop-dead sexy... and you're mine."

Her eyes fluttered closed and sent more tears cascading down her cheeks. He wiped them away and looked at her with genuine confusion as the heat from the fire wafted over them.

"Can you please tell me why you're crying? I really suck at the emotional stuff, and my grandmother always told me that if I ever make a woman cry, then I better damn well know what I did, so that I don't do it again."

"You did make me cry." She opened her eyes and laughed through her tears. "But you better keep it up."

"You want me to keep making you cry?" He looked at her with confusion, which only made her smile broaden. "I don't think I can take too much more of that."

"No." She sighed. "I want you to tell me things like this for the rest of my life, but you have to promise that there will be no more secrets."

"I think I can handle that," he whispered. "So I guess this means you're okay with having a human for a mate?"

"Okay with it?" Marianna hooked her thumbs through the belt loops of his jeans and yanked him against her. She looked at him seductively from beneath a fan of dark lashes as she pressed her warm body against his. "I'm more than okay with it, but I have one question."

Pete held his breath and waited. The fire crackling and the sound of their breathing filled the room as she smiled with that stony look. He slipped one hand to the nape of her neck and released her long, rich brown hair from the confines of the clip. Pete tossed the annoying thing on the couch before lacing his fingers through those smooth locks.

"Take me to bed?"

"I don't think so," he murmured.

Her eyes widened with surprise, and she opened her mouth to undoubtedly tell him off, but before she could say a word he covered it with his. The sweet fragrance of peaches and vanilla flooded his senses as her tongue tangled with his.

He tilted her head, deepening the kiss and angling for more, for every bit of her that she could give. He wanted it all.

She grabbed the front of his shirt and tore it open, sending buttons flying across the room. As he nibbled and tasted her sweet lips, he sighed when her fingernails trailed down his back.

"The bed is too far away," Pete murmured between kisses. He whipped her top off as she kicked off her bottoms, revealing the flawless skin beneath. He looked at her and groaned. "You are gorgeous."

"Shut up." Marianna kissed him as she made quick work of undoing his jeans.

Pete swore silently as her warm fingers wrapped around the length of him. She worked him in her palm as he shucked his jeans. Running her fingers up and down his erection, she kissed and nibbled her way down his neck. Fire, deep carnal need, flashed through him, and if she kept stroking him things would be over before they started.

Tramp barked. Pete forgot the dog was still there.

"No way, buddy," he said between heavy breaths.

"What are you going to do?" Marianna whispered as she rained kisses along his chest. "Throw the poor dog in the snow?" She flicked his nipple with her tongue wickedly and ran her hands over his ass.

"Nope." He slid his hands over Marianna's hips and kissed her shoulder as she ran her nails lightly along his engorged cock. He reached around and slipped two fingers into her hot, wet channel. Her lips parted, and she gasped as he slid them in and out slowly, teasingly. "You're so wet, but I want you wet all over."

"Yes," she breathed. Marianna bit her lip and nodded as she clung to his shoulders and pressed herself against his hand.

Pete picked her up and brought her into the bathroom, leaving Tramp alone on the couch. He kicked the door closed and carried her into the shower. Placing her down, she stood behind him as he turned on the water, assuring it wasn't too hot or too cold. Marianna kissed his back and grabbed him with both hands. One hand brushed up and down his cock in slow, deliberate strokes as the other massaged his balls.

The hot water sprayed over them as Pete braced himself on the tiled wall, and he sank into the erotic effect of her touch. She whispered words of seduction as she took him to the edge of sanity.

No way. Not yet. He wanted this to last.

Pete pushed himself away from the wall, turned, and took her in his arms again. He wanted to taste every bit of her. He spun her around and took both breasts in his hands as she arched back, pushing herself deeper into his grasp. Marianna reached up and ran her fingers through his hair as he rained kisses along her throat. She groaned and writhed against him.

"Please," she gasped. "I want you inside of me."

"Not yet," Pete ground out. "I have to taste you."

He dropped to his knees and kissed the bruise on her round backside, the one she got from jumping from the car. Pete smiled, grasped her hips, and turned her to face him. She looked at him through a heavy-lidded gaze and leaned against the wall, preparing herself for what was coming.

He slid his hands up the slippery skin of her legs and brushed kisses along her inner thigh as she quivered in tense anticipation. He parted her lips, revealing the treasure hidden beneath, and took one long, loving taste.

Marianna's entire body jolted when he put his mouth on her. She grabbed his hair as he dove deep and tasted the most intimate part of her, writhing and moaning as he held her prisoner. Pete licked, suckled, and massaged her to the edge of orgasm.

He stopped short of taking her over the brink and kissed his way up her flat belly, over her breasts, and finally to that succulent mouth.

"If you don't fuck me soon," she growled against his lips, "I'm going to scream."

"That's what I want, Marianna." Pete lifted one of her legs and wrapped it around his waist as he positioned the head of his cock at her swollen entrance. "I want you to scream for me."

In one sure stroke, he speared into her hard and fast. Tight, hot, and wet, she covered him perfectly. Pete moaned as he withdrew and dove in deep again. She clung to him as he pumped into her with smooth, swift strokes. Marianna's cries of pleasure filled the room. She took his head in her hands, brought his mouth to hers, and kissed him deeply as he drove into her at a maddening pace.

She broke the kiss and looked him into his eyes as he sank into her harder—faster.

"*Nos es unus. Materia pro totus vicis. Ago intertwined. Forever,*" she whispered against his lips. Marianna cried out as he plunged deeply and sent them over the edge with one last thrust.

As the water beat down on them, breathing like they'd just run a marathon, they stayed locked in each other's embrace. He was buried deep inside, but neither moved until they realized the water was getting cold. Tramp was whining and scratching at the door.

"At least his timing is getting better." Pete kissed the top of her head and slowly disengaged from the warmth of her body. He shut off the water as she stepped out of the shower. "What was that you said right before…" he trailed off. He snagged two towels, handed her one, and dried off before wrapping it around his waist.

"Nothing." Marianna looked away and used the towel Pete gave her. She shrugged and ran her hands through her long, wet hair. "I don't think it really means anything right now."

"Hey." Pete took her hands and pulled them against his chest, forcing her to look him in the eye. "No more secrets. Remember? What did you say?"

"It was the bonding rite," she said quietly. "It basically means, 'We are one. Mates for all time. Lives intertwined. Forever.' But I'm not sure if it worked," she added quickly.

"So that's it?" Pete asked warily. "You said that phrase while we... y'know... and we're mated?"

"Yes, we're supposed to be, but with the binding powder in place... I'm not sure." Marianna looked at him nervously. "Are you mad?"

"Depends." He narrowed his eyes and tilted her chin with one finger. "Does this mean that we're married?"

"Yes," she said tentatively. "As far as the Amoveo are concerned, we're married." Marianna studied him through watchful eyes. "What is it?"

"I like it." Pete winked and smacked her ass. "You just saved me a bundle on a ring."

Before she could tell him what a jackass he was, he kissed her, opened the door, and tossed her over his shoulder as she wiggled and laughed, trying to escape. Tramp barked playfully and followed them into the bedroom.

"You know what I'm thinking?" Pete said as he tossed a giggling Marianna onto the bed.

"I haven't the foggiest notion." She sat up and removed her towel slowly, baring those magnificent breasts. "You forget that I can't read your energy." She sighed and yanked Pete's towel off his waist and tossed it into the corner with hers. She glanced at his growing erection. "But there are certain things that I can... sense."

Neither noticed when Tramp made quick work of turning the towels into his bed.

"I think we better try it again." He covered her body with his and kissed the corner of her mouth. "I want to make sure that bonding rite worked."

Chapter 10

THE FIRST FEW WEEKS AT THE CABIN WENT BY SURPRIS-
ingly fast. Marianna had never played so many board
games, read so many books, or had so much sex in her
life—and for all intents and purposes—she did it all as
a human.

There had been a few moments when she attempted
telepathy or used her visualization abilities, but it never
worked. She wasn't doing it to try and get away from
Pete; she just wanted to see if she could do it, but to
no avail.

Eventually, she stopped trying and accepted her
human life for what it was. She knew that with Pete as
her mate, eventually, a human life is what she would
have permanently. If being mated to Pete meant eventually giving up her Amoveo gifts forever, then that's
what she would do.

The best gift was having him as her mate.

Pete delighted in showing her the joys of snowmobil-
ing, although she thought that her whole body was going
to vibrate for days afterwards. They explored various
parts of the property, and it was evident that Pete took
pure joy in sharing his home. Tramp came and went as
he pleased, but Marianna missed having him around
when he went off on his excursions.

Pete had been promising her a night in town, and
since he had to check in with Dante again, she finally

got him to agree to go to Flannagan's Bar for something to eat other than their cooking. The only catch was that because so much snow had fallen, they would be going into town on his snowmobile.

"My ass is going to vibrate forever. In fact, I think it's still humming from the ride we took yesterday." Marianna stood next to Pete and stared at the buzzing contraption with a look of contempt. She reluctantly put on the helmet he handed her. "Why can't we take the truck?"

"Well, we could, but this is more fun." Pete smacked her butt playfully and hopped on. "Come on. It's got a headlight and everything, and I think your skin is humming from the other ride we took." He wiggled his eyebrows, and she couldn't help but laugh. When she didn't move to get on with him, he lowered his voice to a challenging tone. "I thought you were a badass."

"Didn't anyone tell you that peer pressure isn't nice?" She climbed on behind him and wrapped her arms tightly around his waist.

"It's not peer pressure," he shouted over the buzz of the engine. "It's good, old-fashioned teasing."

He took off down the snow-covered driveway, and Marianna hung on for dear life. He knew this area like the back of his hand, so she knew she was safe, but that didn't squash the twinge of fear. It reminded her of a roller coaster ride. You were safe, but there was always that small voice in the back of your mind that told you it could go flying off the rails at any second. As she clung to him and watched the trees whizz by, she realized that's what life with Pete was like—an exhilarating ride into the unknown and something new at every turn.

When they pulled up in front of Flannagan's, Marianna smirked when she saw the line of snowmobiles parked outside the bar.

"See, everybody's doing it," Pete teased.

"Very funny." Marianna got off the snowmobile, removed the helmet, and shook out her hair. "My ass is buzzing."

"Let me check." Smiling, Pete looped one arm around her and grabbed her backside. "It's hot, but it's not buzzing."

Marianna laughed and elbowed him playfully as they walked hand in hand into Flannagan's.

The pub was exactly what she expected. The small dark space had a bar at the center with tables scattered around. A deer head with two ladies' bras dangling from the antlers hung above the bar, with a dartboard to the right and an old-fashioned jukebox to the left that rounded the place out.

The pub had several customers, many of whom probably belonged to the snowmobiles outside. The bartender, a big blond, bearded fellow, smiled broadly and waved at Pete.

"Well, I'll be damned. Pete Castro. I heard you were back in town." He shook Pete's hand over the bar, smacked him on the shoulder, and glanced at Marianna. "I'd ask what you've been doing with yourself, but that's probably none of my business."

"Patrick," Pete began with a broad grin, "this… is my fiancée Marianna."

Marianna, too surprised to say anything, simply smiled sheepishly and shook Patrick's outstretched hand. She glanced at Pete, who looked prouder than a peacock and totally comfortable with the fact that he'd introduced her as his fiancée.

"Your fiancée?" Patrick bellowed. He reached over the bar and pulled Marianna into an unexpected hug. "Congratulations," he said, releasing her. "Drinks on the house tonight for both of you. What'll it be?"

"I'd love an Amstel." Pete settled himself on the bar stool. "And for my lovely bride-to-be?"

"Oh, I'd love a gin and tonic, thank you." Marianna sat next to Pete and looked at him through narrowed eyes as she removed her coat and gloves. Patrick moved down the bar to gather her drink. "I have to admit that I wasn't prepared for that," she said quietly, not wanting Patrick to overhear.

"What?" he asked innocently, while keeping one eye on Patrick. "You mean the 'fiancée' thing?"

"Yes." She laughed. "That."

"Well, I wanted to ease you into it. I'm not gonna wait much longer to make it official and marry you for real." He trained his bright blue eyes on her, and they twinkled at her suggestively. "You better get used to it because I don't think I can introduce you to my friends as my mate." He shrugged. "Not that I have many friends—human ones, anyway. My former partner, Doug, wouldn't exactly get the whole mate thing. So wife will have to do."

"You never did tell me why you left the police force."

Pete tensed and grabbed a handful of bar mix from the bowl in front of them. Boy, she wished she could still read energy signatures, but she was getting better at understanding Pete. She'd hit a nerve, and that only piqued her curiosity to know more.

"I worked homicide, as you know." He offered her the snack in his hand but didn't look at her. "A woman and her baby had been hacked up by her ex-husband and stuffed in garbage bags. She had a restraining order and all that crap, but in the end… he still got to her."

Silence hung in the air as she waited for him to continue. He popped the rest of the peanuts in his mouth and brushed his hands off.

"We cornered the son of a bitch in a crack house, and he opened fire on us, but I'm a better shot." He flicked his eyes toward her. "I quit the next day. The guy had a rap sheet longer than my arm. He was a career criminal, a drug addict with a history of violence. That woman tried everything she could to keep him away, but the system failed her and her baby. I'd met Dante on another case, and he'd told me that if I ever wanted a job, it was mine. So I took him up on his offer."

"Didn't you go into law enforcement so that you could get the bad guys and protect people? Why would you quit?"

"I didn't quit." His eyes flashed. "I just switched teams. Working with Dante in the private sector, I'm able to get to these dirtbags before they hurt someone. I decided to focus on prevention, instead of cleanup."

Marianna nodded. Finally, she understood. Pete was a protector. He wanted to keep people safe, keep her safe. That's all he ever wanted.

"Here you go." Patrick placed their drinks in front of them, breaking up their private conversation. "Pete's getting married?" He shook his head, and his words were edged with obvious disbelief. "Brittany is gonna be disappointed."

"Patrick, why do you seem so surprised that I managed to rope Pete into marriage?" Marianna asked, trying to lighten the mood. "Does he have that much of a reputation as a playboy?"

"Not at all." Patrick chuckled and folded his arms over his large belly. "For a while there, I wasn't even sure if he liked girls."

"Hey," Pete said, feigning injury. "I'm merely selective."

"Well, it certainly looks like it paid off." Patrick winked at Marianna. "If you ever get tired of old blue eyes over here, you give me a call."

"I'll keep that in mind," Marianna said through a laugh, before taking a sip of her drink.

"Hey, quit flirting with my fiancée, you big jerk." Pete winked at Marianna as Patrick laughed heartily and made his way down the bar. "Go help your customers."

"Did you come in here with your mom and grandparents a lot?" Marianna surveyed the bar and noticed as several people nodded and smiled at Pete. "You may not be one of the locals, but it seems like you're an adopted son."

"My grandparents used to take me here for burgers and stuff." He peeled the label off his beer and worried it into a ball between his fingers. "Grandpa died before I was old enough to come have a beer with him though."

"What about your father?" She watched him through serious eyes and saw anger flicker beneath the surface. She'd gotten him to open up about part of his past; maybe she could get more. "You never mention him."

"I never knew him," he said flatly. Pete turned his piercing gaze to hers. "He took off before I was born, and it just about killed my mother. By all accounts, before she met him, she was bright, happy, and loved life. Grandpa said that she fell head over heels in love with my father, but then when she told him she was pregnant, he split."

He looked back at the beer in his hands, and anger was replaced by the unmistakable weight of sadness. Marianna's heart broke for him and for the woman she never met. It seemed clear that neither human nor Amoveo were immune to betrayal and heartbreak.

"I never knew the woman that they described. They said she was never the same after my father left, and no matter what I did or said… it was never enough to make her happy." He took a long pull from his beer and shrugged. "She was just broken, I guess. For all intents and purposes, my grandparents raised me. My mother was physically there, but she wasn't… *there*. It took me a long time to realize that it wasn't my fault."

"I'm sorry." Marianna placed her hand over his and brushed her thumb along his fingers reassuringly. "I wish I could've met them, especially your grandparents."

"Me too." He squeezed her hand briefly before releasing it. "I'd better give Dante a call and see if there are any new developments. Grab us that little booth in the corner, the one with the green and yellow tablecloth, will you?"

He placed a warm kiss on her cheek as he stood from his seat, and Marianna watched as he strode to the pay phone. His broad-shouldered frame cut an imposing figure, and the man looked as good going as he did coming. Her thoughts wandered to what he'd been telling her, and a smile played at her lips.

He shared his past, opened up in a way that he never

had before, and then hopped up to make a phone call. Typical man, she thought with a shake of her head. Men were incredibly good at simplifying their feelings and acting like past experiences didn't shape who they were. She wished she could've met his grandparents so that she could thank them for raising such a good man.

Marianna grabbed their things and settled into the small curved booth.

"Looks like Pete finally got saddled." The feminine voice, edged with clear disdain, immediately set Marianna on edge.

She looked up and locked eyes with a freckle-faced brunette, who she could only assume was the infamous Brittany. Dressed in a Flannagan's T-shirt and jeans, notepad and pen in hand, she looked Marianna up and down with the critical eye of a woman scorned. Chewing on a wad of gum, her pale blue eyes were lined with too much makeup and years of unhappiness.

"I'm sorry, but I don't believe we've met." Marianna extended her hand to the woman who shook it weakly before dropping it like a hot potato. "I'm Marianna, Pete's fiancée."

"Yeah," she said tightly. "That's what I heard. Pat was blathering on about it to the guys in the kitchen, but I had to see it for myself."

"And you are?" Marianna asked, trying to be friendly, but knowing that this woman had little interest in being friends.

"I'm Brittany. Pete and I used to... hang out." A wicked smile slithered across her face. "You're a lucky woman." She looked over her shoulder at Pete, who was on the pay phone. "That's one big hunk of man, and if memory serves, he really knows his way around a woman's body."

Marianna hadn't missed her Amoveo abilities over the last week or two. However, right now, she'd give just about anything to shift her eyes into their clan form and scare the shit out of this woman. She wasn't stupid or naive. She knew Pete had other lovers. Hell, she'd had a few of her own. But she didn't need it rubbed in her face, especially by this woman.

She may not have her ability to shift, but she could still play head games with the best of them. The only way to win with a woman like Brittany was to make sure she didn't get to you—at least don't let her see it.

"He sure does. I can assure you that his skill set is second to none." Marianna tilted her chin and smiled sweetly as she surveyed the table before turning her attention back to Brittany. "Do you think we could get some menus?"

"Fine." Brittany's jaw set, and she hissed under her breath as she slapped two greasy menus on the table. "Hurry up. Kitchen's closing early tonight."

"Hello, Brittany." Pete slid into the seat next to Marianna and draped his arm behind her on the back of the booth. Brittany jumped at the sound his voice, and her face flushed. He picked up the menu and had a look. "What's good tonight?"

"Menu hasn't changed here in close to twenty years, Pete, but I'll get you some water while you have a look." She smiled, but the smile vanished when she looked in Marianna's direction. "Be right back."

"You must've done quite a number on her," Marianna said under her breath. "That is one angry woman."

"We dated one summer after high school." He lay the menu down and leaned back in the booth, which creaked in protest. A smile cracked his handsome face. "Jealous?"

"Hardly." Marianna rolled her eyes and pretended to be interested in her menu. "I don't need to read her energy signature to tell that she was obviously holding a candle for you and meeting your *fiancée* snuffed it out in one fell swoop."

"I never made her any promises." He sighed. "We were just kids, Marianna." His eyebrows knit together, and confusion covered his face. "Are you upset about something?"

Marianna lifted one shoulder as she studied the limited offerings. She was annoyed, but not at Pete. She was annoyed with herself for allowing a woman like Brittany to get under her skin. She'd never been jealous in her life, and she knew—intellectually, she knew—she had no reason to be jealous, but she was. It was stupid and juvenile, but she couldn't help it. The notion of another woman touching Pete made her want to tear that woman's hair out.

"What did Dante have to say?" she asked, changing the subject.

"Richard is concerned that their man on the inside might have been discovered. They haven't heard a peep from him in over two weeks, and two more women have gone missing. Both unmated, pure-blood females from different clans, and they're barely eighteen years old."

"It's sick." Marianna shook her head as if she could shake out information about what Artimus was doing. "Any idea where his base of operations is?"

"No." Pete shook his head grimly. "They had several leads, but so far nothing. Richard feels that Artimus is using the advanced shielding that the elders possess to hide him and anyone who's with him."

Marianna nodded and sat back as Brittany strutted by with a tray full of drinks. She didn't miss the lusty look she cast in Pete's direction or the provocative wiggle of her hips as she passed by.

Pete didn't miss that or the look on Marianna's face. "You're not really letting her get under your skin, are you? Don't you think we've got bigger problems?"

"I know. It's silly, and to be honest, I'm surprised at myself." She took a swig of her drink and glanced at Brittany, who was over by the jukebox whispering to another waitress. "I guess I wasn't prepared to answer questions about us or meet old girlfriends. Remember how upset you got with Hayden when he put his hands on me at The Coven?"

Pete's features darkened. "Yes."

"Well, that's how I feel, but you actually slept with her." She put her hands up before he could say anything. "I know it's dumb. I know, but I can't help it… must be a mate thing."

Pete nodded, and a smile broke out across his face. "Must be," he said quietly as he pulled her against him and kissed her head. "I kind of like it. I have to admit that there's something sexy as hell about a gorgeous thing like you getting jealous over a fling from fifteen years ago." The smile faltered, and his tone grew serious. "By the way, Hayden's lucky I didn't take out my gun and shoot him for putting his hands on you."

Looking into those intense blue eyes, she knew he

meant what he said. There was a predatory and protective side to Pete that she knew had the potential to be deadly. She had no doubt that he would kill to protect her, which was frightening and intriguing. That night he'd shown up in the club, he'd instinctively known that she needed him, and it was in that moment everything changed.

"That's when I heard you for the first time." Her voice fell to above a whisper as she stared into those captivating eyes. She sucked in a slow breath, and her lips lifted as she saw desire bloom in his gaze. "That's really the only thing I wish I could still do. Hear you in my mind. Touch your mind with mine while we make love and join with you in every possible way."

"Did you make up your mind yet?" Brittany's irritating voice sliced into their conversation, but neither looked up.

"I'm famished." Marianna held Pete's attention firmly. "I'll have the house special."

"Me too," Pete murmured.

They barely noticed as Brittany huffed away with the menus.

"I *am* famished." She sighed. "But not for food." Marianna leaned into Pete's embrace and brushed her hand along his jean-clad thigh beneath the table. She whispered into his ear as his five o'clock shadow rasped enticingly along her cheek. "I've got a house special for you… if you're interested."

She shifted in the booth and gave a surreptitious glance around the room to see if anyone was watching. Not that she'd care.

"Oh, I'm interested." Pete played with her hair as she snuggled in his arms, and his entire body, hard and taut, hummed against her with anticipation. He picked up his beer and took one long pull, as if trying to put out the flames. "You are full of surprises, aren't you?"

"Must be the bear in me," she whispered as she discreetly undid his belt beneath the table and tablecloth.

He was already hard and sprang from the confines of his jeans easily. Pete tensed and let out a long, slow breath as Marianna wrapped her fingers around him and stroked. She leaned one elbow on the table and smiled wickedly as she brushed her fingertips along the engorged length of him.

His eyes flicked around the room before landing on hers once again. There was something wickedly erotic about touching him this way in the middle of a public place without anyone knowing. It was powerful and intoxicating—a major turn-on. It was like that ride on the snowmobile. One wrong move, and they could be discovered.

"This was the perfect table," Marianna murmured as she sipped her drink casually.

Pete nodded and grunted something that sounded like agreement as she squeezed him and ran her thumb over the swollen head. He leaned both elbows on the table and pressed his folded hands against his lips as she massaged him.

"Brittany." Marianna waved her free hand, flagging her down. Pete stilled, and Marianna smirked as she saw a flicker of panic wash over him. She slowed her pace, but kept her fingers trailing up and down his cock beneath the well-covered table.

"Yeah?" Brittany's annoyance was evident, but her brows furrowed with concern when she looked at Pete. "You okay? You're all flushed and sweating like a pig."

Marianna ran her thumb over him again as she smiled at Brittany. "Actually, that's why I called you over. Pete is feeling a bit… hot." His cock twitched as she flicked her gaze to Pete, who nodded curtly. "Could we please get that dinner to go?"

"Sure." She cast a suspicious glance from Marianna to Pete as she walked away.

Marianna ran her fingernails gingerly up the hot length of him before pulling her hand away completely. She leaned back in the booth and ran both hands through her long hair with a satisfied sigh as Pete discreetly put himself back together.

"Oh, you're gonna pay for that," he said with a wicked grin.

"I should hope so." She winked over the rim of her glass and couldn't wait to see what he'd do to even the score.

———

Pete hauled ass back to the cabin, and Marianna thought at several points they were going to careen into the trees, but in true Pete fashion, they made it back safely. Driving like a man with a mission, he pulled the snowmobile in front of the cabin and skidded to a halt, sending a wave of snow onto the already snow-covered steps.

Marianna took off her helmet and hopped off the blasted contraption. Pete stared at her through serious eyes as he removed his own helmet and tossed it into the snowbank. He didn't shut off the engine, but slid back and patted the empty space in front.

"What?" Marianna shouted over the noise of the engine. "I'm not driving that thing."

"No," Pete agreed. "You're definitely not driving tonight."

With lightning-fast reflexes, he hooked one arm around her waist and pulled her to him. Pete pushed her jacket and sweater up, baring her flat belly to the ice-cold air. She shivered as he licked and nibbled at the tender flesh of her stomach, while he gently pulled her black leggings over her hips. Marianna grabbed his hands to stop him, but he shook his head slowly and made a scolding sound as he flicked his tongue into her belly button.

"It's freezing out here." Marianna ran her fingers through his short dark hair as he rained kisses along the curve of her hip. "What exactly did you have in mind?"

"I just thought of something that might change your mind about riding my snowmobile." He tugged her hips toward him. "Get on."

Intrigued, Marianna straddled the bike in front of Pete, but when she went to sit down, he grabbed her hips and stopped her. She glanced over her shoulder, and he looked up with that cocky grin she'd come to adore.

"Grab the handlebars, and stay like that," he said above the din of the engine. "Do you trust me?"

Shivering from a heady combination of cold, lust, and anticipation, Marianna bit her lower lip and nodded. She leaned forward and gripped the handlebars tightly as Pete pushed her leggings down to expose her bare ass to the winter air and trailed hot kisses along her bottom. Vibrations from the buzzing engine ran up her arms and through her entire body, having a far different effect than usual.

Pete's hand slipped beneath her sweater, flicked

aside her bra, and captured her breast greedily. He massaged and rolled her nipple between his fingers as he reached between her legs, finding her most tender flesh. Marianna gasped as he slid two fingers deep inside and rubbed her clit with his thumb.

Head back and eyes closed, she cried out as he teased her to the edge, and wave after wave of pleasure whipped through her. The frigid winds blew against her hot skin as Pete's touch mixed enticingly with the vibrations of the humming machine. He nibbled and licked at the exposed flesh along her waist as he pushed his fingers in and out of her hot, wet channel. She tried not to move, but she needed more, wanted to take him deeper.

"Please." She moaned and writhed for release. Marianna looked over her shoulder and pushed herself against his hand. "I need you, all of you."

Pete looked at her and placed one kiss on her hip as he made swift work of undoing his pants. She watched as he stroked himself while stroking her at the same time, and Marianna didn't think she'd ever experienced anything more erotic.

She flicked her eyes to his. "Now."

Pete clutched her hips as he stood behind her. Still gripping the handlebars for dear life, Marianna leaned forward, offering herself, and in one swift thrust, he arrowed into her hard and deep. Marianna cried out as he speared again and again with slow, deliberate strokes, taking her to the peak, and finally, over the edge into oblivion.

Still lodged inside her, Pete collapsed and braced his hands on the handlebars on either side of Marianna's. "So," he said between heavy breaths. "Think you'll like the snowmobile any better now?"

Marianna, still breathless, placed a kiss on his unshaven cheek as they pushed themselves off the handlebars, and he slipped from the warmth of her body.
"Something tells me that I'll never look at a snowmobile
the same way again."

Pete shut off the engine as she shivered and pulled up
her leggings. He gave her a hand as she climbed off the
machine onto unsteady legs and swept her into another
breath-stealing kiss.

God, I love this woman.

His voice floated into her mind with surprising ease.
Marianna froze and looked at him through wide eyes.
Had she really heard that? It had been almost a month
since he'd used the binding powder. Could it be wearing
off already?

"What's wrong?" Pete asked.

"Nothing." She kissed his cheek quickly and shrugged.
"Just cold, I guess."

"Right." He studied her carefully as she slipped out
of his embrace and headed for the steps. Pete grabbed
the bags with their food out of the storage compartment
and followed her inside.

"I'll get this on the table," she said, taking the bags
and heading into the kitchen.

While Pete made the fire and she put dinner on the
table, Marianna squelched the guilt of not telling Pete
what she'd heard. She kept telling herself that there was
no use in saying anything until she was absolutely certain.

Lying to herself didn't count, did it?

Chapter 11

THE SUNLIGHT STREAMED THROUGH THE WINDOW, casting an early morning glow in the small bedroom. Pete was sound asleep with his long naked body spooned comfortably around Marianna in a familiar way. She hadn't slept much that night and couldn't stop thinking about the sound and feel of Pete's voice touching her mind.

Tangled up in skin, she snuggled deeper into his embrace and ran her fingertips along his arm that draped over her possessively. Marianna closed her eyes and sighed contentedly, enjoying the feel of his bare skin pressed along hers, and then she heard it.

Marianna.

It was faint at first and sounded muffled and far away, but she recognized it immediately. It was her mother's voice. The warm, familiar sound flitted along the edges of her mind.

Marianna. Her pleading grew louder and resonated through Marianna's mind. *Can you hear me?*

Yes. Marianna reached out and touched her mind with relief. *Yes, Mother. I can hear you.*

Pete said something incoherent in his sleep and tightened his grip. She whispered soothing sounds and kissed his cheek as she slipped out of bed. "I have to use the bathroom. I'll be right back."

As silently as possible, Marianna pulled on her white

pajamas and went into the living room, closing the door quietly, careful not to disturb Pete. She stood at the center of the room and closed her eyes, focusing on following the comforting path to her mother.

I've been so worried. Are you alright? I thought you were like those other girls who've gone missing, but Dante kept assuring me that you're okay. Her voice quivered, and Marianna could tell she was crying. *I can hardly use telepathy anymore since your father died, and I've been so lonely without you.*

I'm so sorry, Mother. Marianna wiped away a tear and struggled to maintain the connection. *I want you to know that I'm alright. I'm better than alright...my mate found me.*

Marianna, that's wonderful. What clan is he from? Marianna...

Her mother's voice faded, as the connection dissolved and vanished.

Mother? Mother, can you hear me?

Marianna tried to reestablish the link, but to no avail. She wandered to the window and stared at the snow-covered woods. She wondered if the connection was lost due to her abilities coming back sporadically or her mother's waning powers.

She glanced at the bedroom door, focused her energy, and reached for Pete's energy signature. Lightning flashed in her mind as his spiritual fingerprint connected with hers. She sucked in a shuddering breath and grinned as her body was energized by him... and something else.

It felt as though there was another layer to his energy—or hers—she wasn't sure why, but she chalked it up to being mated. She knew that all Amoveo's energy signatures changed once they were mated, so maybe that was it? She wanted to try telepathy to reach Dante, but she knew he'd be pissed that her powers were back and worried that Artimus would find her.

Let him, she thought. He'd get a face full of bear claw.

Grinning, and too excited for words, Marianna looked at the snowy trees and frozen lake. As silently as possible, she opened the door and stepped outside. Her grin broadened as she trotted down the steps barefoot and found herself once again unfazed by the cold. The only thing that would make this moment complete would be shifting into her clan form.

After a quick run in her bear form, she'd tell Pete that her powers were back and let him use another dose of binding powder on her again. He'd have to in order to keep Artimus in the dark about where she was, but first she needed one run in her clan form—one little run couldn't hurt.

Marianna trotted through the snow and breathed in the clean, cool air vigorously. She stopped along the edge of the lake, closed her eyes, stretched her arms wide, and whispered the ancient language. *Verto*.

In a flash of static and a rush of energy, the familiar flicker of the shift washed over her skin as her body undulated, stretched, and erupted into her Kodiak bear. With a growl, she fell to all four paws and shook her brown furry body enthusiastically. Reveling in the buzzing energy of the shift, Marianna lumbered into the woods and lifted her snout to breathe in the multitude of scents that filled the air.

Pine. Snow. Wood burning from a fireplace somewhere on the lake. Dirt.

A low satisfied growl rumbled in her throat as she took in each scent. She could smell things in her human form, but nothing like this, and perhaps it took not having the heightened sense of smell to appreciate it. It was as if every scent was ten times stronger, and somehow, each encapsulated separately from the others. She stood on her hind legs, pointed her black-tipped snout to the air, and took in another deep breath.

A new scent captured her attention as a low menacing growl rumbled from behind her.

Tramp.

Marianna dropped to all fours and turned to see Tramp hunched low, hackles raised, and snarling ferociously. The dog growled, baring his mouthful of sharp teeth, and in that moment, she had no doubt he would attack. Marianna stood still, not wanting to frighten him more than she already had. She whispered the ancient language, *Verto*, and in a blink, shifted back into her human form.

"Hey, buddy," she said with a smile. The dog whined, backed away, and shifted his weight nervously from paw to paw. She extended her hand and let him sniff it, to assure him that it was her indeed. It only took a sniff or two before the dog jumped up and licked her in the face happily.

As she ruffled the dog's ears the way he loved, she noticed that extra ripple in her energy signature again.

"Hang on, Tramp. Stop jumping on me for a second." Marianna pushed the dog down gently and closed her eyes, focusing on the unfamiliar signature that pulsed and throbbed, like a heartbeat. It was separate from hers, but linked as well. She intensified her focus and detected not one, but two, distinct signatures.

They were faint and muffled... as if buried or under-water... or...

Her eyes shifted with a tingling snap to her clan form as she discovered the source of the signatures, and all of her breath rushed from her lungs.

Marianna placed two shaking hands on her lower belly.

"Oh my God," she whispered. "Oh my God... I'm pregnant."

Laughing through tears, she rubbed her stomach and closed her eyes again, wanting to listen and feel those beautiful new signatures. Twins. It had to be twins.

"Pregnant?" She laughed again, and her thoughts went immediately to Pete. Would he share her enthu-siasm? He'd already had so many changes, so much to deal with, would he be as excited as she was?

The cold hand of doubt crawled up her back as the sound of Tramp growling again captured her attention. However, before Marianna could ask the dog what was wrong, Artimus's voice tumbled over her shoulder.

"That's something that can be easily remedied."

Marianna spun around and came face-to-face with Artimus, Hayden, and Daniella, a former guardian for the prince who'd defected to the Purists.

"You've been a bad girl, Marianna. Hiding from us like this." He inched closer. "We've been scanning for your energy signature for several weeks. Hayden had almost given up hope of finding you, so imagine how pleased he was when we stumbled upon it this morning."

Tramp started barking at the top of his lungs as Marianna backed away slowly with one hand on her belly. Well, so much for one quick shift not doing any harm.

Pete was going to kill her if they made it out alive.

"It's too late, Artimus." Marianna looked at the three. Fear gripped her heart as she glanced toward the cabin. She couldn't let them get to Pete—he wouldn't stand a chance against them. "I'm already pregnant, so I guess you'll have to find another girl for Hayden."

Tramp barked incessantly and stepped protectively in front of Marianna.

"As I said," he remarked as he grinned and flicked an irritated glance at the dog, "that can be remedied." He snapped his fingers. "Hayden! Daniella!"

The two advanced toward her, but she kept backing off and shook her head. She could visualize herself away, but where would she go? Dante? Her mother? Artimus would follow her wherever she went and going to her family would only put their lives at risk. She'd figure this one out on her own.

"I'm already mated, Artimus." She slipped as she retreated. "The train has left the station."

"Your human plaything and that abomination growing in your womb can be easily eliminated." His eyes shifted into the glowing black eyes of his clan, and a low growl rumbled from his throat. "Don't even think about fighting with me or running because you'll lose. I'm over two hundred years old, and I could tear you to shreds, so be a good girl and come with us."

Tramp continued barking and snarling, but what happened next, happened in a split second.

The dog launched himself at Artimus. Tramp sank his teeth into his arm. Artimus screamed with rage and pain as he grabbed the dog and flung him like a rag doll across the clearing. Tramp slammed into the tree with a yelp and fell in a motionless heap, his blood staining the snow.

"No!" Tears filled Marianna's eyes, and rage flashed through her. "You bastard."

The air filled with static as Hayden exploded into an enormous grizzly bear, and Daniella roared to life as a formidable tiger. Artimus, eyes glowing black as coal with two beasts behind him, stalked her.

"Let's not make this messy," Artimus hissed.

Marianna was about to shift into her clan form and take her chances when she heard Pete's voice.

"Marianna," he screamed as he tore out the back door of the cabin. Pete took the steps in one leap with his gun drawn. Wearing only his jeans he barreled toward them through the snow. "Get out of the way, Marianna!"

The last thing she saw before Artimus grabbed her and visualized them both away was a snarling tiger leaping toward Pete with paws outstretched.

Barking. That fucking dog was barking his head off outside, and through the fog of sleep, Pete's instinct was to snuggle up to Marianna and bemoan Tramp's poor timing—but she was gone. His hand slipped over the smooth sheet, still warm from where her soft, curvy body had slept.

Pete lifted his head and looked around the empty room. He vaguely recalled her saying she was using the bathroom, but that seemed like an awfully long time ago.

"Marianna?" he called out, but was met only with the dog's barking.

In fact, Tramp's barking persisted, frantic and fierce. That dog *never* barked like that—*ever*. Pete threw back the covers and grabbed his jeans from the chair by the bed and pulled them on.

I can't let them get to Pete. Her frightened but determined voice flickered into his mind, sending sheer panic and dread flashing through him.

The binding powder had worn off.

Pete grabbed his gun from under his pillow and ran barefoot to the back door as the barking stopped. He busted open the door, jumped the steps, and landed in the snow, but he couldn't feel the cold. He couldn't feel anything except the desperate need to protect her, and when he saw Marianna cornered by Artimus, a towering grizzly bear, and a fucking tiger—every protective instinct took over.

He would kill them all.

Human. Animal. Amoveo. It didn't matter. He didn't care. They were going to die if they laid a hand on his Marianna. Breathless, muscles straining, Pete aimed his gun at Artimus. "Get out of the way, Marianna!"

The air around her shimmered and rippled like heat coming off pavement. Artimus grabbed her with a smirk of triumph, as Marianna looked him in the eye and vanished from sight.

"No," Pete bellowed as he watched the only woman he ever loved disappear into thin air. Pete squeezed off two shots as the massive tiger snarled and leaped toward him.

Both shots hit their mark, and the beast roared in pain and surprise as it dropped into the snow, skidding to a halt and thrashing at Pete's feet. Moments later, the tiger

shimmered and shifted into a bleeding and pissed off
woman. Swearing like a sailor and clutching her bleeding limbs, she glared at Pete through glowing orange
eyes. Still trying to catch his breath, Pete snatched the
binding powder vial from the pocket of his jeans and
blew the rest in her face.

"I hope you fucking choke," he spat.

He watched as she sputtered, coughed, and winced
in pain from the gunshot wounds in her arm and leg. A
sense of satisfaction came over him as he saw her realize
her powers were gone. Her eyes flickered and shifted to
normal, light brown human eyes full of confusion.

"What—what the hell?" She looked around frantically.

"Those are some nice friends you've got. They pulled
their little disappearing act and left you behind." He
stuffed the empty vial back in his pocket and pointed the
gun at her head. "In case you haven't figured it out yet,
sweetheart, that stuff you inhaled just snuffed out your
Amoveo powers. You're stuck in your human form, so
I wouldn't try anything funny, or I'll add another hole."
He cocked the gun. "Got it?"

The woman nodded furiously and winced as even that
movement brought her pain.

He kept the gun pointed at her. "What's your name?"

"Daniella Trejada," she said through clenched teeth.

"Where did they take her?" A whimpering sound to
his left captured his attention, interrupting his interrogation. "Don't move."

"Is that a joke?" she spat. "I'm bleeding like a
stuck pig."

Ignoring her, Pete moved cautiously toward the tree
line and swore loudly when he saw Tramp lying in

blood-soaked snow. The dog lifted his head and whined as Pete approached.

"Hey buddy," Pete said in soothing tones. He squatted down and stroked the dog's head gently as he ran his hands over his back.

"I can't help you find her, if you let me bleed to death," Daniella yelled.

"Priorities." Pete inspected Tramp's injuries. "You get help *after* the dog."

There was swelling along Tramp's ribs and a large gash on his back from where he hit the tree. With as much care as he could muster, Pete picked him up and carried him into the cabin. He placed the dog on the couch and covered him with a blanket before he grabbed two scarves off the coatrack and went to retrieve the woman.

Pete knelt in the snow next to Daniella, whose color was all but gone from her skin. "If I don't get you inside soon, you're going to get frostbite, and I think you're going into shock." He knelt and inspected the gunshot wounds. "Not that I really give a crap what happens to you, but I need you to tell me where they've taken Marianna."

"I'm not telling you shit," she seethed.

"Yes, you are." Pete grabbed her arm, which put pressure on her wound and had her howling in pain. He leaned close, and his voice dropped to a threatening tone. "If anything happens to Marianna, you're going to wish that I killed you."

He released her abruptly. Daniella winced and let out a cry of pain as Pete moved her leg to look at the wound in her thigh. He didn't like inflicting pain on anyone, especially a woman, but this broad was complicit in Marianna's abduction, so all bets were off.

"It looks like both bullets passed through cleanly." He tied the scarves in makeshift tourniquets on her arm and leg. "That should slow the bleeding, but you'll need an Amoveo healer. I can't take you to a hospital. There'll be too many questions since it's a gunshot wound."

Pete stuck his gun in the waistband of his jeans, grabbed her by her uninjured arm, and pulled her to her feet. Grunting in pain, she put her weight on her good leg and leaned onto Pete. He brought her into the cabin and dropped her onto the couch, which was no longer occupied by Tramp.

"What the hell?" Pete said as he picked up the bloodstained blanket and looked around the small cabin. "Tramp?"

He looked in the bedroom and around the rest of the cabin, but the dog was nowhere. Hands on his hips, Pete searched with genuine bewilderment. The dog was gone.

"How the hell did he get out of here without me seeing him?"

"Lose something?" Daniella asked weakly as she elevated her wounded leg onto the sofa.

"He is not lost."

The unfamiliar baritone resonated through the cabin.

"*What the fuck?*" Pete drew his gun and swung it toward the voice. Heart racing and gripping the gun for dear life, he pointed it at the large man who appeared out of nowhere and stood in front of the dining table with his arms folded over his chest.

"I said—he is not lost." The man's voice rumbled through Pete's bones. "I am not a shifter, like her," he said, sparing a glance at Daniella. "And before you ask, no, I am not a vampire either."

"Since it's daylight, I figured that out for myself." Pete didn't look at Daniella, but based on her silence, he figured she was as surprised as he was. He adjusted his stance and tightened his grip on the gun. "Start telling me who and *what* you are and why the hell you're here, or I'm going to blow your fucking head off."

A grin cracked his face, and his eyes glowed red. "Now, is that any way to speak to your father?"

Chapter 12

A TSUNAMI OF STATIC ELECTRICITY SWAMPED HER, AND the bright shimmer of the morning sun on the snow was swiftly replaced by the harsh glare of fluorescent lighting. Furious and terrified by the last glimpse she had of Pete facing down the tiger, Marianna struggled violently against Artimus's iron grip, but it was no use.

She was outmatched by his age and his size.

"Stop fighting me, Marianna," he growled. "It's futile and boring me."

His black eyes gleamed with pure disdain. Thick, meaty hands squeezed her arms tighter, but she refused to cry out and give him satisfaction. He held her against his barrel chest, but she struggled, wanting to keep some kind of distance between them, but to no avail.

Marianna looked around the room, trying to get her bearings. They were in a hallway with white walls and fluorescent lighting, which reminded her of a hospital. She took in as much of the surrounding area as she could, hoping she might figure out where the hell he'd taken her. She had to keep her wits about her. Losing it now would only hasten whatever plan they had in mind for her and her babies.

Babies. Artimus was going to kill her babies.

She had to get away. Instinctively, Marianna reached out to find the imprinted path to Pete and the cabin, but she was met with an impenetrable barrier. Her eyes snapped to their clan form as she concentrated, but still… nothing.

"As I said"—a satisfied grin cracked Artimus's bearded face—"trying to visualize yourself back to your human lover is a waste of time on two counts. First, as you've confirmed, you can't use our particular form of travel, and if you try to shift, you'll find the same thing blocking your path." He leaned close, his beard scraping her cheek, and whispered into her ear. "And secondly, that human is dead."

"No." She shook her head furiously. "I don't believe you."

"Belief has nothing to do with it," he said flatly. "Your lover is dead. You saw Daniella pounce on him, and we know that no human is a match for one of us. She's probably eating him for breakfast as we speak."

Tears filled her eyes as the weight of her situation settled over her, and Artimus's words ran through her mind. Could it be true? Was Pete really dead? She *had* seen Daniella leap on him, but Pete had his gun, and like he always said, the Amoveo are many things, but bulletproof isn't one of them.

"We'll see," Marianna said through a shaky breath.

She glanced at her surroundings again, hoping to find a way out or a sympathetic face, but the only one she found was Hayden's. He smirked, his arms crossed over his chest, and shook his head as though she were the most pathetic creature he'd laid eyes on.

"There is no point in struggling," Hayden said. "My father has placed a dampening field over the entire compound, which will prevent you from utilizing your powers of visualization and shifting."

"Guess you're not the hot shit you thought you were." Marianna flicked her eyes from Hayden to Artimus and smirked. "Daddy doesn't trust you enough to let you use your shifting abilities either?"

"Shut up," Hayden spat. He grabbed a handful of her hair and yanked her head. She bit back a cry of pain as he tugged harder, forcing her to look at him while Artimus held her firmly in his grasp. "It's you he doesn't trust. You and the rest of the traitors."

Hayden leaned in, his mouth hovering above hers. "But believe me, you'll sing a different tune soon enough. I think you and I will get to know each other much better in the coming days." He grabbed her chin and kissed her on the mouth firmly before releasing her. "Better get used to having the taste of me in your mouth."

Marianna's face heated with fury and revulsion at his touch. Her eyes shifted to their clan form and latched onto his.

"You should keep one thing in mind, Hayden," she ground out. "I don't swallow."

Before he could reply, Marianna hauled off and spit in his smug face.

To her surprise, Artimus laughed and pulled her out of Hayden's reach, but Artimus's rescue came to a halt as he backhanded her across the face. Pain shot through her head. The force made her teeth rattle and her cheek throb. She'd never been hit before, and while the blow brought physical discomfort, it was more humiliating than she'd expected. Tears filled her eyes from the sting, but she refused to let them fall.

Through glowing bear eyes, she glared at Artimus, but he only grinned at her pain. "I don't relish hitting women, but if you ever do anything like that again, I won't stop with one slap. Are we clear?"

Marianna said nothing, but nodded her understanding.

"I think it's time that we take you to see the good doctor."

Artimus dragged her down the hallway with Hayden close behind, and they passed several doors along the way, all closed. There was a clan name above each door, and she cringed when she saw the one that read *Bear Clan* because she had a sinking suspicion that would be her room. Each door had a small, square window, but she wasn't able to look inside.

There were black panels to the right of each with a row of red lights along the top. She wondered what they were, and her curiosity was satisfied when they reached the door at the end. Artimus placed his hand over the panel, which turned the red lights green, and the door opened with a muffled click. He pulled her into a room reminiscent of a doctor's waiting room.

There was a young woman sitting at a computer at the reception desk. Her brown hair was tied back in a tight ponytail, and she was dressed in all black. When she set eyes on Artimus, her eyes flickered to the bright blue of her clan, and she smiled broadly, fading as soon as she looked at Marianna.

"Good afternoon, my king," she said, turning her attention back to Artimus. She bowed her head in deference. "Dr. Moravian is expecting you. Please go right in."

"King?" Marianna said incredulously. "When did you give yourself that title? Richard is Prince of the Amoveo—leader of our people—*not you*. You're a traitor."

"Richard is a weak and pathetic fool." Artimus didn't spare her a glance, but tightened his grip on her bicep. "Thank you, Francesca."

"It's my pleasure." A buzzer sounded, and the door to Moravian's office clicked open.

Marianna knew the girl was a pure-blood, and based on the color of her eyes, she suspected a member of a wolf clan. How could anyone, especially a *woman*, knowingly participate in this sick breeding plan?

The office on the other side of the doorway was far nicer than the rest of the facility. A thick carpet in a rich brown hue replaced tile floors. The eggshell-colored walls had several photographs scattered about, as well as the different degrees that Moravian had earned. There were no windows here either.

The mahogany desk and credenza at the far wall were framed by massive bookshelves littered with books and statues, awards of some kind. Dr. Moravian stood from his high-back leather chair behind the desk to greet them.

"Welcome to our facility, my dear." He grinned broadly and came around the desk with arms outstretched to embrace her, but his face fell when he saw the fading bruise on her cheek. "What on earth happened?"

The doctor took Marianna by the hands, releasing her from Artimus's grasp, and led her to one of the chairs in front of his desk. He helped her into the seat as he inspected the mark on her face. While she was grateful for the empathy, she was leery.

"I guess Artimus doesn't like girls that spit." Marianna winced as Dr. Moravian inspected the bruise.

"We need our participants in the program strong,

Artimus." He walked to a small refrigerator on the other side of the room and removed an ice pack, which he promptly handed to Marianna.

"Thank you," Marianna said, taking the ice pack and watching Artimus for his reaction to Dr. Moravian's kindness.

Artimus, however, seemed unfazed. He simply sat opposite Marianna. Hayden stood by his father, but kept his ugly gaze fixed firmly on Marianna. *You're going to get a lot more than a smack from me, Marianna*. Hayden's thoughts intruded into Marianna's mind sharply. She flicked her eyes at the other two men to see if they'd heard, but they seemed unaware.

Perhaps Artimus's shield wasn't as strong as he thought?

Marianna hadn't been shielding her mind because she assumed it wouldn't matter. She didn't respond, but immediately protected her thoughts from further intrusions. The smug look on Hayden's face told her that he knew she'd heard, but hope glimmered brightly. If Hayden could use telepathy with her, then perhaps she could with Pete or Dante.

Hayden said that she couldn't use visualization or shift, but he didn't mention telepathy. Perhaps it was only inside this facility that she could? She wanted to try to contact Pete, but she had to wait until she was alone.

"You'll want to smack her too when I tell you about a new wrinkle in our plans." Artimus smoothed the lapels of his jacket and looked at Marianna with annoyance. "She's gone and gotten herself pregnant by that human. We'll need to terminate this monstrosity immediately so that we can proceed as planned."

"Let's not be hasty." Dr. Moravian pursed his lips and ran a hand over his goatee as he studied Marianna intently.

"What are you talking about?" Artimus snapped. "We need her to breed with Hayden, and she can't do that if she's already pregnant and with more than one."

"Artimus, please." Dr. Moravian put both hands up in an effort to calm Artimus, but kept his sights on Marianna. "This could be a unique opportunity to study our enemy. Think about it for a moment. The two hybrids we captured both died within a few weeks, and so far, we haven't had any luck finding the others."

"You found other hybrids and killed them?" Marianna asked in a far shakier voice than she intended.

"It wasn't intentional." Dr. Moravian shrugged. "We ran a few tests, to see if they could withstand certain temperature changes, emotional stresses, and so forth. Regretfully, they couldn't. Granted, we found unmated hybrids that weren't aware of what they were, but your situation has given me an interesting idea."

He strolled to his seat behind the desk, sat down, and folded his hands in front of him. His eyes shifted to the glowing eyes of his clan, and a sick smile cracked his face. *There it is*, Marianna thought, *there's the snake I knew was hiding in the grass.*

"If we keep her here and allow her to carry the pregnancy to term, we would have two hybrids to study and experiment on from birth. Imagine what we might learn from them? Perhaps there are weaknesses that we could discover and then exploit in the others we encounter." He leaned back and turned his attention to Artimus. "When she's recovered from that pregnancy, we can continue with our original plan."

Marianna's heart sank. Experiment on her children? Treat them like lab animals? Her stomach tightened, and she thought she might vomit on Moravian's polished desk. The only thing that kept her from losing it completely was that this *plan* would buy her and her babies time.

She looked frantically between the three men, but they remained completely calm, as if what Artimus suggested was a perfectly normal idea.

"Fine," Artimus bit out.

"But, Father—"

"Silence." Artimus didn't look at his son, but merely raised his hand in a clear command. "The doctor has proposed an interesting plan. I'm going to allow it for now. Doctor, please make sure she has a full examination and isn't harboring anything that may cause trouble down the road."

"No fucking way." Marianna hurled the ice pack at Artimus's head and scrambled off the chair toward the door. "You're not touching my children."

Hayden came after her, but Marianna spun around and kicked him square in the crotch. He groaned in agony, clutched his balls, and dropped to the floor in a moaning heap. She grabbed the handle and pulled against it uselessly as the rumbling growl of a bear filled the room.

She swung around, fists raised, eyes wild, ready to kick, scratch, and bite anyone who came near, and she came face-to-face with Artimus in his grizzly bear form. Glowing black eyes filled with hatred gleamed, and his dark brown fur quivered over his tremendous body as he held her prisoner.

Even standing on all fours, he was taller than she was.

His black-tipped snout was inches from hers, and his lips curled back with a low growl as he bared his teeth. Warm, fetid breath wafted over her face as he inched closer. Heart pounding in her chest, Marianna squeezed her eyes shut and pressed her body against the door, trying to get some distance. She prayed that he'd kill her quickly. Better that she and her babies die now than become lab rats for the rest of their lives.

"Now, now, young lady," Dr. Moravian simpered. He sounded close by, but she didn't want to open her eyes to check. She knew Artimus loomed in his bear form; she could feel the intense heat emanating from his body, and his growl surrounded her. "You'll be staying with us for quite some time, so I think it would be in your best interest to cooperate. But for now, we'll help you along."

Before she could ask what he meant, the sting of a needle penetrated her skin as the doctor injected her with something. Cold washed up her arm and through the rest her body with frightening speed, and within seconds, Artimus's growl faded.

As darkness and silence claimed her, only one word went through her mind... *Pete*.

A dull, throbbing headache greeted Marianna as she came out of the drug-induced sleep, compliments of Dr. Moravian. As the haze lifted, she slowly became aware of her surroundings, and the first thing she noticed was that her hands and feet were restrained to the bed. She tugged against the leather cuffs lashed to her wrists and ankles, but to no avail. Her strength had been sapped by whatever they injected her with, or maybe it was the dampening field that Artimus had placed over the facility, but either way, she wasn't going anywhere at the moment.

She cracked her eyes open and tried to lift her head but was greeted with a huge wave of nausea. Marianna shut her eyes and took a few deep, cleansing breaths, hoping to quell the nausea and ease her headache. As her stomach settled, she sought the energy signatures of the twins growing in her womb, needing to connect and know they were still safe.

It took only a few seconds to tune into the beautiful hum of their unified energies. Their signatures were in sync, and someone else might mistake them for one, but not Marianna. Tears of relief pricked her eyes as she confirmed that they were indeed healthy, and well… for now.

Marianna kept her head on the pillow and looked cautiously around the room. The white-walled space couldn't have been bigger than ten by ten. Along the far side of the wall were a toilet and a sink, and directly next to the bed a small table and a chair. The door had that same square window, like the ones she'd passed in the hallway with Artimus and Hayden.

There were no other windows. She didn't know if it was day or night and had no idea how long it had been since Artimus grabbed her at the cabin. Hours? Days? If Pete survived the assault from Daniella, then Marianna knew that he'd stop at nothing to find her.

But what if he hadn't? What if Artimus was right, and Pete was dead?

No. Marianna shook her head as if she could shake away the horrifying thought. He was alive. He had to be. She would know if he'd been killed, wouldn't she? All Amoveo felt the loss instantly upon the death of their mate, and he *was* her mate—human or not—she would know if he had died. Her throat tightened, but she resisted the urge to cry. Tears weren't going to help her or their babies.

"Focus, Marianna," she whispered to the empty room.

Her eyes fluttered closed, and she concentrated on creating a mental link with Pete but was met with that same impenetrable wall. Repeatedly, she sent her energy in search of his, but each time there was no answer... she was alone.

The tears fell freely now as she looked around the sterile room that reminded her of a psychiatric hospital. She laughed through her tears at the irony of it all because if she didn't get out of here soon—she'd fit right in at a loony bin. Hopelessness reared its ugly head, threatening what was left of her resolve.

The sound of the door clicking open captured her attention and sent her heart into overdrive.

She fully expected Artimus, Hayden, or the doctor to come through the door, but much to her relief, it was none of them. A young woman of perhaps twenty came into the room bearing a tray of food and a timid smile.

Marianna watched her carefully as she placed the tray on the table and sat in the chair next to her. Her pale blond hair was swept back in a low ponytail, and her petite frame was hidden beneath baggy, blue hospital scrubs. She looked at Marianna through sympathetic green eyes that seemed oddly familiar.

"My name is Savannah," she said in a sweet, melodic voice. "I'm your daytime caretaker and will be tending to your needs. Now, I could feed you, but I'm sure you'd rather feed yourself."

She peeled back the plastic wrap from the glass of juice and the tray of bacon and eggs.

"So it's daytime?" Marianna asked in a froggy voice. "It's hard to tell with the view from here, and yes, I've been feeding myself for years."

"I'm sure," Savannah replied with a hint of a smile. "You've been here for about twenty-four hours, but the medication they gave you lasted longer than anticipated. We think it's because of your pregnancy, but not to worry, the fetuses are handling it fine. You're only a few weeks pregnant, but they seem healthy."

Reading the confusion on Marianna's face, she continued.

"We did a sonogram while you were sedated to check on the status of the twins. We also ran a few other tests on your vitals and drew some blood. Other than the pregnancy, you're a perfectly healthy pure-blood."

"Who knows what that injection did to my twins," Marianna seethed.

"I can assure you the fetuses are fine. We developed a sedation serum that would have minimal impact on them." She placed her delicate hands in her lap and cocked her head. "Can I remove these restraints so that you can eat, or are you going to start trouble and make me use the Taser in my pocket?" She patted the lump in the pocket of her scrubs.

Marianna weighed her options. She could try to escape, but the truth was that she had no idea where she was, and she was in a completely weakened state. She needed more information before she tried another getaway, and besides, getting Tasered didn't sound appealing.

She nodded and prayed for the strength to hold it together.

Savannah unlocked her wrist restraints with the keys dangling from the cord around her wrist and removed the ankle shackles before helping her to a sitting position. Dizziness and nausea came in another stomach-tumbling wave, but a few deep breaths helped it subside.

"Here." She handed her the orange juice. "I'm sure your blood sugar is low, but this should help."

Marianna accepted it with shaking hands and drank the sweet, cold liquid greedily before handing the empty glass to Savannah.

"I guess you were thirsty?" Savannah laughed and handed her the plate. "I'm sure you're equally hungry."

Marianna accepted it and tried not to be quite as much of a glutton as she'd been with the juice, but didn't have much luck. She was starving and ate the food like her life and the lives of her twins depended on it. Savannah said nothing, but watched her through serious green eyes.

"Thank you." Marianna passed her the empty plate. "Can I ask you a question, Savannah?"

"Of course."

"You seem nice and nothing like the Purists that I've had the misfortune to know." Marianna brought her feet up on the bed, sat cross-legged, and leaned back against the wall for support, but she kept her gaze fixed on Savannah.

"Is there a question coming?" She looked away and made herself busy cleaning the tray.

"Why are you participating?" She leaned both elbows on her knees, watching Savannah's body language and struggling to read her muted energy signature. "How can you be complicit in the violation of our laws and the atrocities they're committing against innocent people?"

"We have to do this," Savannah whispered as she picked up the tray and turned toward the door. Her energy signature fired in nervous pulses. She placed her hand on the black panel, and the door opened with a muffled click. "There is no choice. Our—our race depends on it."

"Really?" Marianna picked up one of the restraints and fiddled with it. "Do I look like a volunteer?"

"It's for the greater good." The uneasiness in her signature grew stronger, and she avoided looking Marianna in the eye as she headed out.

"If it's such a noble cause, then why aren't you getting knocked up? Or that chick I saw in Dr. Moravian's waiting room? You're both pure-bloods." She narrowed her eyes and stared her down. "Why aren't you offering your uterus?"

"We aren't part of the initial trials." Savannah's hands trembled as she tidied the tray and avoided her gaze. "Once all the… kinks have been worked out, then we'll be the first ones in line."

"Kinks?" Bile rose in Marianna's throat.

"Sometimes there must be sacrifice before success."

Savannah repeated the phrase as only a good servant would, but she lacked conviction. Those were words that Moravian and Artimus had probably spewed out, and this young woman was merely repeating them—but she didn't say it like she meant it.

"You don't believe that." Marianna attempted to rise from the bed, but dizziness washed over her again. "I can tell—you lack the conviction of the others—please help me," she said as she crumpled weakly onto the bed. "I know that I'm not the only one held here against my will. I think one of my friends is here too. Courtney Bishop, she's a member of the Coyote Clan, and her family is worried sick." She looked at her pleadingly and whispered, "You have to help us."

Savannah stood in the open door. Her sympathetic green eyes flicked to Marianna's, and she opened her mouth to say something, but snapped it shut abruptly.

"How is our newest resident doing this morning?" Dr. Moravian's overly cheerful voice filled the room just before he appeared in the doorway behind Savannah. He frowned when he saw that she was free of her restraints. "Why is she not in her restraints?"

"She's far too weak to cause any trouble." Savannah tore her eyes from Marianna, and her energy signature immediately hardened. "The patient ate her breakfast without incident. Although I'm quite sure that having my Taser handy helped keep her in line."

"Yes, it would seem that it did," he murmured and kissed the top of Savannah's head with a chuckle. "Leave it to you to think outside the box. See to it that the rest of the caretakers are issued Tasers. Perhaps it will discourage other troublemakers."

Marianna watched the affection that the doctor so freely displayed with curiosity. She looked at the two side by side, and slowly but surely, the pieces came together. Dr. Moravian kissed her on the head again and disappeared from the doorway.

"I'll be sure to take care of it… Father," Savannah said, without taking her eyes off Marianna.

The sound of the door closing echoed through the room and drowned the pounding of Marianna's heart. Savannah's green eyes, tinged with sadness, peered through the small window before vanishing from sight. For the first time since this nightmare started, Marianna felt truly hopeful because she had a strong suspicion that the doctor's daughter was no Purist.

Chapter 13

"WHAT THE FUCK DID YOU JUST SAY?"

The words rushed from Pete's lungs as he blinked the sweat from his eyes that was blurring his vision. Tightening his grip on the gun, he struggled to register what this guy said. His father? This red-eyed guy in the middle of his cabin, who appeared out of nowhere, is claiming to be his father?

He couldn't help but think of what Olivia had said about suspecting he was part demon or part warlock. It was beginning to look like the vampire was right. Crap.

"I said, is that any way to speak to your father?" His eyes glowed bright red, and the smile on his lips grew.

"Really?" Pete cocked the gun and focused his aim. "Then I should shoot your ass on principle alone for being a deadbeat."

"I don't think so." The intruder extended one muscular arm, with his palm facing Pete, and within seconds the gun in Pete's hands went from cold steel to burning hot. Pete swore as it fell from his hands. The man flicked his wrist, and the gun flew across the room. "We don't have time to play the pissed-off-son game."

He calmly turned his attention back to Pete. His irises glowed brighter before flickering back to human blue eyes—eyes just like his. Dressed in all black, he reminded Pete of a commando, and the sheer size of him would intimidate most people.

But Pete wasn't most people. He held his ground and kept his eyes on the man. He knew enough to know that his smartest move right now was to watch and wait.

"Tramp, as you call him, is back home and just fine. He's a hellhound, one of many that I've sent to watch over you." He dropped his hands to his side and bowed his head. "I am Asmodeus, but your mother knew me as Aaron."

"Wonderful." Pete's jaw clenched. "She's dead, so I'm afraid a reunion is out of the question."

"I know." Asmodeus's eyes softened briefly.

"Well, *Daddy,* it would seem that you've got a lot more information than me, so how about you start sharing? You say that you're my father? But you're obviously not a regular guy, and as you already established, you're not Amoveo or vampire. So why don't you tell me what you are?"

Pete looked at him expectantly, put his hands on his hips, and waited.

"Interesting." Asmodeus narrowed his eyes and studied Pete closely. "I didn't expect you to be quite so cavalier."

"Yeah," Pete scoffed. "Well, nothing surprises me anymore."

"You're half demon," he said flatly.

Pete didn't flinch. His stomach dropped to his feet, but he would be damned if he'd show one ounce of fear or surprise in front of this guy or Daniella. He kept his eyes on Asmodeus and waved him on, trying to act like he was more bored than anything else. "And?"

"I am what humans know as a demon—more specifically, I am one of the seven princes of Hell. Each is in charge of one of the seven deadly sins." He cast a grin at Daniella. "Mine is lust."

"Great," Pete snorted with derision. "So my father is a horny devil."

"And hot." Daniella sighed.

"Pipe down." Pete flicked his gaze to her briefly, but she was staring at his father like some moony-eyed teenager.

"I do enjoy coming to earth." Asmodeus's rich, deep laughter filled the cabin as he sat on the edge of the table and folded his arms over his chest. He turned his sharp blue eyes back to Pete. "I met your mother on my last visit, but your conception was most... unexpected."

"I bet it was." Pete inched closer to the fireplace and shifted his body, so he was within reach of the fireplace tools. He ran his fingers over the cool iron, and that alone made him feel safer. "So, what? Do you come to earth and knock up unsuspecting women on a regular basis?"

"No." The smile faded, and face grew serious. "We are permitted a visit to earth once every hundred years for three months. My being here now is not exactly a sanctioned visit. We live as a mortal and experience all of the sins, with particular focus on our own, but it is extremely rare for us to create offspring."

"I see," Pete ground out. "So you fucked your way through the world and happened to knock up my mother? So what does that make me?"

"I met your mother on the first day of my last excursion." His lips tilted. "She was pure joy and had a laugh that could cut through even the toughest of men. I think I fell in love with her before I even saw her. It was that beautiful laugh which captivated me and brought me to her." His eyes flickered red again. "I didn't *fuck* my way around earth—at least not that time. I was utterly besotted by her."

"Bullshit," Pete spat. "If you were so crazy in love, then why would you leave her and break her heart?" His voice rose with years of pent up frustration. "That woman you're describing? I never knew her. I only knew the sad, broken woman that you left behind."

"I had no choice." Asmodeus's eyes glowed brighter as he rose from the table and stalked slowly toward Pete. "I had to leave once your mother found out what I was. I was willing to give up my position and live as a mortal, but she refused me. She forbade me from being a part of your life, so if you want to blame someone for not having a father, you can start with her."

"Go to hell!" Pete screamed.

He grabbed the fireplace poker and swung it at Asmodeus's head, but he wasn't fast enough. Asmodeus grabbed the poker with one hand, Pete's throat by the other, and pinned him against the wall with unnatural strength.

"I do not wish to fight with you," he seethed. His bright red eyes glowed at Pete with a combination of anger and frustration. "I came here to help you, and I am breaking all kinds of rules in the process. If my meddling is discovered, I'll end up having to work as a Peace Keeper here on earth, and I have no desire to do that."

He tossed the poker across the room and loosened his grip on Pete's throat. Pete sucked in a gulp of air and wrestled with the reality of the situation facing him. Looking into his red eyes, he knew that if this man wanted to kill him, he'd be dead already. The only other option was that he was telling the truth and really was here to help.

"You say that you want to help me," Pete bit out. He shoved at Asmodeus, who stepped back and released Pete from his grasp. Pete rubbed his neck, but kept his eyes on his father. "It would've been nice if you'd showed up *before* they took Marianna."

"Yes." He sighed and stepped back, giving Pete the distance he hoped for. "There was no way around that. We are not supposed to get involved in the business of other supernatural races, only humans."

"So you're the devil?" Pete asked warily as he leaned against the wall.

"No. I am a demon. There is no *one* devil, and we are not the purely evil creatures of your human lore." He grinned at Pete's obvious confusion and lifted one shoulder. "We're really just a bunch of troublemakers, and besides, the angels would be out of business if we weren't around."

"I know I'm new to the whole demon thing, but it sounds like you're oversimplifying." Pete leaned on his knees and let out a long, slow breath. "So I'm part demon. I guess that explains the psychic-shielding or whatever. Is there anything in this demon gig that will help me get Marianna back?"

"Yes," Asmodeus murmured. "That's why I'm here." He went to Daniella, who was still lying on the couch, but looked as though she were about to pass out. "However, we need to take care of this first. This shifter is going to expire if we don't stop the bleeding, and it's my understanding that you'll need her alive."

"I thought you weren't supposed to get involved. Wouldn't that be breaking the rules?"

"Well, I *am* a demon."

Before Pete could say another word, Asmodeus knelt and placed one enormous hand over each wound.

"What are you doing?"

Pete moved toward them, but stopped short as a humming sound filled the room. It was muted at first, but soon it grew louder as a bright, orange glow emanated beneath Asmodeus's hands. Thick, dense heat filled the room, causing Pete to sweat, and within minutes the place was like a steam sauna.

The glowing flashed, and the humming pulsed and throbbed, like a heartbeat tumbling through the cabin. Daniella screamed in agony and writhed beneath his touch, but Asmodeus remained resolute. Pete was about to pull him off her because if she died, he'd never find Marianna, but seconds later, everything stopped.

"What the hell did you do?" Pete stood at the end of the couch looking at Daniella, hoping like hell she was still alive. To his relief, her chest moved with the steady breathing of sleep, and he watched as Asmodeus removed the makeshift tourniquets from her arm and leg.

"I cauterized the wounds and stopped the bleeding." He stood and tossed the bloodied scarves on the coffee table before turning his familiar blue eyes back to Pete. "She should be seen by an Amoveo healer, but she's stable for now."

Asmodeus removed the silver ring on his left hand and held it out for Pete.

"No thanks." Pete didn't move but looked at it warily. "I'm not a big jewelry guy."

"It's not a fashion statement." Asmodeus held it out again, and his eyes flickered red. "It will harness your natural abilities and allow you to tap into powers you've only begun to discover."

Pete folded his arms over his chest and met Asmodeus's gaze. "I don't have any powers."

"Yes." He sighed. "You do. Your hunches, as you like to refer to them, are rooted in your natural psychic abilities."

"How do you know about that?" Pete asked with suspicion.

"I told you. I've been keeping an eye on you. Also, Tramp and the other hellhounds I've sent over the years were quite helpful in giving me updates."

Pete glanced at the ring. The silver glinted as he weighed his options. The cold, hard truth was that as far as options were concerned, he didn't have a whole lot, and maybe this would give him a fighting chance at getting Marianna back.

The reality was that he would do anything—*be anything*—if it meant getting her back and keeping her safe.

He'd even make a deal with the devil himself.

"This is the only thing that I can offer you." Asmodeus's deep voice softened. "Please take it. If you insist on battling with the Amoveo, then you are going to need every ounce of power you possess."

Pete swore under his breath, took the ring from Asmodeus, and glanced at him briefly as he inspected it. "What kind of stone is this?"

"Obsidian."

"Obsidian?" Pete smirked and peered at him. "Doesn't that come from volcanos?"

"Yes, it's from the heart of the earth—the under-world—which is where the root of our power is."

"So what?" Pete asked, only half-joking, as he slipped it onto the ring finger of his right hand. "Is this thing going to shoot fire or something?"

It was like a kick in the gut. White light flashed into his mind, and everything started spinning as the air was sucked out of the room like a vacuum. Pete fell to his knees, gasping and straining to get his bearings. Asmodeus tried to help him up, but Pete pushed him away and braced himself on the edge of the coffee table.

"I'm fine," Pete wheezed. "I just need a minute. Jesus Christ, is this ring going to make me feel like that every time I put it on?"

"Jesus had nothing to do with this," Asmodeus said wryly. "The stone in the ring will help you channel latent abilities you may have. If you ditch the ring, then eventually, powers you develop will fade to what they were before." Asmodeus's lips curled upward. "In theory."

"Is there anything that you are *sure* of?" Heat flashed over Pete's body, and suddenly, the room felt about twenty degrees warmer. Was he doing that? Pete sucked in a slow breath and willed himself to keep his temper in check. "As much as this little reunion is warming my heart, I have to get this bitch back to the Amoveo, so we can find out where they've taken Marianna."

"You should be able to use telepathy freely, but I'm not certain about the telekinesis or the ability to manipulate heat." He shrugged casually and glanced around the room. "I suppose you'll have to see how it all shakes out. I have to be on my way, but Tramp will be here in my stead."

"Fucking wonderful." Pete shook his head and rubbed his eyes with both hands. "Is there anything else you can tell me?"

Instead of the deep baritone of Asmodeus, he was greeted with the sharp yelp of a dog. Pete snapped his eyes open to find that Asmodeus was gone, Daniella was still passed out on the couch, and Tramp was sitting at his feet, happily wagging his tail.

"What the hell?" Pete squatted and ran his hands over Tramp's totally healed body. There was no sign of the injuries he'd suffered earlier, not even any blood in his fur. The husky was clean and seemed strong as an ox. "Unbelievable," he murmured through a smile. "I'm glad to see you're okay, buddy."

Tramp yipped and licked his face enthusiastically before sitting obediently at Pete's feet. Pete glanced at the ring on his finger and spun it around with his thumb as he went to the couch and picked up Daniella's limp body with ease. He stilled and noted how much lighter she seemed than she had a little while ago. Looking at her pallid complexion and then down at Tramp, he said, "I guess it's about time to try that telepathy."

Tramp barked his agreement and took his place next to Pete.

"I wonder how Dante will feel about having a demon in the family?"

⁓⁓⁓

Pete stood in the lavish living room of the prince's Montana home and stared out the window at the snow-covered ranch, relishing a few moments alone. He'd forgotten how unnerving it was to be surrounded by Amoveo. Malcolm and William had arrived with their hybrid mates and were getting brought up to speed by Kerry and Dante. Richard's healers were tending to Daniella, who had been passed out for hours. Pete was going crazy with worry over Marianna. He glanced at the mahogany staircase and resisted the urge to run up there and shake the truth out of Daniella.

How had everything gotten so fucked up? He had failed. He failed Marianna and didn't keep his promise. How could she, or would she ever, trust him again?

He'd promised her that the Purists wouldn't touch her, but they sure as hell did. They kidnapped her right in front of him, and he couldn't do a fucking thing about it.

He'd never felt like such a failure in his life.

"You've got to stop beating yourself up." Kerry's voice cut into his internal pity party as she sidled up next to him. "We'll find her."

"Is Daniella awake yet?" He didn't want pity or sympathy. He wanted answers, and the only one who had any was Daniella, but she wasn't coughing up any answers as long as she was passed out. Tramp whined and nuzzled Pete's leg, seeking or offering comfort, Pete wasn't sure which, but he appreciated the gesture.

"Not yet." Kerry stuck a steaming cup of coffee in his face. "Drink this. It'll give you something else to do with your hands than play with that ring."

"No thanks." Pete dropped his hands and stuffed them in his jeans pockets. "I'm wired enough."

"You know," Kerry said before taking a sip of

the coffee herself, "you should stop being such a big baby."

"What?" Pete shot her a deadly glare, and Tramp growled.

"You act like you're the first person to find out that he's a freak." She smirked and glanced at the dog. "This is a house full of freaks. The hellhound is a new addition, but that's fine by me. I love dogs, and I think it's nice that you have a pet."

Pete stilled and speared a glance in her direction. He hadn't told any of them about Asmodeus or his newly revealed heritage. Dante and the others had assumed that the telepathy was a new side effect of his mating with Marianna, and he never bothered to correct them. Hell. He wasn't even sure how he felt about it, so how was he supposed to explain it?

"You knew." Pete looked into her smiling brown eyes, and the knot in his stomach loosened. "You saw something that day when you touched my hand in the elevator, didn't you?"

"Yes." Kerry elbowed him playfully and bumped him with her hip. "You always were a quick study. I saw it then, but I had to let you find out for yourself—you were having enough trouble tackling the whole idea of being Marianna's mate."

Pete smiled in spite of the situation and folded his arms over his chest as he looked at the wintery scene. Tramp barked again, as if asking him, *what's up?* However, much to his relief, the dog didn't actually talk.

"As soon as she wakes up, we'll get the answers we need." Her eyes flickered and glowed to the bright yellow eyes of her panther. "With or without her cooperation."

Daniella is waking up. Dante's voice cut into Pete's mind with an odd familiarity. *The prince has requested we all be present at her interrogation*.

Pete watched as Kerry's eyes flickered to their natural human brown, and a smile curved her lips.

"You heard him too?" Pete asked tentatively.

"I heard the same thing you did… and then some." She winked and linked her arm through his. "Let's go have a little chat with Daniella, or maybe she and I will just hold hands."

Chapter 14

MARIANNA ADJUSTED THE WHITE ROBE AND TIGHT-ened the tie around her waist as she and five other women were escorted, single file, down the brightly lit hallway. Two armed guards, dressed in black fatigues, walked on either side in silence. It was the first time in the past two days that she'd seen anyone other than her captors. She'd tried telepathy with the other women, but if they heard her, they didn't respond, and none attempted to make eye contact.

When she came out of her room and first saw them, she immediately looked for her friend Courtney, but she wasn't among them. She didn't recognize the other girls, but they were obviously held under duress like her. Wearing the same robes, they looked weak and unkempt.

Who knows how long they had been here. Days? Weeks? Months? One woman looked pregnant, maybe four months along, but she looked very sick. She was at the front of the line, and at a few points, Marianna thought she was going to pass out, but when she slowed down, the guard urged her forward with the butt of his rifle.

They'd been walking down a maze of hallways for what seemed like forever. Marianna hadn't seen a single window, which gave her the impression they were in a network of underground tunnels. At first, she'd tried to commit the path to memory and watch for any door, or opportunity to escape, but everything looked the same. And before long, she had absolutely no sense of where they really were.

The hallway turned sharply to the left, and when they rounded the corner, Marianna looked past the women and saw a huge steel door about ten feet ahead. One guard pressed a button next to the door, and a few moments later, a loud buzzing sound filled the hall. He held the door open as the women filed through it obediently.

Marianna glanced up and saw the red eye of a camera clocking their every move.

"Eyes front." The guard behind her jabbed her in the ribs with the tip of his gun.

Marianna bit her lip against the sharp pain in her side and fought the urge to tell him to fuck off. She kept her eyes on the blond head of the girl in front, but her gaze didn't remain there for long.

They were led into a large space with auditorium-style seating filled with about forty Amoveo, whom she could only assume were pure-bloods… and Purists. All stood at their seats. They were dressed in the same black uniform as the guards, and every set of glowing Amoveo eyes were locked on them, tracking their every move as they were led into the room. She could tell by the texture and density of the energy signatures that most of the Amoveo in the audience were already mated, and many were far older than she was.

The collective, dark energy waves of the group battered her relentlessly and brought on another wave of nausea. She focused on putting one slipper-clad foot in front of the other and willed herself not to pass out.

She flicked her eyes to the crowd, and as she got

closer to the front, she finally saw a familiar face, one of the only unmated Amoveo in the room. Savannah stood in the front row, but today she wasn't in her scrubs; she wore the same uniform as the others. Marianna tried to capture her gaze, but Savannah artfully avoided it, and in the process, Marianna saw Hayden standing next to her with his trademark smirk.

She wanted to try telepathy with her, but when she saw who was on stage, she stopped dead in her tracks before she was nudged again.

Artimus sat in large black throne at the center of the stage, flanked by Dr. Moravian and nine former Council members, each seated in smaller versions of the chair he occupied. All members who had declared themselves Purists and abandoned the Council two months ago were staring at her from the stage.

She couldn't believe these people could stand by and watch what was happening. They acted as though they didn't know who she was. Apparently, they'd formed an entirely new government with Artimus fixed at the center as their king.

A massive banner hung behind the group, which read, *Purity is Strength*.

The line of women were brought before the stage and ordered to face Artimus and the others. Marianna held her breath and waited. She half expected the guards to shoot them in some kind of mass execution, but much to her relief, that didn't happen. Both guards stood in front of the stage on either side of Artimus and faced the room, ready in case anyone got out of line.

Artimus's hulking form rose from his chair and he held both hands up to the audience.

"Take your seats, my devoted people." His baritone rumbled through the room, and they silently took their seats.

Marianna took note that neither Artimus, nor the rest of the elders, wore the uniform like the others. They were decked out in usual attire. Suits for the men and elegant gowns for the women, which made them look like a sinister royal court—she expected Artimus to wear a crown.

The stunning blond to his left looked at Marianna with hate-filled eyes. Veronica had been the female representative from the Lion Clan, and until recently, sat at the prince's side for all Council meetings. But now she sat next to Artimus as though she was the freaking Queen of England. Her lips curled into a smug grin, as she looked Marianna up and down.

That's a fabulous robe. Her voice sliced into Marianna's mind with as much condescension as one would expect. *You certainly have found your place in this world, haven't you? Where's your human mate now?*

Marianna didn't respond. She simply looked away and fought the desire to climb up on that stage and scratch her eyes out. Getting upset would only give her some kind of sick satisfaction, and she'd be damned if Veronica, or any of the rest, would get that from her.

Artimus turned his glowing black eyes to the line of women in front. He scanned the group before settling his cold sights on Marianna. "As you can see, we have lost a few more participants in the past week." The hint of a smile played at his lips for a moment before fading. "I know that the unmated females devoted to the cause have expressed interest in participating in the program, and you've been wondering why you haven't been selected. I assure you that there is a valid reason for waiting." He snapped his fingers. "Dr. Moravian, would you please give us your latest findings."

Artimus sat down and turned the floor over to Dr. Moravian, who looked far less comfortable speaking to the group than Artimus did. Marianna watched as he wiped the sweat from his brow with a handkerchief. She sweated right along with him as she waited for him to explain what happened to the other *participants*.

His voice carried easily over the crowd. "We have had trouble with the initial test subjects with this new breeding initiative. We had three more participants expire over the past week, and until we find out why this is happening, I would prefer not to risk the lives of the true believers."

A murmur broke out among the crowd behind Marianna, and their collective energy signatures pulsed with nerves and fear. The doctor motioned to the guards, who quickly escorted the young pregnant woman from the front of the line and brought her to the foot of the stage.

Weak and shaking, she didn't fight, but stood there meekly. Her eyes, vacant of emotion, stared at the ground, and her hands remained at her side—not over her rounding belly. It was as if she didn't know she was pregnant or didn't care. She reminded Marianna of a zombie—totally disengaged.

The murmuring of the crowd grew louder.

"As you can see," Dr. Moravian said, gesturing to the poor girl, "this one is viable, and if all goes smoothly, she should birth a pure-blood for the Lion Clan in the next five months. Unfortunately, the test subjects from the Wolf, Tiger, and Cheetah Clans expired."

The murmuring grew to a dull roar.

"But our participant from the Coyote Clan has been successfully impregnated. She is watched closely in the medical facility, which is why she is not here today."

Marianna's heart went into her throat. Courtney. The Coyote Clan *participant* had to be Courtney, and for the moment, she was still alive. Dread clawed at her as she wondered how exactly she'd gotten pregnant. It must've been artificial insemination, but she couldn't help but wonder if one or more Purist men like Hayden had tried the old-fashioned way.

She swallowed the bile that rose in her throat and looked at the vacant expression of the pregnant girl from the Lion Clan. This girl had been traumatized—there was no doubt about that—and she strongly suspected that it was in more ways than one.

Her gaze flicked back to Artimus, who was staring with pure hatred in his eyes. Marianna didn't flinch and returned his glare with equal fervor before turning her sights back to the doctor.

"It is quite unorthodox for us to allow nonbelievers into our sanctuary, but Artimus felt it was important for you to know how hard we're working to bring you the future of our race. We will not stop until we have found the answers to keeping the Amoveo line pure."

The group broke into thunderous applause and raucous cheers, which was why it took everyone a minute or two to realize that the pregnant girl had fainted.

Dr. Moravian jumped from the stage, and Savannah rushed from her seat to help the poor creature. Troubled rumblings quickly replaced the applause, and Marianna watched as the doctor and Savannah tended the girl.

The girl's body convulsed wildly, and her eyes rolled back in her head, as a pool of blood spread beneath her. Savannah attempted to hold her still as the doctor tended to her, but moments later she went still. Marianna watched in horror as a rivulet of blood trickled toward her across the white tiled floor. She covered her mouth to keep from screaming, but she couldn't stop the tears as they fell down her cheeks.

"Damn it!" Dr. Moravian rose slowly from his place next to the motionless girl and looked as bewildered as anyone. "She's dead. I don't understand why this is happening."

The crowd broke into a frenzy of arguments as the energy signatures of the group flared violently around the room. Marianna sobbed quietly as the doctor wiped blood off his hands with the handkerchief from his pocket. She looked at the broken, bleeding body of that girl and knew that if she didn't get out of here, she was going to die too.

Through the shouts and murmurs, Marianna's attention was caught by Savannah, who sat on the ground with the dead girl's head in her lap. She stroked her hair as tears fell freely down her face. She glanced up and captured Marianna's eyes with hers. *We have to stop this.* Her teary voice touched Marianna's mind on a whisper.

The bone-shattering bellow of a bear thundered through the room, and everyone fell silent.

Artimus had shifted into his grizzly bear form and was standing on his enormous hind legs at the center of the stage. He fell to all fours, kicked his chair, and growled ferociously as his glowing black eyes glared at the crowd. The other Amoveo stood and kept their shifted, glowing eyes on Artimus. Despite their best efforts to look authoritative, the only thing they managed to do was look scared.

Artimus roared again and reared to his hind legs. All Amoveo onstage bowed their heads and fell to one knee. Veronica peered at Marianna with that smug look as she took to her knee in deference to her leader.

Veronica, your offering from the Lion Clan has not been successful. Artimus's voice blared into their minds. *Failure will not be tolerated.*

Without warning, Artimus whipped to his left and snatched Veronica by the throat with his powerful jaws. He picked her up like a rag doll as she kicked and flailed helplessly in his grasp for a few seconds. With a sickening crunch, he bit through her neck. Blood sprayed onto Marianna and the others as Veronica's blond head was severed from her body and fell to the stage with a wet thump.

"No!" Dr. Moravian screamed. "Artimus, she is a pure-blood."

Artimus dropped her limp body, and Marianna watched with horror as blood dripped from the edge of the stage. She lifted her shaking hands and looked in disbelief at the splatters that marked her—blood, which up until two minutes ago, had been pumping through Veronica's veins. The gory scene was an assault on her senses and her sanity.

Now she's an example. Artimus, with blood dripping from his muzzle, spun toward Dr. Moravian, who flinched but said nothing else. *Get the body back to the medical lab, and take her apart until you figure out what's going wrong.* The deep baritone of his voice slammed into their collective minds as he turned to face the rest of the room. *All of the devoted will go back to their dwellings within the compound. You will revisit your lists. The participants you are bringing us are weak, and that is unacceptable. Veronica's offering was unworthy and wasted our time and resources. Each clan must bring me at least one more participant for the program.*

Artimus shimmered and shifted back to his human state; eyes still glowing he looked out over his followers. Marianna glanced at the other women in line, and while some were crying quietly, none looked at Artimus or said a word. She wiped the tears away and turned her defiant gaze to Artimus, wanting him to know that she wouldn't be broken by him—or anyone.

"If you cannot find more suitable specimens, then you will suffer the same fate as Veronica. I will not allow *anyone* to soil our bloodlines with weakness and failure."

The room hummed with silence and thickening, nervous energy waves. Artimus used fear and intimidation the same way dictators and tyrants in human history had. Fear was a powerful tool for men like Artimus.

His deep voice rumbled through the room. "The entire facility is on lockdown for the next forty-eight hours. No one leaves. We will gather here in two days, and you will provide me with the names of your clan's new offering. Then I will send the retrieval team to collect them. You are dismissed."

With a rush of static, Artimus uttered the ancient language and vanished.

—◆—

Marianna sat on the bed in her barren room and waited.

Legs crossed, she rubbed her belly and sent soothing energy waves to the two babies in her womb. She knew it was still early in her pregnancy, but she already loved them because they were part of her and Pete.

He still didn't know about the twins she carried, and she thought that perhaps that was better for now. If something did happen, if Artimus changed his mind and forced her to terminate the pregnancy, then at least Pete would be spared the loss. He couldn't miss what he never knew he had.

Tears stung her eyes, but she wiped them away. Crying wasn't going to help anything. Marianna shook her head and steeled her resolve. She *would* get out of here, and Pete *would* know about his babies. She smiled. *Their* babies.

Savannah normally came to her room with meals around this time, and now, more than ever, she wanted to see her. Her suspicions about Savannah's feelings were confirmed earlier at the gathering, and there was no mistaking it once she'd touched her mind to Marianna's.

Savannah was her best shot at getting out of this place alive.

The door clicked open, and Savannah's warm green eyes met hers. Dressed in her usual blue scrubs, she came in bearing food. The door shut behind her, but Marianna didn't miss the guard's face in the window as he watched Savannah set the tray on the side table. His stone cold expression vanished as he walked away, presumably to check on another *volunteer*.

"That was quite a gathering," Marianna said quietly. "Does Artimus make a habit of murdering people at his meetings?"

Savannah stilled for a moment before taking the stethoscope from around her neck and checking Marianna's vital signs. It was obvious that she was deciding what, or how much, to say. Marianna cooperated as Savannah did her usual rundown of blood pressure, heart rate, and lung functions. She worked quickly and efficiently, wrote in the small notebook she carried, and handed Marianna the plate with the sandwich.

"I—I've never seen anyone killed like that," she whispered. Her pale green eyes were filled with fear. "My father is terrified of Artimus. I think, at first, he truly believed in what Artimus was doing, but things have gotten completely out of control." She glanced to the doorway, but it remained free of onlookers. "Father said that he's threatened other former Council members and their families with death. Until today, I don't think anyone truly believed he'd do it. If people wouldn't defy him before… they definitely won't now."

"I couldn't keep this down if I tried." Marianna leaned forward and put the plate back on the tray. "Do you know where my friend Courtney is? She's the Coyote Clan female that Artimus said was pregnant."

"Yes." She pushed her pale blond hair off her face and flicked her eyes to Marianna's. "The insemination worked, but I think it's because of the donor they used." Her voice dropped low, and her eyes widened. "Her mate is here, held captive like you are. He's been heavily drugged. I don't think either are aware of what's going on. Apparently, the male was here posing as a believer, but was discovered to be a spy for Richard and the rest of the Loyalists. He was caught trying to escape with Courtney. He said she was his mate, but Artimus and the guards overpowered him. The only reason they didn't kill him was because they wanted to use him to impregnate Courtney. They'll keep him alive until she delivers—then dispose of both."

"So, she's actually pregnant with the child of her mate," Marianna said slowly, putting it together. "But they did it through artificial insemination and the rest of the followers don't know that. Do they? I would bet that Courtney and her mate don't even know she's pregnant."

"Yes," Savannah confirmed, but her eyes grew stormy. "Although, rumor has it that Hayden tried to impregnate her the *old-fashioned* way."

Marianna swallowed the sickening lump in her throat, and she could barely force herself to say it out loud. "He—he *forced himself* on her?"

Savannah said nothing but nodded as one large tear rolled down her cheek. Looking at this young girl, Marianna realized that she was as much a prisoner here as the rest. She knew another woman had been victimized, and there was nothing she could do to stop it. The only thing she could do was offer glimpses of compassion in a storm of cruelty.

"It's not your fault." She scooted closer to the edge of the bed and took Savannah's hands in hers. "Please, you have to take me to her. Maybe the three of us can figure out how to escape."

"No." Savannah shook her head vehemently and packed up the tray. "They keep her guarded on a constant basis. Besides, Artimus has placed a shield over the entire compound, and those armed guards are on orders to shoot to kill. I want to stop him as much as you do, but there's simply no way. He's older, stronger, and I don't know what he'd do to my father if I helped you."

Marianna sat quietly and studied Savannah. She knew that if she pushed too hard, the girl would run, and maybe even stop coming to see her. She decided to change the subject to ease the tension.

"Where exactly are we anyway? I haven't seen daylight since I got here."

"That's because we're underground." She sniffled and wiped at her eyes with the back of her hand. "This entire facility was built from a network of caves in the mountains of Utah. So you can forget about escaping."

"Artimus mentioned that the others have dwellings here." Her brow knit with concentration. "Are they underground as well?"

"Yes. I don't think that most people realized what they were getting into." She glanced at the door and lowered her voice. "I've told you too much already."

"Wait." Savannah started to get up, but Marianna grabbed her arm, urging her to sit down. "What about this shield that Artimus has? Do you know how we can disable it?"

"No." She rose from her seat, for good this time. "He's one of the oldest Amoveo, almost as old as Prince Richard. I would imagine that Richard and his wife Salinda may be the only ones who can get past it, but they'd have to find us first."

"Savannah, please." Marianna's voice dipped to a desperate whisper. "Think about it at least?"

Savannah placed her hand over the panel, and the

door clicked open. As she disappeared, her gentle voice touched Marianna's mind. *Stay alert. Hayden has made no secret that he wants you for himself.* Her sympathetic eyes appeared in the window of the doorway briefly before vanishing. *I'm sorry.*

Chapter 15

PETE STOOD AT THE FOOT OF THE BED AND LEANED ON the bedpost as he stared at their uncooperative guest. Daniella lay there weak, but no less defiant. Her hazel eyes, full of hatred, avoided their gazes as she stared at the ceiling.

Richard stood to the right of the bed with his arms crossed over his chest, his glowing, golden eyes fixed on Daniella. Dante stood with his arm around Kerry's waist in his usual protective manner, but both looked no less irritated by her unwillingness to talk. William, a member of the Gyrfalcon Clan, and his hybrid mate, Layla, stayed toward the back, observing the situation with their typical distance.

"I gotta hand it to you," Pete said quietly. "You're surrounded by a room full of Amoveo, and you're not giving up an inch. That's a pretty ballsy thing to do, considering you've got zero powers right now." He leaned closer and whispered harshly. "How does it feel to be stripped bare? Stripped down to the essence of the very thing you hate? *Human*. That must really gnaw at you."

Her eyes flicked to his briefly, and that's when he saw it. *Fear.*

"I'm not human." She tugged the covers to her chin and closed her eyes. "It's just a spell."

"Maybe," Pete said, pushing himself off the

footboard. "But I don't think Artimus would see it that way, would he?"

"That's a valid point, Pete." Richard's deep voice caught the girl's attention. His eyes glowed brighter as he stared at Daniella. "Perhaps we should let her leave? I wonder how welcome she'd be with Artimus and the rest of the Purists now? Not only did she fail in killing you, but she managed to get hit with a binding powder."

"He—he would help me." Daniella's eyes flew open, and her face twisted in fear. "He'd know it wasn't my fault."

"I can tell by the look in your eyes you don't believe that for a second." Richard glared at her. "We all know that Artimus is anything but merciful."

"I'm not saying anything." Daniella looked back at the ceiling, her jaw set.

"I have to admit that I am more than a little disappointed in you, Daniella. You were a guardian, a caretaker of my ranch and those who stayed within it. Including my family." The prince's voice hardened. "Your brother, Dominic, is still furious with you for your betrayal, but you should know that he still works here as a guardian."

"Dominic is here?" Something flickered in her eyes, which were still locked on the ceiling. Sadness? Regret? Pete wasn't sure, but it left as quickly as it came.

"He is," Richard confirmed. "I asked him to come and see you, but he refused."

"Fine with me," she seethed. "I've got nothing to say to him or any of you."

The room fell silent, and Pete watched Richard's glowing eyes flicker and return to their human blue eyes.

"Kerry," Richard said without taking his powerful gaze off Daniella, "I realize that your gift of sight is usually limited with Amoveo, and normally you only see our clan animal, but do you think you'd be willing to see if you can get more from this traitor?"

"I would be happy to." Kerry grinned and flicked her eyes to Pete briefly. "But I may need some help from Pete, if he's willing."

"Me?" Pete crossed his arms over his chest and fought the tension that settled in his neck. "I don't know what kind of help I could be, but I'll do whatever you want."

"Then it's settled." The prince stepped back and gestured to Daniella. "She's all yours."

"I'm not telling you shit." Outright terror came over Daniella's face as Kerry moved toward her, and she shook her head vehemently. "No matter what you do to me."

"I'm not going to hurt you." Kerry sighed dramatically and put her hands on her ample hips. "That's not my style."

Kerry sat on the edge of the bed as Daniella tried to move away.

"Stay still," Dante growled. His amber eyes glowed brightly as he shifted to a protective stance next to Kerry.

"Don't mind him." Kerry patted Dante's arm and smiled at Daniella. "Tarzan, here, is overprotective."

"Let's hold hands, okay?" Kerry wiggled her fingers at Daniella, who cast a confused look at Kerry's outstretched hand. "It's not going to hurt or anything. Honest."

When Daniella didn't comply, a low growl rumbled in Kerry's throat, and her eyes flickered brightly to the yellow cat eyes of her clan. "Now."

Daniella licked her lips nervously and placed her hand in Kerry's.

At first nothing happened. Everyone in the room held their breath as Kerry sat quietly holding Daniella's hand, but a few seconds later Kerry's body jolted as the connection was made. Dante stepped back, giving her the space he knew she needed, and Daniella's eyes fluttered closed as their connection deepened.

"Pete," Kerry ground out. "Take my other hand." Eyes still closed and her body humming with tension, her left arm flew out toward Pete. At first he stared at it in disbelief as the words sputtered from her lips with obvious effort. "I don't—have—time—to—debate—this."

They all looked at him, and Dante waved him forward. "I've never seen this happen before, but you should do what she wants."

Pete came around the foot of the bed, said a silent prayer, and placed his hand in Kerry's.

The vaguely familiar kick in the gut was immediately followed by the time-warp sensation he'd experienced when he first put on the ring. Propelled through a vacuum of time and space, he found himself standing in the midst of a series of passing images.

He was flying over the mountains and diving into caves and tunnels. Darkness was swiftly replaced with bright, artificial light, and he was whipping through rooms that reminded him of a hospital. He saw women restrained to beds and bodies operated on. Artimus lorded over a room of glowing eyes. Chanting. Screaming.

Marianna's smiling, brown eyes filled his mind and faded with the faint cry of a baby.

The time-warp-like vacuum sucked him back to the present in a rush of heat and swirling light. Gasping for air, Pete released Kerry's hand and dropped to the ground on all fours. The cool, solid wood floor beneath his hands was a welcome relief from the nauseating spin of the vision. Pete grabbed the side of the bed and pulled himself to a standing position; falling to his knees felt remarkably undignified.

He rubbed the sweat from his eyes as he let out a slow breath, and when he finally opened his eyes, he found everyone staring at him—everyone, except for Daniella, because she had passed out again.

"What?" He ran a hand through his hair. "Did I bark like a dog or something?"

Kerry, still sitting on the edge of the bed, smiled through weary eyes. "No, but thanks for pinch-hitting with me."

"What do you mean?" Pete flicked his eyes around the room, wondering what the hell they were all thinking. "What did I do?"

"Normally, when I touch another Amoveo, I only get an image of their clan animal." She took Dante's hand as he pulled her from the bed and wrapped her in his arms protectively. "I had a hunch that your power might help me break through to another level and get past that initial image, and it did."

"I'm glad it helped, but I have no idea what we just saw." He shoved his hands in his pockets, hoping he didn't look and sound as uncertain of himself as he was. All this demon stuff was going to take some getting used to. "It felt like some kind of bad LSD trip. Just a bunch of weird, jumbled images."

"I know." Kerry grinned and leaned further into Dante's embrace. "It's like that at first, but the more you use the gift, the better you'll get at understanding it."

"We'll see." Pete rubbed his thumb against the silver of the ring. "I want to know where Marianna is and get her back. She's all that matters."

"We followed the path of Daniella's memories, and you helped me do that." She turned to the others. "Marianna's not alone. Artimus has several Amoveo females held captive at his compound. I saw at least three missing girls, but I think there are more. Unfortunately, we were right about the breeding program, but Marianna isn't going to be much help."

"You're goddamned right." Pete's jaw clenched, and heat crawled up his back.

Kerry's eyes widened, and she cocked her head. "You don't know, do you?" she murmured.

"Know what?" The knot in his stomach tightened. He looked from Kerry to Dante. "What's going on?"

"You're going to be a father."

Pete blinked.

"What?" He took a step back and grabbed the bedpost again for support. "She's pregnant? Marianna's pregnant with my baby?"

He kept saying it as he tried to wrap his brain around it. He was going to be a father? Heat flashed, and the air grew thick. His sweaty palm slipped on the post as he glanced at the smiling faces of his friends.

"Well," Kerry said as she scrunched up her face. "It's more like *babies*. She's having twins."

"Twins?" The word had barely escaped his lips as the world went dark, and he fainted.

———•———

Pete sat on the couch in the living room with a scowl on his face and an ice pack on his head.

"It's not funny," he grumbled to Dante and William. "I was dizzy from that freaky vision, that's all."

Tramp sat dutifully next to Pete and placed his head in his lap. Pete rubbed the dog's ears, wishing he could rub away his own humiliation as easily. He'd never fainted, and the first time, he did it in front of a room full of Amoveo. Nice.

"I think the lump to your ego is bigger than the lump on your head," Kerry said as she handed him a glass of water. "Shit happens. You've had a lot of revelations in the past twenty-four hours. Discovering that you're half demon and going to be the father to twins—that's enough to make anyone faint."

"Not me," William said evenly. He stood ramrod straight by the window in his usual uptight way.

"Stick it, birdbrain." Pete growled as he removed the ice pack and handed it to Kerry.

Layla laughed and swatted her mate on the shoulder. "You better not give him a bad time, William, or I'll start telling stories."

William straightened his tie and cast her a contrite look. "That's unnecessary. I'm merely stating a fact."

"That's quite enough." Richard's authoritative voice silenced the room. He sat in the wingback chair next to the fireplace; his large blue eyes regarded all of them. "Let's get back to business."

William bowed his head and wrapped his arm around Layla. "Of course."

"We know that Artimus is holding Marianna and the others in some kind of underground compound in Utah. We also know that according to Daniella's memories, there is a shield in place, which prevents anyone other than Artimus from utilizing most of their powers."

"That's correct." Kerry nodded somberly. "Based on what we saw, I can use her imprinted memories and get us to just outside the entrance of the compound, and I should be able to draw up a map of the facility. However, once we go in there, we're all at a disadvantage. Unless we disable this shield, we won't be able to shift or use our visualization skills."

"What about telepathy?" Pete asked. "I've tried to talk to Marianna that way, but I haven't had any luck. I thought maybe it's because I'm new at it."

"No. I tried telepathy as well," Kerry said. "I think that once we're inside we can, but we can't through the shield."

"I would agree with that assessment," Richard replied. "The informant that we had in place was able to use telepathy sporadically. But a few weeks ago, it stopped altogether."

Pete was curious to know who this informant was, but he had a feeling that it wasn't something Richard wanted to share. All he cared about was getting Marianna back—Marianna and his unborn children. Children? Pete ran his hands over his face. What kind of father would he be if he couldn't keep their mother safe?

"Given that we will likely be at a disadvantage, it

would be wise to bring as many weapons as possible." Richard turned his serious eyes to Pete. "It's my understanding from Dante that you have a rather large stockpile of guns and ammunition. We would be most grateful to utilize as much as you can spare."

"You read my mind," Pete said evenly. "There's plenty to go around."

"Excellent." Richard nodded. "I will attempt to disable the shield once we are there, but we cannot afford to waste more time. We could call in others, but I think that it's best if we go in with a small, focused group." He cast a somber gaze to Pete. "If Marianna is pregnant, that will not sit well with Artimus's plan, and I would imagine that he'll terminate the pregnancy."

"Like hell he will." Pete rose slowly from the couch, and his eyes burned. "Dante, it's time for you and birdbrain here to use your vanishing act. Let's go get some guns, so I can blow that motherfucker's head off."

Everyone looked at Pete as though he'd grown an extra head, but before long a smile played at the corners of Richard's mouth. "Looks like the demon is ready for a fight."

Pete's brow furrowed, and he was about to ask Richard what he was talking about when he caught a glimpse of his reflection in the mirror above the massive mantelpiece.

His eyes burned red, just like Asmodeus's.

He probably should've been freaked out, but instead, he felt something far more surprising—power. He barely recognized his own reflection. As his blood pumped through his veins and his eyes glowed red, only one word went through his mind.

Marianna.

The guard held Marianna by the arm and dragged her down the hallway with little concern for whether he was hurting her. He refused to tell her where he was taking her and wouldn't even utter a word. She recognized him and realized that she'd seen only two guards the entire time. Tweedle Dee and Tweedle Dum.

Could it be possible that Artimus had only two armed guards in the whole compound? Maybe fear was a better security system?

Marianna suspected that the Amoveo who'd followed Artimus had reservations about him from the start. However, after he'd ripped off Veronica's head in the auditorium, she doubted that anyone would speak against him or defy him.

As they rounded the corner, the guard practically ran over Savannah.

"Watch where you're going, you imbecile," Savannah snapped in a tone that Marianna hadn't ever heard.

"Apologies." The guard bowed his head. "I'm taking the patient to the medical lab as your father requested."

"I'll take her from here." Savannah grabbed Marianna's arm but didn't look at her. "Artimus wants you to tend the patient hallway as your associate is keeping watch over the living quarters of the true believers."

"Perhaps I should speak directly with Artimus. I don't think—"

"You're not paid to think," Savannah snapped. Her eyes shifted to their clan form and glowed brightly at the guard. "Artimus is in a meeting with my father and would be most upset to be disturbed. Besides, I'm sure you don't want me to inform him you're questioning his orders. Do you?"

"No, ma'am." He flicked his gaze from Savannah to Marianna. "Are you sure you can handle her?"

"Quite sure." Savannah arched one pale eyebrow and removed the Taser from her pocket. "I suggest you get back to your post before Artimus comes looking for you."

The guard gave her a curt nod and went on his way. Marianna watched him disappear around the corner and said nothing as Savannah walked her down the hall toward the medical labs. At least, she thought it was the labs, but the truth was that she wasn't sure. The two times she'd been there, she'd been heavily drugged.

They came to a bright red door that seemed vaguely familiar, and without saying a word, Savannah placed her hand on the panel next to it. The door opened with a muted clicking sound and she proceeded to lead Marianna into a large room that resembled a hospital. To the left there was a birthing suite, several pieces of medical equipment, and a sonogram machine.

A nurse with mousy brown hair sat at a desk along the center of the back wall. She looked at them through scrutinizing eyes. Marianna could tell by the woman's dense energy signature that she was a mated pure-blood from the Fox Clan. She stood from her chair and looked at Marianna like she was a bug that needed to be squashed.

"Where's the guard?" the woman snipped as she looked past them to the door. "You should not be walking with this one unattended. She gave your father and Hayden quite a bit of trouble when she first arrived."

"I can handle myself, Iris." Savannah led Marianna to the curtained area to the right. "My father wanted to run some comparison tests on this one and the woman from the Coyote Clan. He's curious to see if there are any differences between the hybrid pregnancy and the pure-blood."

"Yes," Iris sniffed. "He mentioned that to me, but I assumed that *I* would be running the tests."

"Well, you assumed incorrectly. Why don't you go ahead and take a break. This shouldn't take long, and I'll escort her to her room when I'm finished."

Savannah pulled the curtain aside, and Marianna's hand went her mouth as she let out a muffled cry. It was Courtney. She was either asleep or sedated and strapped to a hospital bed in only a white bra and underwear. She had electrodes stuck all over her body, and the steady beep of her heart monitor filled the room.

"Fine." Iris snatched a folder off her desk and stuck it in Savannah's face. "Be sure to write down all of your findings." She shot an angry look at Marianna. "I need to use the ladies' room, but I'll be back shortly—so don't get any ideas, missy."

Marianna barely heard her because she couldn't stop looking at her friend. Courtney's sandy blond hair splayed over the pillow and looked like it hadn't been washed or brushed in days. Marianna's throat tightened, and as soon as Iris was out the door, she went directly to Courtney's side and took her hand in hers.

"Court?" She sniffled as tears fell onto the sheet. She brushed stray strands of hair off Courtney's face. "Can you hear me?" *Courtney?* She reached out to her friend's mind but was met with a dark void. This woman, always full of life and often heard with a loud, raucous laugh, lay in the bed looking almost dead.

"They're keeping her completely sedated." Savannah stood at the foot of the bed and kept her voice low. "So far the pregnancy is fine, but I don't how much longer it will be. Here," she said gently. "Come sit on this bed next to her, and let me get some data."

Marianna wiped the tears from her eyes and placed a kiss on Courtney's forehead. She did as Savannah asked and sat near her friend as Savannah pulled a cart over and attached sticky sensors in the same places that Courtney had them.

"I'm going to collect the data like my father asked." She attached the last two sensors beneath Marianna's shirt. "Just lay back, and stay quiet for a few minutes. This won't hurt you or the babies. They want to track your information and compare it with Courtney's."

Marianna complied and stared at the bright lights in the ceiling as tears fell freely down her face. Hopelessness reared its ugly head, threatened to swallow her whole and suck her into the abyss. She'd allowed hope to glimmer and trick her into thinking Savannah was going to help, but clearly that wasn't the case. Was this how she'd spend the rest of her life? Like a lab rat in a maze?

Savannah removed the electrodes without saying a word and took notes in the folder that Iris had given her, before helping Marianna to a sitting position.

"Boy, you really had me fooled," Marianna said bitterly. She tugged the sleeve of her shirt down and turned her furious eyes to Savannah.

"What do you mean?" Savannah asked as she checked Courtney's vital signs.

"When you took me from the guard in the hallway," she seethed. "I thought you were helping me get out, but you're a good little girl for daddy, aren't you?"

Before she could answer, the door clicked open, and Iris huffed in with a large cup of coffee.

"We're finished here, Iris." Savannah didn't spare a glance to Marianna as she handed the folder off. "I'll leave it to my father to analyze the information. It's time for me to get this one back to her room before dinner."

"Fine by me." Iris took the folder and shot Marianna a look of contempt. "I still don't know how you could do it."

"Do what?" Marianna asked as she hopped off the gurney with Savannah's help.

"Sleep with a *human* and let him impregnate you." She shuddered as the words escaped her lips and made a sound of disgust.

"Well, that makes us even," Marianna ground out. "Because I don't know how you can declare your allegiance to a psychopath. Better watch your step, Iris. Veronica was a devoted follower, and look where it got her."

Iris's complexion paled at the mention of Veronica's name, and Marianna tried to suppress the grin, but it was no use. Getting under this bitch's skin was a small victory, but she'd take it.

Iris turned her back on the two and settled herself at her desk. "Get her out of here."

Savannah walked Marianna to her room in silence. Tweedle Dee was back at his post in the hallway as usual, but he barely spared them a glance when they walked past him to Marianna's room.

Savannah escorted her in and motioned for her to sit on the bed. Still furious, Marianna complied, but remained silent as Savannah took out her stethoscope and once again checked her heart rate. She glanced over her shoulder at the door as she jotted more notes into her notebook.

Marianna watched her intently, but she avoided her gaze as she finished her usual tasks. Savannah took something from her pocket, leaned past Marianna, and slipped it beneath her pillow before she left the room in silence.

The door shut with a gentle click. Savannah's bright green eyes peered through the window. *Be ready.* Savannah's voice touched her mind as her face disappeared from view. *We're getting out of here tonight so get some sleep. You'll need as much of your strength as possible.*

Marianna sat motionless on the bed, uncertain if she'd heard her correctly. She slipped her hand beneath the pillow, and a grin cracked her face as she wrapped her fingers around Savannah's Taser. Relief and hope washed over her, and in that moment, she knew that she would get out alive.

Marianna lay on the bed and rested her head on the pillow, with the precious gift beneath, as she closed her eyes and waited for sleep to claim her.

Chapter 16

PETE DOUBLE-CHECKED THE FOUR AMMO MAGAZINES attached to the specially designed utility belt and loaded his Beretta with the ease of experience. Satisfied with his supplies, he holstered his gun and checked on the others. Layla and Kerry opted not to carry weapons due to their inexperience, but Dante, Richard, and William were stocking up just as Pete had.

"Are you sure that you two don't want a weapon?" Pete asked Kerry and Layla.

"Absolutely." Layla tied her curly red hair into a ponytail as William hovered nearby. "I hate guns, and the last thing that we need are nervous trigger fingers added to the mix. Kerry and I have gotten stronger in our human form since our mating, and we've been schooled in hand-to-hand combat over the past few weeks. Once Richard gets the dampening shield down, we can shift and provide backup in our clan forms."

"Agreed." Kerry winked. "I'm far more confident fighting in my panther form, but thanks to Dominic's crash course in ass-kicking, I should be able to hold my own." Kerry took a folded piece of paper from her back pocket and handed it to Pete. "Here, I drew us a map of the compound from Daniella's memories."

Pete unfolded the paper and scanned the hand-drawn diagram intently, doing his best to commit as much as possible to memory. He laid the map on the dining room table as the rest gathered around.

"This hallway here," Kerry said, pointing out a short corridor, "I think this is where they're keeping the prisoners, and this larger room looks like some kind of meeting space. The halls and rooms to the left are the living quarters. Then, on the other side of this network of hallways, is the medical facility."

"It's a fucking maze," Pete murmured. "If we make a wrong turn, we could get lost in there forever." He turned his serious eyes to Richard. "How confident are you that you can get past this shield on your own?"

"He won't be on his own." Salinda's melodic voice floated into the room and captured everyone's attention instantly. She stood in the doorway of the dining room dressed in the same all-black, combat-ready outfit as the rest. Her dark hair was swept back in a tight ponytail, and looking at her shapely body, it was hard to believe that she'd had a baby a couple months ago.

"Absolutely not." Richard's eyes shifted and glowed brightly at his wife. "It's not safe, and you should be here with our baby daughter."

"First of all," Salinda began calmly, "you should know, after three centuries together, that I don't take orders. Secondly, I love you, and what kind of mate would I be if I allowed you to do this on your own?" Her pale brown eyes shifted into the amber eyes of the Tiger Clan and shined as she slowly moved toward her husband. "Dominic is here guarding the property and will assure that Daniella doesn't leave. And as for our sweet baby girl Jessica, she is staying with Malcolm and Samantha until our return. Actually, Samantha was thrilled to have an opportunity to practice her mothering skills, since her own baby is due in a couple months."

"I'd argue with you, but I know it wouldn't get me anywhere." Richard hugged his wife and placed a kiss on her head before handing her one of the nine-millimeter handguns.

"Thank you." Salinda tucked it into the waistband of her pants and smiled at Pete. "Using our energies to disable the dampening field will be more effective and far faster than if Richard does it alone."

Pete nodded and looked pointedly at each couple that stood around the table. They were about to go in there and risk their lives to get Marianna back. His throat tightened with an unexpected wave of emotion because he couldn't remember the last time he felt like part of a family. He'd been a loner—and alone—for so long that he'd practically forgotten what it felt like to belong.

"I realize that this probably goes without saying," Pete said quietly, as he folded the map and tucked it into his pocket. "But I want to thank you for helping me get her back. You don't have to do it, and you're putting your own lives at risk."

When he looked up again, all six stared at him through the glowing eyes of their clans, and for the first time, he wasn't unnerved. In fact, he was comforted. He knew that they would stop at nothing to retrieve Marianna and the others held by Artimus.

Kerry held out her hands and nodded. "I'd say it's time for a jail break."

The seven held hands and completed the circle. Eyes closed, they joined energy signatures as they tuned into Kerry and the imprinted path that she took from

Daniella. Pete held on and kept his mind fixed on Kerry as they took him along for the ride.

He saw bright light and felt a slight breeze. The scent of raw earth, fresh snow, and pine filled his nostrils. Static electricity flared in a prickling wave, and was instantly followed by a frigid blast of arctic air.

Biting wind whipped over his face as he squinted against the freezing air and dropped the hands of his companions. They were standing in snow halfway to their knees with towering pine trees on either side, and twenty feet in front loomed the rocky side of a small mountain, and other than the seven of them, there wasn't a soul in sight.

Richard's voice touched their collective minds. *William, take flight, and check the surroundings for guards that might be outside the entrance of the cave. Layla, Kerry, and Dante, take your clan forms, and scan for energy signatures, or see if you can pick up familiar scents. We'll meet at the mouth of the cave once we have an all clear. Salinda and I will work on penetrating the shield. If we can create a weak point, then that's all we'll need to break through.*

Pete took his Beretta from the holster, and just feeling the weight in his hand made him more at ease. He held his breath and waited for the group to shift and set the plan in motion. They whispered the ancient language, and in a rush of static and a ripple of heat, the others shifted into their clan forms in one massive power pulse.

William shifted into his gyrfalcon and soared into the air with a few powerful pumps of his enormous wings. Pete waited as he soared effortlessly and circled the area like a stealth bomber silhouetted against the moonlit sky.

Layla's spotted cheetah burst across the snow in a blur and disappeared in the trees. Kerry's sleek panther loped into the dark night, and her glowing yellow eyes twinkled over her shoulder as her familiar teasing tone touched their minds. *Make sure you cover our asses, Castro.*

Pete merely nodded and kept his gun at the ready. After what seemed like an eternity of waiting in cold and silence, the others sent back the all clear. Pete, Richard, and Salinda crouched low and silently made their way to the mouth of the small cave. Dante, still in his fox form, had gone into the cave to see the layout and find the actual entrance to the compound network.

As he trotted out, his glowing amber eyes were the first thing they all saw. Once he emerged, he shifted into his human form and hunkered down with the others.

"There's a door about fifty feet in," he said, keeping his voice low. "It's designed to look like the cave wall, and there's some kind of panel next to it."

"I think it's heat-sensitive," Kerry said. "In the vision, I saw Artimus put his hand on it." Brow furrowed, she looked at Pete. "It must be rigged to open only to certain people's heat signatures, but I bet you could pick that lock."

"Me?" Pete shifted his weight and rubbed the silver ring. "How?"

"Asmodeus told you that part of the demon thing is being able to manipulate heat, right? So maybe you can trick the sensor into thinking you're Artimus?" She shrugged. "It's worth a shot."

"I'll give it a try." His mouth set in a tight line, and he checked the magazine in his gun before slamming it back in place. "If that doesn't work, then I'll just fucking shoot it."

"Stick to the plan," Richard directed. "You go to the patient rooms first, and if she's not there, then you go to the medical facility. If you see any missing women, grab them, and take them with you as well. Salinda and I will stay here and focus on creating a tear in the shield. Once we've broken through, we should be able to use telepathy, and then you can visualize yourselves, and anyone you can rescue, back to the safety of the ranch."

Richard put his hand into the middle of their circle, and the rest immediately followed, clasping their hands, one on top of the other. Eyes glowing, they looked at Pete, waiting for him to add his hand to the group. Dante nodded, and even William tipped his head in encouragement. On a silent prayer, Pete placed his hands on the others as they whispered the ancient language in unison. "*Iunctus.*"

He knew what it meant. They were proclaiming their unity, their vow to be a united front until the end. Pete looked back and whispered, "*Iunctus.*"

"In for a penny, in for a pound," Pete murmured as he started into the entrance of the cave and waved the others to follow. He adjusted his grip on the gun and stopped for a moment as he waited for his eyes to adjust to the dim light.

Pete snagged the small flashlight from his belt and pressed his finger to his lips, signaling the others to be silent. Leaning against the rough wall, Pete cupped the end of the flashlight and kept it shining along the floor, trying to light the way discreetly. The further they went in, the narrower the passage got, and Pete struggled against the growing sensation of being buried alive. The moist dank air filled his nostrils, and he was surprised by how warm it was within the cave.

It's about five more feet on the right. Dante's voice cut into his mind. Pete didn't answer, but nodded his understanding. He stopped and holstered his gun as he felt along the wall, searching for the disguised door. The rough surface, slick with moisture, rasped beneath his fingers, and he eventually found an unnaturally straight groove in the rock.

Pete reached to the left and felt around until he found a smooth, rectangular surface, which had to be the heat-sensitive panel that Kerry had mentioned. Sweating and anxious, Pete placed his palm over the cool surface and focused on Artimus. He pictured the smug bastard's face and the expression when he'd disappeared with Marianna.

Heat raced down his arm as the soft click of a lock opening echoed through the passage. A rush of warm air blew over them, and a stream of bright light lit the cave as the door disappeared slowly into the wall.

No time to register what he'd done, Pete snatched the gun from his holster and pressed himself against the wall next to the opening doorway. Half expecting an army of Amoveo to come flooding out, they all braced themselves and waited.

No one came.

Pete peered around the corner and found the hallway empty. Before entering, he took note of the space. It was a small entry that led to two hallways. In the far left corner was a camera with a blinking red light scanning the entrance. Pete snagged the silencer from one compartment on the belt and quickly attached it to his gun. Knowing he'd get only one try, he intensified his focus and took out the camera with one stealthy shot.

He pulled back and waited to see if anyone was going to come running around the corner, but the only thing he heard was the crackling and hissing of the destroyed camera. He signaled to the group, and they all followed him across the threshold into the compound.

The door slid shut silently behind them, and he noticed the subtle shift in the demeanor of his companions. The dampening field was obviously in place, and they felt the effects already.

Pete took out the map as the others gathered around. "If we take the hallway to the right," he whispered, "then that should take us to the patient rooms, and the hallway past that is where the medical labs are."

"Stick to the plan." William's cool voice cut into the discussion. His glowing dark eyes latched intently onto Pete. "You, Dante, and Kerry go to the rooms where we suspect they're holding the women. Layla and I will go to the medical labs and see if any are held there."

"The faster we can do this, the better. If you turn off here," Pete said, referencing the map, "then you should be able to take this corridor to the labs."

"Understood." William nodded curtly.

"Don't take any chances." Pete turned his serious gaze to each of them. "If it moves, and it's not one of the women we're looking for, shoot first, and ask questions later. It's only a matter of time before they figure out we're here—if they haven't already. Check every corridor for cameras, and if you spot one, shoot it out."

They nodded as Pete tucked the map into his pocket

and checked the magazine in his gun. He held his gun in front of him as he checked around the corners of the hall to see that they were clear. Finding the halls empty, he signaled for the others to follow and silently made his way down the sterile corridor.

Game on. Dante's voice touched their minds, and he could sense their relief. Even if they couldn't shift, at least they could communicate with each other while inside. If he could hear them, then Marianna could hear him.

As Pete led the way down the white hallway, he reached out to Marianna with his mind and prayed that she could hear him.

I'm coming for you, Marianna.

―〰―

The sound of the door to her room opening woke Marianna from a light sleep. She squinted against the fluorescent lighting as she came out of her slumber. Marianna rubbed her eyes, expecting to see Savannah, but instead, was greeted with Hayden's lecherous, leering face just inches from hers.

He was on top of her before she could reach the Taser beneath her pillow. He straddled her, pinning her legs with his, as he held her arms on the bed along either side of her head. Marianna screamed and tried to buck him off, but it was no use—he was far stronger than she was.

"I've been waiting for this for a long time, Marianna."

Hayden leaned down and tried to kiss her, but she thrashed her head and held her mouth closed. Hayden licked the side of her face. She squeezed her eyes shut and shrank from him, but there was nowhere to go but deeper into the pillow. She could feel the lump of the

Taser beneath the pillow and her frustration grew. So close, and yet so far.

Savannah. Marianna reached out to her, praying she'd hear. *Please help me. It's Hayden. He's trapped me in my room.*

I can't. Savannah's voice sounded as desperate as her own. *I'm with my father and Artimus in the meeting hall. They know that—*

Her voice cut off abruptly, and Marianna tried to connect again, but she was met with silence. Tears pricked her eyes as Hayden dug his fingers into her wrists. His eyes glowed with the unmistakable glare of evil.

He wanted to hurt her.

"Scream all you want. No one will hear you, and even if they did, they wouldn't care. But go ahead," he whispered. His beer-tainted breath filled her nostrils, and her stomach roiled in protest. "I want you to scream for me."

"Fuck you," Marianna ground out between clenched teeth. "Get off me, Hayden!"

Hayden tugged her arms and crossed her wrists, one over the other, pinning them above her head with one of his massive hands. Marianna's wrists burned in his grip, and she turned her face away, grimacing as he kissed her neck. He shoved his hand beneath her shirt, grabbing her breast and squeezing it to the point of pain. Marianna fought the urge to cry out as she struggled beneath him, trying to get away.

I'm coming for you, Marianna. Pete's faint voice brushed along the edges of her mind.

Marianna's breath rushed from her lungs as his energy signature connected. Had she heard it, or was it an illusion? *Pete?* She reached out to him, tentatively at first, terrified that she was hallucinating. *Oh my God. Is that really you?*

"You're mine," Hayden hissed. One hand brushed the top of her crotch, but he stopped when alarm buzzers blared and red lights flashed through the compound. "What the hell?" Hayden sat and looked at the door through confused eyes.

The door to her room swung open, and the guard barged in frantically.

"The compound has been compromised, sir. We have intruders, and they're heading this way."

"Get down to the medical lab, and protect the host," Hayden barked.

"Yes, sir." He disappeared through the door, and as Hayden climbed off Marianna, she saw her window of opportunity—and her revenge—in sight.

With her glowing eyes on Hayden, she slipped her hand beneath the pillow and curled her fingers around the Taser. Body shaking with adrenaline, she watched and waited for the right moment.

"Don't go anywhere," he spat.

Hayden adjusted his pants as he went to the door and placed his hand on the sensor panel.

As the door clicked open, Marianna scrambled from the bed, raced up behind Hayden, and jammed him in the neck with the Taser. His body shook violently as he made a gurgling noise and dropped to his knees. She screamed with rage and pushed it harder against his neck as he crumpled into a heap on the floor.

Blind with anger, she removed the Taser and kicked him square in the face. He howled in pain, and blood spurted from his nose. Marianna scrambled to get out, but Hayden grabbed her ankle and yanked her into the room and down to the floor. The Taser fell from her hand and clattered out of reach.

He dragged her to him, straddled her on the cold tile floor, and backhanded her across the face. Pain exploded behind her eye, and everything started to spin as she struggled to stay conscious. She smacked and clawed at him blindly, kicking desperately, as she tried to get out from under him.

"You fucking bitch," Hayden screamed.

Blood and spittle clung to his chin as he sat on top of her, trying to undo the fly of his pants. Marianna swung with all her might and punched him square in the crotch.

He roared in pain and smacked her again. Nausea swamped her, and her head felt like it was going to crack open like an egg as she tried to escape.

Just when she thought he would overpower her completely, the muffled sound of a gunshot whooshed through the room. A hole bloomed in Hayden's forehead, and blood splattered as he collapsed on top of her.

Shaking and crying, Marianna shrieked and scrambled away as two strong hands scooped her up and pulled her from the floor. Eyes closed, she flailed and screamed as she was pulled against a familiar, strong body.

"Marianna," he murmured in her ear and held her close. "It's me. It's me, baby."

Recognition fought its way through the thick shroud of horror. Marianna opened her swollen eyes and found herself looking into the concerned eyes of her mate.

"Pete." His name rushed from her lips on a shaky breath. She touched his unshaven cheek with one bloodstained hand, as tears flowed freely down her face. "You came for me."

"You bet your ass I did." He captured her lips with his before raining kisses over her face. The sweet taste washed through her like the calm after the storm. Pete pulled her into his arms, tangled his fingers in her hair, and kissed the top of her head tenderly. "I'm so sorry I couldn't get here sooner." His voice, barely above a whisper, broke Marianna's heart.

"You're here now." She squeezed her eyes shut and wrapped her arms tightly around his waist. "I don't know what would've happened if you hadn't gotten here."

She buried her face in his chest and breathed him in. Sobbing, she allowed her exhausted, beaten body to lean into him for support. The alarm blared through the compound, and the red lights flashed urgently, but she could barely hear it above the pounding of her own heart.

"Pete," Dante's urgent voice interrupted their reunion. "We've got to check these other rooms. Layla and William went to the medical suite, and we still haven't heard from Richard."

"Courtney." Marianna looked frantically at Pete and then to Dante and Kerry. "Courtney Bishop. She's pregnant, and they're keeping her sedated in the medical lab. It's the room with the red door," she added urgently. "There are two armed guards, and I heard Hayden send one down there."

"Got it. We'll tell William and get the others." Dante and Kerry disappeared into the hallway.

"Are you okay?" Pete looked at Marianna. "I mean, the babies? Are they okay?" He placed one large hand over her lower belly and furrowed his brow as he glanced from her eyes to her tummy. "Can they hear this? Amoveo babies, I mean?"

"You know?" Marianna held his hand to her belly, and more tears fell as she looked into his loving eyes.

"Kerry told me."

"I'm sorry," she whispered. "I wanted to tell you myself, and I only realized it that morning that Artimus—" She choked on the words.

"Shhh." Pete pulled her into his arms again and stroked her hair. "I'm just grateful that you and the babies are safe." He kissed her head and murmured, "We have to get the hell out of here."

We've broken through the barrier of the shield, but I'm not sure for how long. Richard's deep voice rang into their minds in one collective message. Confused and more than a little surprised, Marianna looked at Pete and was about to ask him what was going on when a massive wave of dizziness sent her wavering in his arms.

"What's going on?" His brow furrowed as he gave her a worried look. "Marianna?"

She wanted to answer him and reassure him, but before she could form a coherent sentence, the darkness swallowed her, and she fainted.

Chapter 17

Just as Richard's message touched his mind, Dante shot open the door of yet another patient room. He expected to find one of the missing girls, maybe even a girl that he didn't know, or possibly, another empty room.

The last thing he expected to find was his friend Steven.

It's Steven. He shouted to the others as he went to his friend's side. Drugged and shackled to the bed, he was barely recognizable. Kerry came up next to her mate and helped him as he frantically removed the shackles from Steven's wrists and ankles.

The air filled with a crackling rush of static as Richard and Salinda materialized in the room behind them.

"What the fuck is he doing here?" Dante seethed as Richard pushed past both.

Richard dragged Steven's limp body from the bed and threw him over his shoulder.

"*He* was our informant." He turned his glowing, golden eyes to Dante and kept his voice in control, but Dante could sense how unnerved the prince was to find Steven here. Richard would never forgive himself for allowing one of his people to be harmed as a result of something he requested.

"Get the other women, and get the hell out of here now, but you'll only be able to take one person at a time. We weakened the shield, but did not completely destroy it. In fact, I'm not even sure how long we can keep it in a weakened state. There must be something else, something within the rock of the mountain, that's interfering with our shifting and visualization abilities."

Richard uttered the ancient language, but instead of vanishing smoothly as he always had, his image sputtered and sparked like a light about to go out. Finally, in one burst of static, he and Steven were gone.

Dante, frustrated and wanting an answer, went into the hallway with Kerry and Salinda. He shot out the other doors and kicked them open, but in all the other rooms, they found only three missing women—all shackled as Steven had been. Salinda and Kerry visualized themselves back to the ranch, each with one of the victims, and Dante grabbed the last girl before running to check on Pete and Marianna.

He stuck his head in her room to see Marianna passed out on the bed and Pete sitting next to her. Pete whipped his gun up and trained it on Dante before realizing who it was.

"Whoa—" Dante held up one hand and stood in the doorway with the passed-out girl over his shoulder. "I've got to get her to the ranch. I'll be back for you soon. Sit tight."

Pete said nothing. His eyes glowed bright red, and the temperature in the room skyrocketed as he stood and took a protective stance beside Marianna and nodded his understanding.

Dante uttered the ancient language. His image sputtered and blinked before finally disappearing.

∼∿∼

He didn't know how long Dante had been gone, but it felt like forever, and Pete couldn't wait longer. He holstered his gun and scooped Marianna off of the bed. Her limp body molded against his, and he tried not to think about how ill she looked—pale and weak—all that did was make him crazy.

Just as he was going to leave, William's stoic voice filled his head. *We disposed of the guard outside the medical lab. The lab is empty, but it looks like someone was kept here until recently.*

A rumbling growl suddenly filled the room and chilled Pete to the bone.

"Artimus," he whispered. Pete slowly laid Marianna on the bed and wrapped his fingers around the butt of his Beretta.

Pete yanked the gun from his holster, spun around, and fired two shots, but a massive, clawed paw swatted it from his hands and sent it flying across the room. Pete stumbled backward as Artimus stood on his hind legs in his grizzly bear form and bellowed into the air, towering over Pete.

Marianna moaned on the bed behind him, and every protective instinct Pete had went into overdrive. His eyes burned as he pulled the dagger from the sheath of his belt and launched himself into the arms of the bear. Heat raced over his skin, and his body hummed with newfound power as he stabbed Artimus over and over. Screaming with rage, Pete sank his dagger deep into his flesh, causing him to roar in agony and rage.

Artimus wrapped Pete in a bone-crushing hug and sank his teeth into the muscles of his shoulder. Burning, white-hot pain seared the left half of Pete's body as he stabbed at Artimus, but with one swift stroke of a clawed paw, he swiped at Pete and sent him to a bleeding heap on the floor.

Artimus, bleeding from various stab wounds, breathing heavily and weakened, dropped to all fours and growled as he sniffed Pete's broken body. The room went in and out of focus as Pete struggled to stay conscious. He leaned on the bed, wanting to be near Marianna if he would die. Wheezing and squinting as blood dripped into his eyes, he leaned his head back on the bed as Marianna's hand brushed his cheek, and her voice drifted into his mind, *I love you*.

Artimus's black eyes, dead and void of emotion like a shark, glared at Pete as he let out a bone-shattering roar. Artimus raised his paw to deliver what was sure to be a final deathblow, but the room filled with familiar static as William and Layla materialized behind Artimus.

Pete watched through blurred vision as Layla, in her cheetah form, snarled and pounced on Artimus's back, but she was shrugged off and swatted away. Her spotted body slammed into the wall with a high-pitched shriek as she shifted to her human form and lay motionless on the floor. William bellowed in rage at the sight of his mate wounded and fired at Artimus.

The shot missed. Artimus jumped on William and wrestled him to the ground, sinking his jaws into William's shoulder. Pete coughed up blood and watched helplessly as Artimus attacked his friend. He spotted his gun across the room, but given his weakened state, it may as well have not been there at all. He'd never be able to get to it and was losing more blood than he knew he had.

We're fucked.

You are not thinking like the son of a demon. The ring burned and branded itself into his skin as Asmodeus's voice rumbled into his mind. *If you can't get to it, then you bring it to you.*

Hell, it was worth a shot.

Pete grunted as he lifted his shaking hand toward the gun. He took every last ounce of strength he had and focused on willing it to him. His eyes burned; scorching heat zipped through his body as the gun flew into his hand. With his last ounce of strength, Pete swung the gun and pointed it at Artimus, who had his teeth buried in William's shoulder.

William locked eyes with Pete over Artimus's brown, furry form. *Shoot him.* William screamed in agony as he grabbed Artimus by the ears and yanked him as hard as he could, tearing his teeth from his flesh, and giving Pete a clear shot in the process.

"You're still not bulletproof, motherfucker," Pete whispered before squeezing off two rounds.

Artimus's hulking body fell and shifted to his human form as he hit the floor in a bloody mess. What was left of his head created an enormous pool of blood.

He watched as William, bleeding and weak, went to his mate and gathered her limp body in his arms. He leaned against the wall and cradled her in his lap as he winced in pain. "Nice shot," he ground out through shuddering breaths.

"Thanks, birdbrain." He grunted as the gun slipped from his fingers and clattered onto the tile floor. Marianna's hand grazed Pete's cheek, and her voice whispered in his mind as the room slipped out of focus and the world fell silent.

—◈—

Richard, Dante, and Kerry had materialized in the room moments later and let out a collective gasp at the sight. The room was an absolute bloodbath.

Artimus and Hayden lay dead on the floor. William and Layla were badly wounded, but conscious, and had called their friends for help. However, when Richard set eyes on Pete, he feared there was little they could do. Marianna, barely conscious herself, sat on the floor with Pete's head in her lap, and she was covered in blood— Pete's blood.

Flesh had been torn from the left side of his neck and shoulder, and it looked as if he'd lost more blood than they could replace. Pete's breathing was shallow and erratic, and his color was a pallid shade of gray.

Demon blood or not—he was dying.

Richard squatted to look closely, but he knew that even their Amoveo healers could do little to save him. He shot a grave look to Dante and shook his head.

"Please help him, Richard." Marianna looked at Richard through tear-filled eyes as she stroked Pete's hair. "You can't let him die."

"I'm sorry, Marianna." Richard's jaw set, but his voice was gentle. "His injuries are too severe, even for our Amoveo healers."

"Typical." Asmodeus's voice boomed like a thunderbolt. He stood in the doorway with Tramp sitting at his feet. The dog's eyes glowed bright red, just like Asmodeus's.

All eyes were fixed on the stranger. The man was massive—larger than any Amoveo man or Pete. His jet-black hair framed a familiar pair of eyes, which were locked on Pete. Marianna held Pete tighter and linked her energy signature to his as it ebbed and waned.

Is that who this man is, she wondered? Is he death personified, coming to claim her mate?

"Marianna." Kerry was the first to break the silence. "I'd like you to meet Asmodeus. One of the Seven Princes of Hell—and Pete's father."

"No time for introductions, I'm afraid." He crossed the room in a swift blur and placed both hands on Pete's injuries. Heat wafted from Asmodeus, and his hands glowed red as he cauterized the wounds and lifted Pete from Marianna's lap effortlessly. He winked and said, "That will stop him from losing more blood, but let's take him to see your friend, Olivia. Shall we?"

"Oh my God," Marianna breathed. "Of course." She smiled and laughed through her tears. "Olivia can turn him."

Marianna scrambled weakly to her feet and took Pete's limp hand in hers. She suspected that making Pete a vampire would cause problems, but she didn't care. Demon. Human. Vampire. All of the above? It didn't matter. Nothing mattered, except making sure that he survived—one way or another.

Richard and the others eyed Asmodeus warily, but no one made a move to stop him.

"If Olivia turns him, he'll never be fully accepted by our people or the vampires," Richard said quietly. "You're opening Pandora's box. He won't belong in any world. Not human, Amoveo, or vampire."

"He'll belong with me," Marianna said firmly, as her eyes glowed. "He's my mate and the father of our unborn children. After everything he's done, we owe it to him to at least try."

"And here I thought you were a progressive and open-minded soul, Richard." Asmodeus made a *tsking* sound as his eyes flared, and his voice dropped to a growl. "He will be more powerful than any of you can fathom."

Tramp barked, trotted to Marianna, and sat at her feet as they all vanished in a burst of fire and smoke.

"I hope she knows what she's doing," Dante murmured.

—∿∿∿—

As the smoke cleared, Marianna found herself standing in the living room of Olivia's private apartment beneath the nightclub. The muffled pounding of music could be heard faintly from above. Asmodeus lay Pete's limp body onto the black leather sofa and stepped back. Marianna sat next to him. She lifted his head and cradled it gently in her lap as he moaned in pain. Tramp yipped and sat at Asmodeus's feet, but he didn't take his eyes off Pete.

"Shouldn't you call to your friend?" The words had barely escaped Asmodeus's lips when the heavy wood and steel door flew open and slammed shut, seemingly by itself. Olivia whisked into the apartment in a blur of red and a gust of wind. Fangs bared, eyes flashing, she stopped short of attacking Asmodeus when she saw Marianna and Pete.

"I'd ask you how you're doing, but that would probably be a galactically stupid question." Olivia's nostrils flared as she breathed in the pungent aroma of blood. Her fangs retracted with a snap, and she glanced at

Asmodeus as she straightened out the jacket of her navy Ralph Lauren suit and smoothed her red curls. "Do I even want to know who you are?"

"Probably not," he said as he looked her up and down and grinned. "But I know who you are—or more importantly—*what* you are."

"I know what you are too," she said with a fang-flashing grin. "Demon."

"My son needs your assistance, *vampire*."

"Your son?" Olivia blinked and turned her attention to Pete. "I *knew* Pete had some demon blood, but royal demon blood... now *that* is unexpected."

"Please, Olivia," Marianna pleaded. "It took me forever to find him... don't make me live without him. You can turn him, can't you?"

"Shit." Olivia sighed. She looked from Marianna to Asmodeus, and finally, to Pete. "Does the prince know about this? And what about your brother? How will he and the Amoveo feel about having a vampire mated to one of their own?"

"I don't care." She ground the words out between clenched teeth, and her eyes glowed. "All I care about is Pete."

"We're wasting time," Asmodeus bit out.

Olivia nodded and knelt in front of Marianna and Pete. She picked up his arm and pushed the blood-soaked sleeve of his shirt to his bicep, exposing the tender flesh of his inner arm. "I know you said that you don't care about what the other Amoveo think, and I can respect that." She leaned both elbows on the couch and lowered her voice. "But what about Pete?"

Olivia's large green eyes latched onto Marianna's

as she searched them for the answer. Marianna's heart caught in her throat because she hadn't thought about that. All she thought about was herself—her feelings about living without him—but she never thought about how he'd feel living as a vampire.

Pete groaned, and his eyelids fluttered open as he said something incoherent, and his body twitched.

"Pete… please." Marianna leaned close and brushed tender kisses along his forehead. *Pete,* she whispered his name as she touched his mind with hers. *Please don't leave me.*

"If I do this—" Olivia whispered intently. "If I turn him, then he is vampire, and his allegiance will always be to the Presidium. Mate or no mate." She kept her narrowed eyes fixed on Marianna. "Having a vampire for your mate will be no less complicated than being mated to him as a human—probably more."

Olivia turned her attention to Pete. "Are you up for this, Mr. Hottie? Actually, you're not that hot right now." Her lips curved. "It's more like Mr. Oh-Shit-I-Got-My-Ass-Kicked."

He struggled to speak, and his body shook with effort as two simple words rushed from his lips. "Bite me."

"The Presidium will have a fucking field day with this one," Olivia said wearily.

Marianna watched as Olivia bared her white fangs and sank them into the vein on the inside of Pete's elbow. Her long, pale fingers gripped his arm like a vice as she drank deeply. Her body shuddered as she took one long last pull before coming up for air.

Marianna noticed that for the first time, Olivia's cheeks were pink, and her green eyes sparkled brilliantly.

"Son of a bitch, that tastes great." She gave Marianna an apologetic look. "Sorry. I don't have live feeds often, and I've never tasted anything like this before. If he tastes this good as only half demon, I think that the pure demon blood would send me into a fucking pleasure coma."

Marianna reached out and grabbed her friend, who wavered on her knees and looked like she might pass out herself. Olivia shook her head and sucked in a few steadying breaths.

"I'm fine. Just a little blood drunk, but it should pass in a minute. Damn." She let out a whistle and gave Marianna a sidelong glance. "You two had quite the fun month at that cabin… I'll never look at a snowmobile the same way again."

Marianna's face heated with embarrassment as she kept her gaze fixed firmly on Pete.

"Not trying to be a Peeping Olivia, but I can't help it. Blood memories, sorry." Olivia grinned as she sliced her own wrist with razor-sharp fangs. She placed the bleeding wound over Pete's mouth and lifted his head as she let the dark, ancient blood flow into his mouth.

Olivia looked to see what Asmodeus thought, but he said nothing. Tramp trotted to the couch, jumped up, laid over Pete's legs, and let out a low whine.

"There's a dog on my sofa." Olivia shook her head. "The only thing harder to get out than bloodstains… is dog stink."

Tramp growled, and his eyes burned red.

"Excuse me." Olivia sighed and rolled her eyes. "Hellhound stink."

Olivia removed her wrist from Pete's mouth, and

Marianna watched as the wound closed completely seconds after. The ivory skin of her wrist looked fresh and unmarred. Olivia stood wearily and sat on the edge of the coffee table as she pulled Pete's sleeve back down.

"Now," she said on a sigh, "we wait. He'd already lost a lot of blood before our blood exchange so... we have to wait and see. She turned to Asmodeus. "So what's your story?"

"Thank you for helping my son, *vampire*."

"It's Olivia." She zipped around Asmodeus and came up behind him in a barely visible flash. He didn't move, but stood motionless with his muscular arms crossed over his broad chest, as he allowed her to inspect him. Olivia grabbed his head and tilted it to one side as she took a long sniff of the skin along his neck. Fangs burst into her mouth, and her eyes fluttered closed as she breathed in his exotic aroma.

"Holy shit." Olivia sighed as she released his head and stepped away in an almost drunken stupor. A smile curved her full pink lips. "You smell like the best fuck I ever had... and then some."

"Yes," he mused. He lifted his muscular shoulders and watched as she moved around him slowly this time. "That sounds about right."

"You are the Demon of Lust," she said through a shuddering breath. "Sweet Jesus, what do the others smell like? I almost had an orgasm from one whiff."

"Belphegor, the Demon of Sloth, smells like shit, so I doubt you'd be getting any orgasms from him." The smile that played on Asmodeus's lips faltered, and his eye glowed bright red as he lost his patience.

"I'd be happy to school you further on the rest of the brotherhood at another time, but it's time for me to take my leave."

Marianna stroked Pete's hair as she gave Asmodeus a weary smile. "Thank you."

Asmodeus bowed his head and vanished in a cloud of smoke.

Chapter 18

THE SWEET AND FAMILIAR SCENT OF PEACHES AND vanilla filled Pete's head as he emerged from the deepest sleep of his life. As the fog lifted, he heard the distinct rhythm of three heartbeats.

"Pete?" Marianna's melodic voice surrounded him. "Can you hear me?"

Pete's eyes flew open as the bloody memories of his encounter with Artimus swamped him. Images flashed through his mind. Marianna trapped beneath Hayden as he attacked her. A massive bear claw slashing him to pieces. Artimus's head being blown to smithereens. Marianna passed out on the bed.

Then… darkness.

"Marianna," he shouted as he sat up in the bed and reached for her instinctively.

Well, he'd meant to sit up in bed, but instead, he found himself clinging to the ceiling above an unfamiliar bedroom.

"What the fuck?" Pete looked frantically around the room beneath him. Another memory crept in—he had told Olivia to bite him. Apparently, she did.

"I guess it worked." Olivia elbowed a concerned Marianna and waved to Pete. "Come on down from there, and have something to eat."

Bewildered and more than a little embarrassed, Pete let go of the ceiling and landed silently on two feet, as sure as a cat. Wearing only sweatpants, he slowly stood to his full height, keeping his gaze intent on Marianna, who looked at him through wide brown eyes.

"What happened?" He didn't move, unsure of exactly what was going on.

"Drink this," Olivia said as she held out a coffee mug.

Pete didn't take it at first because he was too busy filtering out the array of sounds and smells. The ticking of the clock on the other side of the bedroom sounded like it was inside his head instead of twenty feet away. He could hear Tramp's panting from the living room, and the three heartbeats he heard were coming from Marianna and the babies in her womb.

The world was brighter, sharper, and louder than it had ever been before. He didn't think it would be possible, but Marianna was more beautiful. His body hummed with power—and he was starving.

Whatever was in that mug smelled like bacon, eggs, and French toast all rolled into one. Pete snatched the mug from Olivia's hand and sucked back the warm liquid like his life depended on it. Warmth rushed through his veins, and power surged.

He swiped at his mouth and held it to Olivia. "More."

"I'm your maker, not your mother." Olivia smirked and walked to the door of the bedroom. "There's a full pitcher of blood on the dresser, and if you need to warm it up, the microwave is in the kitchen."

"Olivia?" Marianna looked nervously from Olivia to Pete. "That's it? Don't you need to do vampire training or something?"

"Not right now." Olivia smiled, baring her fangs. "He'll have to be trained for the first year of his new life. As his maker, he's my responsibility, but you two need time to get reacquainted. He didn't try to rip your throat out when he woke up, so he's not suffering from a bad turn."

Pete's eyes widened. "I'd never hurt her."

"I didn't think you would, but until the change is complete, we never know." She lifted a shoulder. "Usually, when someone is changed, they're the same person they were before. If you were an asshole as a human, you're an asshole as a vampire. A good guy is a good vampire... usually."

"Right." Pete swallowed and flicked his gaze to Marianna. She stared at him wide-eyed with her hands on her belly. Clad in a simple tank top and yoga pants, she looked more gorgeous than ever, but the look on her face brought him pause. Was she afraid? Of what he'd become? The truth was that he didn't really know what he was. "I'm not exactly the usual vampire though. Am I?"

"Nope. Actually, it'll be interesting to see what effects your demon blood has on you as a vampire." A grin cracked her face. "Okay, kids. He's got a full supply of blood and should be fine for right now. Besides, it's daytime, and I'm fucking exhausted. By the way, don't be surprised if you can't sleep. You've been asleep for two days while the change took place, so it'll take you some time to get used to your new system."

"Thank you," Pete murmured.

The women watched as he took the pitcher from the dresser and drank greedily, directly from it. He never dreamed that blood would taste good—hell—good didn't cover it. It was fan-fucking-tastic. He drained the pitcher dry and wiped his mouth with the back of his hand.

"I should've known," Olivia said through a laugh. "You're that guy who drank milk right out of the carton when nobody was watching, weren't you?"

"Sorry." Pete gave them a sheepish grin and placed the mug and pitcher on the dresser. His face grew serious, and his dark eyebrows furrowed. "Thank you again, for saving my life."

"Yeah." Olivia sighed. "Well, I didn't save your life... I changed it. You and Marianna will stay with me over the next few weeks while you get used to our world. You'll register with the Presidium records keeper and be introduced to the members at their next meeting. If I had to make a bet, I'd say that they're going to want to recruit you as a Sentry."

"One of their soldiers?" Marianna asked. "Aren't they executioners?"

"Sometimes," Olivia said casually. The concerned look on Pete's face caught her attention. "Relax, big guy. They aren't a kill squad or anything. They're basically vampire cops." She rubbed her neck and closed her eyes wearily. "We've got ground to cover, and you've got a lot to learn, but right now, I'm going to my room."

The door clicked shut as Olivia left Pete alone with Marianna. An intense hunger gnawed at him, and it kicked into high gear as Marianna's familiar scent filled his nostrils. He closed his eyes as he took in the distinct aroma, and suddenly, a pair of fangs burst into his mouth. He ran his tongue along the smooth surface, but winced as he drew blood when he touched the sharp points.

Marianna gasped. "Are—are you still hungry?" she asked in husky whisper as her heart rate picked up a notch. The seductive beat filled his head and made every single inch of him hard as stone. "I could get more from the kitchen, if you'd like."

"I'm most definitely hungry," he murmured. "But not for food."

A split second later, in a blur of flesh, he was across the room and had effortlessly scooped Marianna into his arms. Her brown eyes shifted into the dark, glowing eyes of her clan, and her lips parted on a sigh as she linked her arms around his neck.

"What did you have in mind?" She arched one dark eyebrow, and her lips curled into a sexy grin.

"Something like this," he murmured.

In a rush of wind, he laid her out on the bed and stripped the sweatpants from his heated body. Pete settled his body over her and kept himself raised with his hands pinned on either side of her head. He stayed there for a few moments, taking in every curve, every gorgeous inch of his mate.

Pete linked his pinky finger beneath the strap of her top and pulled it down, baring her neck and the beautiful curve of her shoulder. He trailed butterfly kisses along the smooth skin as he pulled the other strap down and tugged the top to her waist. He cursed softly as he took in the sight of her bare breasts.

Marianna threaded her fingers through his short hair as he brought one caramel-colored nipple into his mouth and suckled. She moaned and held him as he lavished attention on her sensitive breasts.

He moved further down, but lifted his head when he

reached her belly, and placed a sweet kiss there before dragging her pants from her body. The knowledge that his children were growing in her womb made him love her more than he thought possible.

Marianna lay naked and wanting, looking at him through hooded eyes as he kissed his way over the curve of her hip, wanting to taste her. The bruises and swelling from Hayden's attack had faded from sight, but Pete wanted to make sure he washed that day from her memory.

She sighed contentedly as he licked and kissed his way up her body and finally settled over her again. Her skin felt like warm silk beneath his lips, and the sound of her heartbeat surrounded him. He captured her mouth with his and tangled his fingers in her long, dark hair.

He lay there, kissing her and reveling in the touch of her tongue along his. *I love you, Pete.* Her voice touched his mind and heightened his pleasure. There was something wildly erotic about joining her body *and* her mind.

He broke the kiss and gave her a wicked grin. *I want you on top.*

A moment later, he was on his back, Marianna was straddling him, and he was buried deep inside. She gasped with surprise as his fingers gripped her hips and urged her to move. Marianna closed her eyes and threw her head back as she started to ride him.

Slowly at first, she rotated her hips as he held her, and let out tiny gasps of pleasure. She lifted her arms over her head and arched her back, which only accentuated those spectacular breasts. Pete sat up and wrapped his arms around her as she rode him faster and took him deeper into the warmth of her body.

Heat flickered over his skin, and his eyes burned as he

grabbed her breast and took it into his mouth. Marianna reached behind her and took his balls in her hand as she feverishly writhed in his arms. Pleasure flared through him, and as the orgasm crested, Pete's fangs burst into his mouth.

Without thinking or realizing what he was doing, he gathered her hair in one hand and tilted her head as he sank his fangs into the tender flesh of her neck. The moment he pierced her skin, they climaxed together hard and fast. Marianna screamed as she raked her nails across his back, and he moaned as her sweet blood flowed into his mouth and splashed down his throat.

Lights flashed behind his eyes, and it felt as if every cell in his body buzzed with electricity. Marianna's blood made that stuff in the pitcher seem paltry. She tasted like summertime and sex. She tasted like home.

He drank for only a moment before releasing her, but any pleasure he felt was swiftly replaced by guilt, as he saw the puncture wounds he'd made and the blood that trickled down her neck. However, to his amazement, the holes closed before his eyes and faded as if they'd never been there.

Marianna, her face buried in the hollow of his neck, was shaking and breathing like she'd run a marathon. Her body was limp, and for a second, he thought she'd passed out or he'd taken too much blood.

"I'm so sorry," he whispered. God, he felt like a monster. "Marianna?"

"That-was-un-fucking-believable," she said through hitching breaths. With his body locked inside hers, she sat up in his arms and looked at him through confused eyes. "What on earth are you sorry for?"

"I—I bit you." He flopped back on the bed and threw one arm over his face. "I drank your blood, Marianna."

"Yes, you did." Marianna climbed off him and snuggled her naked, sweaty body against his. "I suppose that goes with the territory, but you didn't hear me complaining, did you?"

"No." He put his arm behind his head and forced himself to look her in the eye. To his great relief, the only thing he saw there was love and trust. "I could've hurt you or the babies."

"You would never hurt me or our children." She draped herself over his chest and ran her fingers through his dark chest hair. "Everything will be fine. Actually, better than fine."

"What do you mean?"

"You're immortal now." She flicked her gaze away and bit her lower lip.

"Your powers—" A smile cracked his face as he realized what she was talking about. "You shouldn't age now either, right?"

"Yes. Well, at least I think so but I guess we'll just have to wait and see." She flicked his nipple with her tongue and grinned mischievously. "Think of all the fun we can have along the way." Marianna nuzzled his neck and pulled the covers over their naked bodies. "I'm surprised that you're still so warm. Olivia's skin feels much cooler."

"Maybe that's one of the side effects of having demon blood."

"Maybe." She kissed his cheek and whispered, "I'll take you any way that I can get you."

They lay in one another's arms in silence as Pete

listened to the sound of Marianna's heartbeat and the two softer pulses of the babies. They were faint, but he could tell they were strong and healthy.

"It's a boy and a girl," he said quietly.

She lifted her head to look at him, and a smile curved her lips. "How do you know?"

"I just know." He wrapped one long lock of hair around his finger and rubbed the smooth strands with his thumb. "What kind of father can I be to those children, Marianna? I can't take them out to the playground on a sunny afternoon or take them to school. The whole bursting-into-flames-in-sunlight thing makes that problematic."

"That will not be a problem for you." Asmodeus's thunderous voice burst through the room.

Pete flew from the bed, naked as a jaybird, and grabbed Asmodeus by the throat before realizing who he was. Marianna shrieked, clutched the covers over her naked body, and gaped at them.

"Don't you believe in knocking?" Pete seethed as he dropped his hand from his father's throat. He snagged his discarded sweatpants from the floor and dragged them over his hips.

"I don't use doors." Asmodeus sauntered to the over-sized chair in the corner and made himself comfortable. "I don't know what you're upset about. I waited until you were finished," he said with a wink at Marianna.

"What are you doing here?" Pete folded his arms over his chest and stared at his father. "And what do you mean… it won't be a problem for me?"

"Sunlight." Asmodeus sat in the chair and crossed his legs with his usual air of arrogance. "Your demon blood will allow you to be a Daywalker—to a point. You shouldn't attempt to sunbathe, but you will tolerate a certain amount of direct sunlight." He grinned, and his eyes burned red. "This will work to your advantage with the Presidium. There are only a handful of vampires who are Daywalkers, so this will make you quite a valuable commodity to them."

"So these other... Daywalkers," Pete began cautiously. "They're like me. They've got demon blood?"

"No." He ran one large hand over his dark beard. "They are vampires who found their blood mates—it's extremely rare. At any rate, I wanted to make you aware, so you could use this information to your advantage when you meet members of the Presidium. If they give you a hard time, it will be a useful bargaining chip."

"Are you sure?" Marianna asked. Pete cast a glance at Marianna and saw that she seemed as surprised and relieved by this revelation as he was. "Pete can go out in the daytime?"

"Does a bear shit in the woods?" Asmodeus replied with a mischievous grin.

"That's not funny." Marianna narrowed her eyes.

"I thought it was rather witty," he mused. "Well, I have to go now. I've already interfered far more than acceptable, and if the rest of the brotherhood find out, there'll be hell to pay." He stood and added, "Literally."

"Hey." Pete closed the distance between himself and Asmodeus in the blink of an eye. He lowered his voice and bared his fangs. "I appreciate the heads-up, but stay out of my bedroom, and no more spying on Marianna and I. The next time you pop into my room uninvited and invade our privacy... I'll drink you dry."

Asmodeus's eyes brightened, and his jaw clenched as he stared Pete down. Heat filled the room, and for a moment, he thought things were going to get ugly. However, when a huge grin cracked his bearded face, and his shoulders shook with laughter, Pete was too stunned to say or do anything.

"That's my boy," he said with a loud laugh. "I'll be seeing you around."

Then in a cloud of smoke and flash of fire, he was gone.

Marianna sat on the couch in the living room of Richard and Salinda's ranch and stared into the roaring fire. Pete sat with his fingers linked with hers. It had been over a month since Pete had been turned and Artimus had been killed, but it felt like a lifetime.

The moon cast an eerie light over the melting snow on the fields of the Montana ranch, and Marianna couldn't help but wish they were back at Pete's cabin. Her gut instinct to run away and hide from trouble began to rear its ugly head, but she squashed the urge to visualize herself out of the mess.

"Any word on where Dr. Moravian might have taken Courtney?" Pete asked.

Marianna glanced at Pete and brushed her fingers along his ever-present five o'clock shadow. He knew how desperate she was to find her friend, and as always, his only concern was for her happiness.

"Not yet," Dante chimed in from across the room. He and Kerry sat side by side on the other sofa and looked as concerned as she felt. "When we went back to the compound to see what information we could gather, everyone was gone, and all the computers had been wiped clean."

"Understood." Richard nodded solemnly and looked intently at each. "Have any of his former followers attempted to come back into the fold of their clans?"

"The two Purists who defected from the Council returned to the Falcon Clan with their mates and asked for forgiveness." Standing ramrod straight by the windows, William smoothed the lapel of his jacket. "I suggested that they speak with you directly."

"My aunt, Bianca, said that there was one Cheetah Clan member who returned with her mate and asked to be forgiven." Layla shoved her hands in the back pockets of her jeans and blew a bubble with her gum. "I don't think most folks are feeling forgiving at the moment."

"Forgiveness is one thing," Richard said quietly. "Trust is quite another."

"What about Steven?" Dante said tightly. "He still hasn't come out of the coma. There's a part of me that thinks it's actually merciful he's like this. When he wakes up and finds his mate pregnant and abducted, well, that may send him back into a coma."

"When I connected with him, I found that his current state is somehow linked to what's happened to his mate." Kerry chimed in. She looked at Richard and continued. "Steven is a healer, and this coma seems more like a perpetual dream state than a brain injury. From what I can tell, he's keeping himself on the dream plane so that he can stay connected with her."

"I'd like you to communicate with him, and see whether we can get him out of it. He can't help her if he stays where he is." Richard ran a hand through his long dark hair. "In the meantime, we'll look for her. The bottom line is we owe it to him to find Courtney so they can have a proper mating. He's in this situation because he was acting on orders from me." His voice dropped low. "I will not rest until we find her and bring her to him."

"I thought that perhaps I'd connect with Savannah, but so far, I haven't had any luck," Marianna added. "She was going to help me get out, and if she hadn't slipped that Taser under my pillow, I don't want to think about what Hayden would've been able to do."

Marianna shivered at the dark memories of that night. Pete held her tighter and placed his other hand over her rounding belly. He didn't say anything, but his actions spoke volumes.

"The only piece of hope I've got is that Savannah is still working with her father and doing it so she can protect Courtney." She locked eyes with Richard. "I know that she's not a Purist, Richard. If she's alive, then she's with Courtney."

The room filled with static, and Salinda appeared next to her husband with their infant daughter in her arms. "Your daughter wants her daddy to tuck her in," she said as she handed the smiling child to Richard.

Marianna watched as their leader was instantly reduced to a big heap of mush as his daughter wrapped her tiny fingers around his much bigger one. The chubby, blue-eyed cherub gurgled happily as she looked at her father. Marianna held Pete's hand against her belly and smiled.

He glanced at her as his mind brushed hers. *I want you all to myself, so let's make a graceful exit.*

"One more thing before you go," Richard said with a grin.

Marianna's face heated with embarrassment as she realized that he must've heard Pete. He'd gotten a much better handle on the telepathy, but he wasn't always great at shielding it from others. The prince adjusted the child in his arms and turned his attention back to Pete and Marianna.

"I've been in contact with the Presidium's New York czar, and he's agreed to allow you to work as a sentry and a liaison between our races." He glanced at Marianna and then to Pete. "If that's acceptable, of course."

"I'd be honored," Pete said. He stood and shook Richard's hand. "However, if it's all right, I'd like to take Marianna home to get some rest."

"Yes," Richard said through a smile, casting a knowing look to his wife. "We'll reconvene here next month to review new developments. Dante and Kerry will look for hybrids that may still be out there. William and Layla will follow new leads that pop up regarding Courtney or the doctor's whereabouts, but I imagine I can count on you if we need extra assistance."

"You can count on both of us." Marianna rose from her seat and linked her arm around Pete's waist. She winked at her brother. *No more running…I promise*, she whispered. Dante smiled and winked back.

Marianna whispered the ancient language, static flared with a gentle breeze, and within seconds they were back at her apartment in New York City.

Before she could say a word, Pete dropped to his knees and kissed her slightly rounded tummy. He pushed her sweater up and kissed her belly button as he cupped her bottom.

He peered at her with those arctic-blue eyes and grinned as his fangs burst into his mouth. He spun her around so that her ass was in his face, and she giggled as he splayed his hands over her stomach and kissed her butt.

Smiling, Marianna looked over her shoulder. "What exactly do you think you're doing?"

"I'm kissing your ass."

"Really?" She arched one dark eyebrow. "Kissing is nice, but I'm in the mood for a bite."

Marianna laughed at the surprised look on his face and slipped from his embrace. Still laughing, she ran to the bedroom as she visualized her clothes away and jumped onto the bed buck-naked.

In a flash, Pete was naked and tackling her. He wrapped her in his arms and slipped inside her on a sigh. Tangled up in skin, he drove into her with slow, loving strokes and held her gaze as he sank into her again and again. As the passion coiled deep inside, Marianna turned her head and gave him access to the tender skin along her throat.

"Not yet," he whispered.

Marianna groaned and urged him faster, wanting to make him lose control and chase the orgasm to the edge. To her disappointment, Pete disengaged from her body.

"Turn over," he rasped.

Marianna complied and turned onto her belly. Pete grabbed her hips and pulled her so that she was on all fours. She looked over her shoulder and wiggled her hips enticingly. That was all the encouragement Pete needed.

With one swift stroke he drove deeply inside. Marianna gasped with pleasure as he speared her again and again. Still pumping her, Pete held her hip and brushed her long hair aside. As the orgasm crested to the top, Marianna quivered in anticipation, knowing what was next.

Yes. Her voice, rich with pleasure, touched his mind as he sank his fangs into the side of her neck, and they tumbled over the edge together.

Sated and gloriously exhausted, the two lay with their limbs entwined, and Marianna didn't know where he ended and she began. As she drifted to sleep in the arms of her mate, the energy signatures of their unborn children surrounded her like a blanket. This was what she'd been looking for all her life. No more running. A smile curved her lips.

Unless, of course… she was running after their children.

Look for *Unclaimed*,
the fifth book in the Amoveo Legend series,
coming December 2013 from Sourcebooks Casablanca

In the meantime, read on for an excerpt from *Undenied*,
an Amoveo Legend novella, available for free
from DiscoverANewLove.com

And take a sneak peek at *Tall, Dark, and Vampire*,
the first book in an exciting new series from Sara Humphreys,
coming August 2013 from Sourcebooks Casablanca

Undenied

A GROWL RUMBLED IN THE BACK OF BORIS'S THROAT AS he struggled to keep his irises from shifting into the glowing yellow eyes of his clan. He gripped the tequila bottle in one hand and snatched a glass with the other before pouring a shot and sliding it across the bar to his unwelcome patron.

His instinct was to shift into his Tiger form and rip Hayden's throat out, but since he had a bar full of humans, that wasn't likely to happen, and Hayden knew it. Hayden threw the shot back and slid the empty glass across the bar to Boris. As a member of the Bear Clan and the son of a high-ranking Council elder, Hayden had to be tolerated—unfortunately.

"What do you want, Hayden?" Boris asked as quietly as possible.

He moved to the far end of the bar and motioned for Hayden to follow. The last thing he needed was more rumors flying around about him or his place. Ever since the incident with his sister, business hadn't been booming, and discussing Amoveo politics within earshot of humans was unwise. The existence of their race had remained secret for centuries, and he'd rather not be the one to let the proverbial cat out of the bag.

He hit the volume button from the jukebox remote. He could speak with Hayden telepathically, as all

Amoveo could, but he didn't care for the idea of allowing this asshole into his head.

"My father asked me to come and speak with you." He took the seat at the very end and kept his voice low. "You know that our race is under attack from within, and we need to gather as many true believers as possible before we can make our move."

Boris stilled and gritted his teeth against Hayden's dark energy signature. It slithered around the bar like a snake and set him on edge. All Amoveo had a signature, a spiritual fingerprint that distinguished them from everyone else, and Hayden's was dark and thick. Aside from being a spoiled, self-entitled tool, he also had a mean streak a mile long, and Boris couldn't stand him.

"You're barking up the wrong tree. My sister got involved in this crap, and look where it got her." He shifted his body so that his back was to the rest of the bar and fixed his intent gaze on Hayden. "Dead. That's where."

"Your sister was a patriot," Hayden seethed. He grimaced and dropped his voice to just above a whisper as he leaned both elbows on the bar. "Are you telling me that you would encourage mating with humans and add more hybrids to the mix?"

"There's nothing to encourage." Boris crossed his arms over his broad chest. "You know as well as I do that our matings are predestined, so there's little choice in the matter."

"We are not supposed to mate with humans," he seethed. "It's going to be our undoing."

"Listen." Boris poured him another shot and leaned onto the bar with both hands, getting right in Hayden's face. "All I'm telling you is that I want no part of politics. All I want to do is run my bar and be left alone. Got it?"

Hayden narrowed his dark beady eyes and leveled a suspicious gaze at Boris. "You haven't found your mate yet, have you? You're in your midtwenties, so the clock is ticking. I hope you're not thinking that your predestined spouse is a hybrid freak like the ones that Dante and Malcolm have shacked up with."

"No." Boris stilled and looked away, busying himself with cleaning behind the bar. "I am positive that my mate is not a hybrid."

"I see." Hayden nodded and made a sound of understanding. "Good. Because I'd hate to see you put yourself in a dangerous position. We've got a civil war brewing, and you don't want to be one of those hybrid sympathizers when it happens. Better to be unmated and fight with us than to allow this cycle of birth-defect breeding to continue."

Boris said nothing and hoped that Hayden would be satisfied with his lie. The truth was that he had found his mate—and she was not a hybrid—she was one hundred percent human.

At least, that's what he suspected.

He'd found her in the dream realm years ago, the way all Amoveo found their predestined mates, but he'd never been able to see her. At first he thought she was from a different clan, and that's why it was difficult to connect. There were, after all, ten animal clans among his people. But after several years of not being able to connect, he realized that she was likely human.

He didn't exactly know how he knew it... he just

did. After listening to Hayden and his hatred, the last thing he was going to do was tell him. The hybrids and their Amoveo mates were under attack from men like Hayden, so God only knew what they'd do if they found out his mate was a human.

He'd rather never connect and die alone than put her life at risk.

He could already feel his powers slipping away. He walked in the dream realm less as the days passed, and his skills of visualization and shifting took more and more energy. He knew that if he didn't claim his mate and connect with her by his thirtieth birthday, all of his powers would fade away until they were nothing but a distant memory. At that point, death would be merciful.

Hayden tossed back another shot, stood from the stool, and threw a twenty on the bar. He glanced at the row of pictures along the stairway that led to the upstairs dining area and stopped to stare for a few minutes. Boris watched him intently, and every cell in his body went on high alert.

"Your sister was quite a piece of ass," he said through a heavy sigh. Hayden turned to face Boris and gave him a smug smile. "Too bad I didn't fuck her when I had the chance."

Rage flashed over Boris's skin at the crude comments about his sister. He leaped over the wooden bar with a growl, grabbed Hayden by the throat, dragged him through the crowd, and tossed him into the street as stunned patrons looked on.

"And don't you ever show your goddamned face in my place again!" he yelled. Seconds later, he watched Hayden plow into a young woman as she rounded the corner. The poor thing tumbled to the ground in a heap and gaped at Hayden, too surprised to say anything.

Hayden screamed something at him, but he didn't hear it because he was completely transfixed by the disheveled creature sitting on the sidewalk. Boris wanted to apologize and tell her how sorry he was, but just as he was about to offer her a hand, the familiar sound of bracelets jingling stopped him dead in his tracks.

He'd heard that sound countless times in the dream realm as he'd looked for his mate. While he'd never seen her, he had heard her voice, and it was always accompanied by that jingling.

Boris froze, and all reason left him when her voice reached out and touched his mind with the gentlest of whispers. *Worst day ever.*

His instincts had been right.

His mate was a human. She was here, and she was pissed.

Tall, Dark, and Vampire

THE MUSIC POUNDED LOUDLY THROUGH THE CLUB AS IT reverberated through Olivia's body. She walked the dance floor, taking note of the various humans writhing with one another amid the pulsating lights. She stuck out like a sore thumb, since she was the only one wearing a black Armani suit, not the leather or spikes of her faithful patrons.

Olivia waved at the regular customers peppered throughout the club and allowed herself a moment of pride. The Coven had become one of the most popular dance clubs for the Goth set in NYC, and she had worked her ass off to make it happen.

She liked it here and had no desire to leave, but the drawback of immortality was that moving on eventually was an annoying necessity—can't stay somewhere for thirty years if you don't age. Although, the prevalent use of Botox among humans certainly helped explain her lack of facial wrinkles.

Olivia scoped out the club and marveled at how far society had come—and yet not.

Humans who loved to dress like vampires, or what they thought vampires looked like, flocked to this place every night as the sun went down. Except Sunday—she closed the joint on Sunday, since the place used to be a church. She figured it was the least she could do. Olivia grinned and shook her head as she watched the humans wooing one another in their *vampire* garb.

Ironically, most vampires did not dress like horror-movie rejects; many adopted the fashion of the era they lived in, but not all did. Vincent, for example, liked the Victorian era so much that he still adorned himself in a top hat and ascot, although she thought it looked ridiculous. Vampires retained their individuality at least.

Imagine if they knew this club was owned and operated by an actual vampire who preferred silk and cashmere to leather and spikes. Olivia had to wear the leather sentry uniform every day for a century and loathed the idea of wrapping herself in it again.

I'd be a sad disappointment to them.

Olivia climbed onto the DJ's platform and gave Sadie a pat on the back. Sadie was one of the best spinners out there, living or undead, and Olivia's oldest, most trusted friend. She was dressed much like the patrons of the club, except Sadie actually *was* a vamp, and the girl had a serious passion for leather and lace.

"Hey, boss. Feels like a lively crowd tonight." Sadie winked and smiled. "No pun intended."

Sadie was the first vamp she had ever turned. Olivia and Vincent were traveling through a largely unsettled part of Arizona and picked up the distinctly potent scent of blood. The Apache Indians had been attacking settlers at that time, not that Olivia could blame them, and Sadie's family had been among their victims.

Sadie was barely alive when she found her. The faint beat of her heart called to Olivia, and before she even knew what she was doing, she turned her. It was an instinctive need to save her, to help this poor girl who had lost everything, left seemingly alone in the world.

Vincent, of course, was less than pleased, and that was the beginning of the end for them.

Sadie winked and adjusted the headphones around her neck. "You're just a sucker for hard-luck cases. Face it. You would rescue the world if you could."

"Not the *whole* world," Olivia said dramatically. "Just the ones who really need it."

"I sure needed it," Sadie said with a warm smile.

Olivia swallowed the surprising lump in her throat before looking back at the crowd. Sadie had tried to thank her on several occasions, but Olivia never let her get the words out. Deep inside she felt as though she hadn't saved Sadie or the others. Perhaps the vampire hunters of the world were right. What if vamps really were damned to burn in hell for eternity? Would anyone thank her then?

Another loud, bass-driven song tumbled over the crowd as Sadie's voice floated into her head. *Hey, boss. I see our VIP table is full again tonight with your boyfriend and his crew.*

Olivia threw an irritated glance over her shoulder at Sadie and shot back. *He's not my boyfriend. He just wishes he was. What a termite.* She could hear Sadie stifle a giggle as she navigated the crowd and made her way to Michael's table.

How long has it been since you got laid? I forget. Olivia did her best to ignore that last jab from her friend. Other than Vincent, Sadie was the only one who knew that Olivia had been celibate since becoming a vampire. *Don't you think you've tortured yourself long enough? I never knew this Douglas guy, but if he really loved you the way you say he did, would he want you to spend eternity alone?*

I'm not alone. Olivia threw a wink over her shoulder. *I've got all of you, and sex is overrated anyway.*

Damn. Sadie's laugh jingled through Olivia's mind. *Now you're just talking crazy.*

Olivia shook her head and smiled. Her heart had been stolen long before Vincent made it stop beating, and besides, even if she did have her heart to give, Moriarty certainly would not be a candidate.

Michael was a greasy little worm who used his family's reputation to get what he wanted. He came to The Coven every Saturday night with his gaggle of dirtbags, and Olivia could smell his fear and feelings of inadequacy a mile away. He'd been trying to get into her pants for months now, and apparently, was still trying, even after a multitude of rejections.

She felt his eyes on her all night and had managed to ignore him, but now, it was time to play the game. She had to placate the little weasel. Jerk or not, he was a customer—a customer who spent a lot of money in her club.

Olivia flashed the most charming grin she could muster as she approached Michael and his motley crew.

"Hey there, hot stuff." He leered, and his lips curved into a lascivious grin. "I was wondering how long it was gonna take you to get your sweet ass over here."

She wanted to bite his face off. What an asshole.

"Hello, Mr. Moriarty," she said through a strained smile. "Are you gentlemen finding everything satisfactory this evening?"

"I'd be doin' a lot better if you'd come here and sit with me."

Olivia smiled tightly and looked at him like the

black-haired little bug he was. "Well, *gentlemen*, I hope you'll let me buy the final round here. It's almost last call."

She motioned to the waitress who covered the three VIP tables opposite the bar. Suzie, one of only two humans who worked at The Coven, came over quickly, but Olivia sensed her anxiety long before she arrived at the table.

"Sure, baby." He leered. "You can buy me a drink."

Olivia wanted nothing more than to glamour this guy into dancing naked in the middle of the club with only his socks on, but the image alone would have to be enough to get her through.

"Suzie. Please get our guests their last round." She flicked her gaze back to Moriarty. "On the house, of course."

"Yes, ma'am." She looked like a skittish lamb surrounded by wolves. She almost hadn't hired Suzie due to her naive nature, but Olivia was a sucker for hard-luck cases. Suzie was straight from the farm and as green as the fields she hailed from. By hiring her, she figured she could at least keep an eye on her.

Olivia nodded and said a brief good-bye before working her way to the front door. The place was starting to thin out, since it was just about last call. The tension in her shoulders eased as soon as she set eyes on the only other human who worked at the club—their bouncer Damien.

Damien, unlike Suzie, knew what Olivia and the others were. He was what some referred to as a *familiar,* but Olivia hated that term. It seemed like a dirty word, laced with innuendo and ill intent. Most humans who worked with vampires did it out of love and friendship.

However, Damien wasn't just a friend—he was more

like family. He was the only human who knew what Olivia was and kept her secret, and not because he had to, but because he genuinely cared. She'd met him when he was a boy, spending most of his nights on the streets and clearly heading down a bad path.

She'd heard his cries one night, and even though it was against Presidium rules to interfere with humans and their problems, she couldn't help it. That cry of a young boy in the dark overrode any rules she was supposed to follow, and before she knew it, she was plucking him from what was sure to be a deadly situation.

She planned to rescue him from the local drug dealer and send him on his way. Yet the second she looked into the soulful, brown eyes, she was hooked. At first, she told herself that she would only check on him for a few nights to be sure he was safe, but those few nights turned into weeks, and then years. Since vampires couldn't have children, Damien was the closest she'd ever have to a child, and she loved him as if he was her own.

"Moriarty's still here?" Damien had barely finished the question, when Michael appeared in the vestibule with his posse.

"We were just leaving, big guy." Michael gave him a smack on the back as he walked to the enormous stretch limo waiting at the curb. Olivia put her hand on Damien to keep him at bay. She couldn't blame him for wanting to go after him, because she wanted to punch the little bastard's lights out too.

"You know, Olivia, one day that guy is gonna get what's coming to him," Damien said quietly as the limo pulled away. "I just hope I get to see it."

"You know what they say, babe," she said quietly.

"Be careful what you wish for. Besides, his money is as green as anyone's."

"I realize you're not into live feeds like most of your *crowd*, but boy, does that guy deserve to be dinner or what? I know you can handle yourself, but I don't like the way he speaks to Suzie or any other woman for that matter."

She rubbed her temples absently as various patrons pushed past as they left. Live feeds were always best, but Olivia tried to avoid them. While the live feed was most rejuvenating, it was also the most dangerous. Live feeds were like a drug. The more she did it, the more she wanted it, and each time it got harder and harder to stop. Besides, blood memories came with it, and she wasn't interested in anyone else's baggage. She had quite enough of her own shit to deal with.

As she turned to go back inside, an oddly familiar voice floated over, and the scent of the ocean filled her head.

"Excuse me. Can you tell me where I can find Ms. Olivia Hollingsworth?"

Olivia stopped dead in her tracks, and the tattoo on the nape of her neck burned. Her fangs erupted, and little licks of fire skittered up her spine, as one note of that smooth, velvety voice banished all self-control. She closed her eyes and willed her quaking body to settle.

It can't be.

Terrified and hopeful, Olivia steeled herself with courage she'd forgotten she had. She turned around, ex-cruciatingly slowly, and found herself face-to-face with the man of her dreams and the love of her life.

The problem was he'd been dead for almost three hundred years.

Acknowledgments

Many thanks to everyone at Sourcebooks who work their buns off to get my books published. Thanks especially to Cat and Deb for the editorial expertise. To Danielle Jackson for her publicity with pop and to the art department for creating such gorgeous covers. Thanks to my agent Jeanne Dube for her tireless support and to Sheila McLoughlin for her beta-reading brilliance.

I have to extend a huge shout-out to Jason and Jennifer Nickelsen for sending me all those great pictures of the cabin at Schroon Lake and for answering my endless questions about the area. So glad we met all those years ago at Marist! Beer on me next time.

Thanks to the gals and guys on my street team, Sara's Angels, for their ferocious support and positive attitudes. Thank you for working to get the word out about the Amoveo Legend, both on the street and in cyberspace. You rock, and I am so grateful to have you in my corner.

Thank you to my husband Will and my four sons. I love you all very much. You are my happily ever after.

Dream on…

About the Author

Sara Humphreys graduated from Marist College with a degree in English literature and theater. She started her career as an actress, with credits including *Guiding Light, As the World Turns*, and *Rescue Me*. She specializes in public speaking, presentation development, and communication skills training. But she has loved romance novels and sci-fi/fantasy worlds for years, beginning with *Star Trek* (she had a huge crush on Captain Kirk). She is now married to her college sweetheart, with whom she has four boys and two "insanely loud" dogs. They live just outside of New York City, a perfect inspiration for where things go bump in the night.

Sara's fascination with sci-fi/fantasy eventually grew into a love for all things paranormal, including ghosts, shapeshifters, and the undead. She considers herself a hopeless romantic and a sucker for happy endings.

Sara's first manuscript caught the eye of a major national bookseller, who championed her publishing career. Sara utilizes her acting skills during her writing, using sense memory recall and creating backgrounds for her characters so they have a history. Even for shapeshifters, she researches the animals and utilizes their natural traits in her characters who take on their forms.

You can find information about upcoming books on her website: www.sarahumphreys.com